'You're expecting me to ravish you?'

His body pressed down on hers, subduing it. 'To be sure, I'm tempted. You're comely, and I like a woman with spirit.'

'I would not have thought you cared about the sort of woman you defiled.' Constance retorted furiously. 'Likely you've ravished hundreds of women.'

'Not hundreds,' he said unsteadily, 'and never one who talked as much as you.'

June Francis was born in Blackpool during the war, but bred in Liverpool. Her father taught her the alphabet from a signwriters' book of lettering, and told her stories from memory; so passing on a love of storytelling. Although she always wanted to write she did not begin until her youngest son started school—greatly encouraged by her husband. She has had many articles published, as well as short stories broadcast, but her first love has always been the historical novel. History has always been a passion with her—due, she says, to an incurable curiosity about the past. Her other interests are walking, cycling and swimming. She has been happily married for over twenty years, and has three sons. The eldest, who is at Oxford studying Classics, also wants to be a writer.

June Francis has written three other Masquerade Historical Romances; *The Bride Price*, *Beloved Abductor* and *My Lady Deceiver*.

FATEFUL ENCOUNTER

June Francis

MILLS & BOON LIMITED
ETON HOUSE   18-24 PARADISE ROAD
RICHMOND   SURREY   TW9 1SR

*First published in Great Britain 1989
by Mills & Boon Limited*

© June Francis 1989

*Australian copyright 1989
Philippine copyright 1989
This edition 1989*

ISBN 0 263 76385 4

*Set in Times Roman 10 on 11 pt.
04-8904-79246 C*

Made and printed in Great Britain

CHAPTER ONE

'I MUST have been mad to let you talk me into this, Constance,' muttered Robin Milburn moodily, huddling inside his woollen houppelande, which glistened with moisture. 'I know we've come a good distance, but it's not too late to change your mind.'

Constance de Wensley cast a glance at the tree-smothered hills wreathed in mist, and swallowed an exasperated sigh. It had been fine that morning when they had set out. Placing a hand on her kinsman's arm, she smiled up into his plump, but pleasantly boyish face. 'Look upon this as an exciting venture into the unknown, Robin!'

He grunted. 'This isn't the unknown! We know that somewhere along this road the forces of King Richard II were attacked and your husband Milo was killed.'

Constance's dark brows puckered. 'You are forgetting that the kings and chieftains of the native Irish have been swearing fealty to Richard for the last few months. Matters are bound to improve.'

'And you're forgetting what the guide told us in Dublin—that the king of Leinster and his allies have not departed from the mountains, as they swore to do in January. Despite all the agreements made between the English and Irish, I doubt much has changed since Milo's father fled with him twenty-five years ago. This is a dangerous land, and I should never have allowed you to accompany me.' He made a noise in his throat. 'Look how it started in Dublin, with your maid breaking her ankle slipping on the gang-plank,' he grumbled. 'We had to send her home on the next ship.'

5

'Oh, Robin, don't be such a crosspatch,' she replied impatiently.

'But your father will be furious! We should have waited for him,' insisted Robin.

'He would have been an age. Likely he is still in London consulting with Sir Richard Stury—who is, as you know, a member of the Privy Council. They have hopes of bringing before Parliament a document stating the Lollard views and aims calling for reforms in the church. You know how dear that is to Father's heart. He will have no thought for me until he returns to Yorkshire, where my stepmother is with my twin half-brothers.' A shadow crossed her oval face.

'And then he'll be in a fury when he's told what you've done, and will make for Ireland post-haste. And who'll get all the blame? Me.' His anxiety showed in his blue eyes.

'I shall tell him that the blame is all mine.' She smiled coaxingly. 'When has Father ever stayed angry with me for long?'

'Since the twins were born and pushed your nose out of joint,' he replied promptly. 'That's why you wed Milo de Wensley in the way you did. A penniless son of a dreamer of an Anglo-Irish minor nobleman! You could have done better, Con, despite those brothers of yours. Your father would have still provided you with a handsome dowry, even though you were no longer the heiress you were before Henry and John were born.'

'Do you not think I don't know that!' she said vehemently, her fingers tightening on the reins. 'But I made my bed, so I had to lie in it. Do not think that I haven't regretted it often. Things happened that I have never spoken of to anyone. And I have no intention of speaking of them now—so don't look at me like that, Robin! Best to forget the last four years of my life with Milo, and to look ahead to the future.'

'Then why come to Ireland?' He wore a bewildered expression. 'It seems madness.'

She hesitated. 'Can't you understand why?' He shook his head. 'Then this I will tell you, because I think you might understand, being a younger son with no property to call your own. Milo's land over here, left to him by his father, is now rightfully mine, so I do not now have to beg my father for anything.'

'You wouldn't have to beg from him,' he said in a distressed tone. 'Your father is strict but fair—and he loves you, despite the times you have wilfully disobeyed him.'

'You never heard what he said when he caught up with Milo and me after we ran away!' She moistened her mouth, and swallowed. 'I know he has forgiven me for the pain I caused him and Philippa,' her voice was low, 'but my stepmother and the boys are his life now, and I have no part of it. Sometimes I feel that he has completely forgotten my mother.'

'How could he?' Robin noted the proud Castilian features of her countenance. 'Each time he looks at you he must be reminded of her, but my mother told me she caused quite a rift between your father and his brother. A Spanish maid in the train of Constanza, Duchess of Lancaster, whom they both loved.'

She smiled slightly. 'It is hard to believe that Father married her without permission—and that Uncle Hugo spent years barely speaking to him, until he met Aunt Rose.'

'Even that caused a scandal!' Robin chuckled. 'She was Philippa's maid, and Philippa was his betrothed, with whom your father fell in love.'

'He wouldn't have married her, though, had my stepmother not been so determined to marry Father—and it has worked out, and they are happy. But I can't go back and live with them. In this way, I may perhaps build my own future.'

'But I can't stay indefinitely,' said Robin. 'Sooner or later I shall leave, and so will the king with his forces. What then?'

'I shall worry about that when the time comes,' she said calmly. 'Now let us catch up with the others. Did that man Brandon not say that there was a town within a few miles? I'm starving.'

'Ay.' He grinned suddenly. 'I think Master Brandon has a fancy for you—and he's a member of the Earl of March's household.'

She frowned, but could not quite hide a smile. 'Hush, Robin, he might hear you. Let's catch up with them. And let's pray there's something hot and meaty when we reach the town. Despite its being April, it's damnable cold now the mist has come down.' She pressed her knee against her mare's neck, and immediately she responded.

As they rounded a bend, Constance's gaze took in a new vista sweeping up from the road to the Wicklow Hills. Her heart gave a sudden lurch, as she thought she saw movement. Her eyes strained through the mist that swirled tantalisingly, parting here and there to reveal a boulder or tree, only to conceal them a moment later. Her fingers tightened on the reins, and her pulse jumped. 'Robin!' He turned to face her. 'There are men in the hills—I'm certain.'

He pushed back the wide-brimmed beaver hat, revealing thick brown hair, and his head slewed round to follow her pointing hand. 'You're mistaken. But, no, sweet Mary, I think you're right!' He shouted to the other riders a little ahead, and obediently they responded, and several faces turning up to the hills.

An axe suddenly hissed in the misty air, to find a target in a tree on the other side of the road. There was a concerted gasp, and without more ado, the riders spurred their horses on to speed ahead of Constance and Robin. 'Time these horses had a good gallop,' they said in unison.

Constance sent a swift estimating glance to the hills to see that the leading man was not far away, but after that, she dared not look again. So intent was she on trying to catch up with Robin's stallion that the thud of feet drawing closer did not register at first as a threat. Then a man shot into sight, running like a deer alongside her. The mare swerved away from him, and for a moment she thought he would be left behind. Then unexpectedly he was up behind her, one arm about her waist as the other stretched to pluck the reins from her gloved hand. Furiously she struggled, swaying perilously on the side-saddle that had been made fashionable by Richard's dead Queen Anne. Catching sight of a lean profile, barbarously moustached, she lashed out and caught him a blow on the chin. His eyebrows shot up, but he ducked her next blow, then he was pulling the reins to force the mare round and off the road. Still she fought him, leaning back in an attempt to throw him off balance, but he pushed against her so that her nose hit the horse's mane, bringing tears to her eyes. The beast was brought to a jolting halt, and before she could realise what he was about, he had unfastened his damp mantle and blinded her with a fold of it, successfully muffling her cries of angry frustration.

He dismounted, and placed her on the ground. She sought for an opening in the clammy folds of the garment, scared, but furious at being treated in such a manner, and at last managed to free her head. Then her arm shot out, but her feet became entangled just as she was pushing herself up, and she fell. Eventually she extricated herself, and saw that he had his back to her and appeared to be unbuckling her saddle. Her eyes sought for a weapon, and her fingers found a rock. She was struggling to lift it, when he turned, with her saddle in his hands.

The slightest of smiles tugged at his mouth as he dropped the saddle. Her throat tightened, and she stilled.

His smile broadened, angering her further. Suddenly she had her fear under control, and lunged at him with the stone held high, but its weight was too much for her, and they both fell in a tangle of arms and legs beneath her trembling mare.

His breath hissed between his teeth as he sent the rock tumbling, then he dragged her fully on top of him. Terrified of the mare's flaying hoofs, she did not move as he heeled and elbowed his way backwards with a speed that amazed her, and which took them from beneath the mare and to safety.

He collapsed, his chest heaving, and for several seconds her relief at escaping injury was so great that she did not move. Then, lifting her head, she saw the fury in his face. Hurriedly she rose to her knees, but he seized her arms and pulled her back on top of him. She gave a scream as he rolled her over, imprisoning her beneath him. He flung a string of unintelligible words at her, which sounded so dire that she wilted beneath their force. Then his mouth came down over hers with a ruthless ferocity.

Her body stiffened with resistance, preparing for the violation that she was certain would follow, and she punched at his face. He wrenched his mouth from hers and slapped her lightly. She gasped, and began to tremble, but the spirit that had never been subdued beneath Milo's cruel domination fought within her, and she slapped him back. 'How dare you touch me, you barbarian!'

As he caught her wrist, his sharp pale grey eyes were staring into her face with an intensity that almost mesmerised her. He raised himself slightly to run his gaze over the tightly-fitting dark blue cote-hardie. Her veil had worked loose, and her black braids had cascaded from their confining loops about her ears to tickle her cheeks. She forced herself not to flinch beneath his scrutiny, noting that his good looks were marred by a thin white scar snaking down past his left eyebrow, so that the skin was puckered slightly.

His lips formed words in English. 'You will come with me.'

'I will not,' she responded, attempting to pull her hand away. 'You must release me.' She was surprised that he spoke English.

'Release you? I did not run like the devil to let you go so easily.' He smiled, touching her chin lightly with his fist, before lowering himself on to her again. She struggled to throw him off, her apprehension mounting, but it was useless. He kissed her again with an enthusiastic fervour that sent shock rippling through her body. Tears welled in her eyes. Robin had been right; she was a fool to have come to Ireland, knowing the dangers.

He raised his head and looked down into her eyes. 'There is no need to cry,' he said, resting his hands on her breasts. 'Who are you?'

'What difference will it make if I tell you?' she replied, her voice unsteady. Her fear was no greater than at the times Milo had bedded her with all the finesse of a beast in the fields.

'None, but we need to know your name.' He moved a hand to wipe a tear from her cheek. 'If you are someone important, all the better.'

'Do you keep a list of all the women you ravish?' she said vehemently, attempting to throw him off again.

'You are expecting me to ravish you?' His body pressed down on hers, subduing it. 'To be sure, I'm tempted! You're comely, and I like a woman with spirit.'

'I would not have thought you cared about the sort of woman you defiled,' she retorted furiously. 'You're the kind of man who cares about a woman's purity only if she's your sister or your betrothed. Any other woman is a target for your attentions. Probably you have ravished hundreds of women!'

'Not hundreds,' he said unsteadily, 'and never one who talked as much as you. You don't look English,' he flicked one olive cheek, 'but you talk like an Englishwoman, and not one from Dublin or any part of the Pale. I'm glad of that! And from appearance—and the feel...' she gasped as he felt the material about her thigh, 'you are not poor.'

'My father's a wool-merchant. If you were considering a ransom, you will get more money if you do not despoil me,' she said.

'A wool-merchant!' He brought his scarred face close to hers. 'Is he very rich?'

She moistened her mouth. 'Not really rich,' she lied. 'And he's in England, but he has an agent in Dublin. But if you hurt me—or aught else—I doubt he would be prepared to pay much. After all, I am only a daughter, and not worth as much as a son.'

'It makes no difference if you're a woman—because it's not for a ransom that I want you.' His mouth touched hers lightly.

'No!' she cried vehemently, attempting to push him away.

He shrugged, and got to his feet, pulling her up with him. 'You're coming with me.'

'No! I...' She stopped abruptly. Robin was just behind, and for an instant she could not think what to do. As it was, she did not have to do anything because her kinsman acted swiftly, bringing a piece of wood down on the man's head. As he fell, she wrenched her fingers from his hold, and jumped aside.

'It appears that I came just in time,' said Robin with grim satisfaction. He knelt beside the man, and rolled him over. 'I don't think I've killed him.'

'It would serve him right if you had,' she declared tersely, smoothing down her skirts with an unsteady hand. 'I'm glad you came when you did. He was just going to take me away.'

'Are you all right? He didn't...?'

She shook her head. 'When did you realise I wasn't with you? Where are the others?' Her cheeks were pink.

'Almost immediately. Can you ride? We'll lose sight of the rest of them if we don't make haste.' He sounded uneasy.

'I can ride.' She gazed at the man, noting that his chest was rising and falling. A groan escaped him. 'Let's go,' she said quickly. 'He's stirring—and there were others with him, don't forget.'

'I haven't forgotten.' He stared at her flushed face. 'How did he manage to catch you?'

'He ran after me.' She made to pick up her saddle.

'No, leave it,' Robin ordered suddenly. 'I can hear someone coming. Let's go! I left my horse on the road.'

Constance dropped the saddle, picked up the man's mantle and flung it over her mare. She dragged herself up, sparing one last glance at the Irishman, and she thought his eyelids fluttered. 'He's waking,' she cried. 'Let's go!' Robin ran to the road, and she followed swiftly.

'Let's pray the rest of them can't run as fast he could,' said Robin drily, as he pulled himself up into the saddle.

She made no reply, being intent on listening for signs of pursuit. When there came the slightest sound of voices muffled by the mist, her glance met Robin's for a moment, and then they set out to put as much distance as possible between them and the owners of the voices. Soon the only sound to be heard was their own breathing and that of hoofs drumming on the earth.

The mist swirled; its clammy streamers chilled her face, and the cold seemed to seep into her bones. Still they went on, not daring to slow down. After a while, Robin called a halt. There was no sign of the party they had travelled with in the belief that there was safety in numbers. 'This is futile,' he muttered. 'We have no notion of where we are.' The lines of his face expressed his misery.

'What can we do but go on?' Her voice sounded loud, and she could not prevent herself from glancing swiftly over her shoulder.

'I don't know,' he said disgruntled. 'I told you this was madness.'

She ignored that remark. 'All roads lead somewhere. Surely, sooner or later, we shall arrive at a town?' She attempted to force a note of optimism into her voice.

He grunted. 'I suppose you're right. But I wish this damned mist would lift. We could be anywhere!'

Constance made no reply, convinced that the mist would be with them for the remainder of the evening. She had experienced the same sort of weather on the Yorkshire fells, where she had spent part of her childhood. Her thoughts drifted with the swirling mist. Had it been like this last autumn, when Milo had been caught in the ambush? He might never have returned to Ireland if Richard II of England had not insisted on all absentee landlords born in Ireland joining him in an attempt to resolve by force the problems in that land. Perhaps the man could have been one of those involved in that ambush? Her body burned, almost feeling the weight of him again. She questioned again her decision in coming to Ireland.

'I wonder what we'll discover when eventually we find Milo's manor? Could it be as his father was wont to talk about it?'

'Unlikely,' was Robin's grumpy response. 'Nothing is ever exactly as people remember. Distance lends enchantment—you want to remember that.' He stilled his horse with a steady hand, attempting to pierce the grey curtain. 'I think it's getting darker.'

She nodded, thinking she heard something in the sudden silence.

'Let's go on.' Anxiety sharpened her voice.

When it was that they strayed from the road, Constance was never sure, but suddenly their mounts were slithering. Immediately she slid from her horse, only to find herself ankle-deep in muddy water. Her eyes closed briefly in distaste, and taking the bridle, she somehow managed to force the mare out of the marshy ground. At last she felt firm turf beneath her feet, and soothed the animal with soft words. In the moment it took to achieve all that, she lost sight of Robin.

She cried out in panic, and an answer came from somewhere to her left. She could not help considering that 'Over here!' was not helpful.

'Where exactly are you?' she called.

'Never mind!' cried Robin. 'Keep talking, and I'll find you somehow.' His voice now seemed to come from behind her.

'What should I say?' she retorted, rubbing her cold hands together

'What does it matter?' The mist muffled the words so that they did not sound like Robin's.

Taking a deep breath, she launched into, 'Did I ever tell you about the Fiann? They were a band of warriors who lived an almost spartan life and were led by one Finn MacCumail. Can you still hear me?' The words burst from her as the mists seemed to encircle her in an island of silence.

'Keep talking,' came the voice. 'I'm coming.'

Her brow creased. 'Running was part of their training. That man reminded me of them. They had to run, and if caught by the other warriors, they were disqualified.' How silent it was! Her glance swept wildly in a circle. 'Robin!' she yelled.

'Con—stance!'

The sound was faint and far off, and filled with anxiety. Throwing caution aside, she stumbled in its direction or what she thought was the right direction, taking one careful step after another. Three paces—

four—five—six, and still no Robin. But she was on firm
ground. Another step and another, and suddenly she was
floundering. Panic seized her, and she tried to step back,
but slipped and fell. She shuddered as the cold mud
oozed between her gloved hands and soaked her skirts,
penetrating to her buttocks. How she hated it! There
had been a day on the fells when a sheep had been unable
to free itself from a bog. She gritted her teeth and attempted to rise, only to slip again. A sob burst in her
throat.

'Keep still, woman!' Her recognition of the voice en-
sured not only her stillness, but silence. 'You'll never
get up like that, to be sure.' His lilting voice held a hint
of satisfaction. Instead of crying, now she had an over-
whelming urge to scream, but remained silent. 'Perhaps
you'd like me to help you out? And, maybe, if you asked
me nicely, I'd do it.'

'If you have come to gloat...!' she said furiously.

'Why should I gloat? Unless you managed to hit me
from behind? But I don't consider that's possible now.'

'You know it isn't possible,' she muttered unsteadily.
Her teeth were beginning to chatter. 'How did you find
me? Where is... Robin?'

'Maybe, now, *he*'s in the bog?' His laugh chilled her
blood. 'And maybe it is that you'd like to join him?
They say this bog is haunted by a *fomor*. But perhaps
you don't know what a *fomor* is, your being English and
all?'

She swallowed. 'If you've thrown Robin in the bog,
I'll...I'll...'

'You'll what? Go down after him? Or will you try to
persuade me to drag him out?'

'He was only doing what any man would do to protect
his kinswoman!' Her voice rose. 'Surely you wouldn't
punish a man for that?'

'So he's your kinsman. What would be his name?'
She heard the splash of water.

'Robin Milburn. He isn't in the bog, is he?' Panic shook her voice. 'Please, you haven't let him sink?'

'No, we haven't. What are you doing, woman, wandering Ireland in the mist? Your kinsman should have more sense than to bring you here.'

'I wanted to come.' Her bottom was quite frozen, and she was frustrated because she knew she had to have his help. She doubted that she could move without it. 'And I do know what a *fomor* is, and I can almost believe that there is one here.'

'Is that right, now?' His voice was against her ear as his arms slid about her. He dragged her upright.

'Ay!' she said stiffly. 'And if I'd a penny's worth of— of sense, I would *never* have come to Ireland.' She was too chilled to resist when he humped her up in his arms in front of him, her legs dangling, and proceeded to carry her backwards out of the mire. He set her down on firm ground before turning her to face him. 'There now; you are well and truly rescued. Do I not get any thanks? A kiss, perhaps?' There was a hint of laughter in the face that appeared ghostly in the mist.

She lifted a filthy hand to thrust aside a dangling muddy braid. Then she had cause to rub her nose, only to recoil from the stench. 'I—I stink! It's all your fault!' she stammered. 'If you hadn't caught me and hounded us, this would never have happened. You are a barbarian! A bullying—heartless—pagan!' She sniffed back her tears.

There was a pause before he spoke. 'Is that right?' he said in a seething sarcastic voice. 'Twice I've saved your miserable life, and a word of thanks wouldn't come amiss.'

'Thank you! Why should I *thank* you? I could have been in Naas having a hot meal if you hadn't chased me and almost raped me.'

'Almost raped you!' He ground his teeth. 'If my intention had been rape, woman, you'd have been well and truly raped by now. I wouldn't have wasted my time listening to your ceaseless bleating.'

'I don't bleat!' She glared at him, her body stiff with cold and rage.

'You never stop talking—chatter, chatter, chatter.' He folded his arms across his chest. 'And I thought Irish-women talked!'

'You don't have to stay and listen. I'd much prefer it if you went.'

'I'll go, then.' He turned and walked away.

She stared after him, noting the height of him and the broad sweep of his shoulders in the ochre-coloured tunic. Already the mist was swallowing him up. Fear over-whelmed her as the silence made itself felt. 'Don't go! I didn't mean it!' She stumbled hurriedly in his wake, even as he turned.

'Changed your mind, have you?' His smile caused her to clench her fists. 'Scared of the *fomor*?'

'I'm not scared! And, besides, I think you mentioned the *fomor* only to frighten me.' A shiver set her teeth chattering.

'How do you know? Some say the *fomor* still walk the land. Half man, half demon—one-eyed—claw-footed. They can kill with a blow of their mighty tails.' He stood very close to her. 'Could you face one here alone without my protection?' His chest brushed her breasts.

'I—I don't believe in—in them.' She shivered again, and stepped back, not wishing him to believe that she trembled because she was scared of him, or his talk of *fomors*.

'Never disbelieve that which you can't prove doesn't exist. Ireland is a land where magic and the miraculous have rivalled each other since Patrick came.' His hands shot out suddenly to seize her shoulders. 'You're cold!' He rammed her hard against him, enveloping her in his arms. 'Frozen little Englishwoman, you need my warmth.'

She struggled violently. 'I don't need anything from you, except to know what you have done with Robin.' Yet, as she resisted, her weariness was as overpowering as his presence.

'Forget your kinsman—he'll come to no harm. Think of yourself. It is too dark now even for me to find a way. We'll have to spend the night by the bog till dawn. It would be warmer and safer if we stayed together.' His breath warmed her forehead, stirring her hair.

'Stay with you! Do you think I'm mad?' She fought against the cold and the tiredness that gripped her, forcing her head upright.

'You are mad if you think you can last the night without my help.'

'I don't trust you.' Her voice was muffled. 'My husband was killed by the Irish here in the hills.'

'You are a widow, then, not an innocent? So why balk at spending the night with me? Because, whether you trust me or not, you have no choice. My mantle... you took it?' He released her abruptly, so that she almost fell.

'On my mare.' She swayed, completely disorientated in the cold blackness.

'Call her, then.'

Shivering now without his warmth, Constance sought to penetrate the darkness. 'Maeve, come to me, my lovely!' A whinny sounded, sending warmth flooding through her. She continued to call, and suddenly there was a damp furry nose against her shoulders. Tears pricked her eyes, and a great lump clogged her throat.

'Good girl!' She felt his hand brush her shoulder and the next moment the warmth of the mantle was about her and he was close to her again. 'You have given your horse the name of an Irish queen—why?'

'Because-she-is-Irish-and-has-the-heart-of-a-queen.'

'That's a good enough answer. But you need something else to warm you. I have a small flask of whiskey. You have tasted whiskey?'

'Once. My—my husband's father g—gave me some.'

'He has lived in Ireland?'

'Once—a long time ago.' She started as his fingers brushed her cheek.

'Here, drink this.' The flask touched the side of her mouth. She reached up and took it. His fingers covered hers, steadying the flask as she sipped cautiously. 'He is Anglo-Irish, perhaps?'

'He was.' A spasm of coughing took her as the fiery liquid hit the back of her throat, and she thrust the flask away.

'No! You must drink some more.' He thrust it back at her. 'It is the best remedy I know for warding off the cold.'

'Then I shall drink,' she responded, adding to herself; Then, perhaps, I shall not long for your warmth so much in this desolate place.

'Good.' There seemed to be a smile in his voice. 'Your husband's father? He is dead?'

'Mmm!' She swallowed a mouthful of the liquid. It tasted vile.

'And your husband, he is dead also?'

'Ay.' Another mouthful burned its way down her throat.

'Then why are you here in Ireland?'

'You ask a lot of questions, Master Barbarian!' She held the flask out to him, thrusting it against his chest, which was only a few inches away. 'And I told you earlier that my husband was killed.'

'To be sure you did.' He took the flask.

'I did!' she exclaimed, the mockery in his tone angering her.

'So you did. Who was your husband?' The words murmured so close to her ear caused her to step back. 'Why are you in Ireland?'

'Questions ... questions! Why do you ask so many questions?' she said rather breathlessly.

'Because I want answers.' He moved closer again. 'And if you want to see your kinsman alive again, it would serve him best if you satisfied my curiosity.'

'You—You will not kill him, surely?'

'Sweet Jesu, woman, I'm not a barbarian! But my kinsmen have no love for the English.'

She clutched at his tunic. 'You must not let them harm him! My father would pay a ransom. Believe me! It is my fault he has been captured. I it was, who persuaded him to come with me to seek my husband's estate.'

'Your husband's estate?' His fingers toyed with hers.

'My husband, Milo de Wensley.' She winced as his fingers tightened suddenly. 'I have come to claim what is mine now. Does that satisfy your curiosity enough?'

CHAPTER TWO

'WELL ENOUGH,' the Irishman said lightly, his grip on Constance's fingers slackening. 'But it is cold and the night is coming. I consider my mantle should be shared between us.'

'A—And how do you—consider we should do—that?' Her throat was suddenly dry, and her head spun slightly.

'Well, I did not propose to tear it down the middle! I thought that we could wrap ourselves in it and make ourselves comfortable on the ground. We would not do too badly that way.' His arms went round her before she could move away.

Her heart began to beat uncomfortably fast. 'I—I'm not sure that's a good plan.'

'Is it that you're a craven after all, Mistress de Wensley? I give you my word that you can trust me. The word of an Irish barbarian.' His hands were beneath the mantle round her waist. 'What say you?'

'I suspect I have no choice.' His closeness was having a peculiar effect on her knees. She felt quite weak, and had to clutch at his tunic again.

'Of course you have a choice. Either you share my mantle with me—or you sleep alone without it.' He was pulling it about him now, and there was room enough for both of them.

A garment big enough to fit rogues and vagabonds—where had she heard that before? Her eyes closed, since trying to see his expression in the dark made her feel as if she were swaying. 'That is no choice,' she murmured, 'and I do not trust you, barbarian!'

'You expect me to behave like a barbarian?'

'Ay,' she whispered, struggling against the lethargy enfolding her.

She felt as though she floated when he lowered her to the ground. Even the dampness caused her no real discomfort. The real Constance seemed to be separated from her body huddled close to his. When he kissed her, it was as though it were happening to someone else. It was a long time since that person had been kissed. Pictures drifted in and out of her mind; memories of Milo's father's tales mingling with stories of old Ireland—of *fomor* and the Fiann, devils and men. She awoke for a moment, and moaned softly when his lips teased her nipple. He hushed her and kissed her hungrily. For an instant her mouth clung to his, and she was remembering the dreams she used to have about the old heroes of Ireland. They were poets, who knew magic. They had the choice of the prettiest girls in the settlements, and this man was a warrior who had chosen her as his mate. Their kisses became quite frantic and she no longer felt cold. They were lying in a golden meadow and he was whispering words of love. How long since she had been loved? She reached up and brought his face down; she could not see him properly, but her fingers could feel the outline of his nose, and his lips, before they claimed hers. Then they were moving in harmony together like horses galloping across the meadow towards the sun. She gasped with delight as the sun came out suddenly in a blaze of golden glory. It was quite unbelievably blissful. Afterwards, they were at peace, her head resting on his chest. Legend said much about the Fiann warriors. She dreamed that the Irishman fought for her, challenging the demon that haunted the bog. It carried a huge sickle, which it swung so threateningly that she awoke with a start.

Pale stars gleamed overhead, and the grey of dawn was in the east. The faintest light gleamed on little brown streams that trickled running paths through the treacherous ground. She sat up, shivering as the mantle slipped from her shoulders. Pulling it more closely about her, she looked for its owner, but there was no sign of him, or of her mare. She peered in a frantic circle about her. Now that the mists had evaporated, she could see the Wicklow Hills as clearly as though stamped in wax. Had he gone back to them, riding her horse? Fury erupted inside her and she scrambled to her feet.

When the mantle slipped to the ground, she became aware of the state of her clothing. It was stained, and reeked of the bog, and she was still damp. Something felt wrong! Her hand went to her breast to discover that all the buttons were in the wrong holes. Earlier a silver button had worked loose, and she had placed it in her pouch. With shaking fingers she refastened the buttons as hot colour stained her cheeks. What had happened last night? Her heart felt as if a hand squeezed it. Where was that barbarian with her mare? Where was Robin? Why had she been left alone here? What *had* those dreams of heroes and monsters fighting meant? And there was more—she was sure there had been more!

Her fears still gripped her, but as she watched the sun turning the brown streams orange and pink and gold, another picture came into her mind. She compressed her trembling lips. A kiss he had asked for saving her life— for rescuing her from a demon. Had he taken more? Her fists clenched. She had been defenceless, so had he taken advantage of her lack of resistance? What was the good of standing still, wondering what had happened. There was nothing she could do at present to right any wrong against her person.

Help! She had to get help for Robin. How far was the town Master Upton, the guide, had mentioned? If she could find her way there, she would be able to secure help from the authorities. Her eyes searched the ground. She could not rid her thoughts of the barbarian. There were hoofprints in the damp earth, and her gaze followed them, like a muddle in one area, before they became more distinct and easy to follow. She began to walk, hoping they might lead her to the road. She headed towards a mound, skirting the bog, but the prints took her not up the slope, rather round it; and then, treading carefully through undergrowth for a moment, she lost the trail, before finding it again in a patch of mud. Through some trees she went and then across a damp meadow. In the distance, she caught the gleam of water.

Slowly she walked towards the river, but there was nobody there, and the trail stopped. Perhaps the mare had crossed the water? She gave a sigh, and sank down on the river bank. How quiet it was, as though the whole landscape had been deserted by man! She was thirsty and filthy, and would have a drink, and wash as much as she was able.

Discarding her cote-hardie, she placed the mantle on the bank beneath a group of willows. Her stockings were ruined, as were her shoes, and she put them in a clump of nettles, long dead, and not yet growing fully. In the shadow of the willows, she entered the water in her shift. She gasped with cold as the water deepened, but she determined to rid herself of the stench of the bog.

She was rinsing her hair when the noise of a horse's hoofs sounded. Her breath caught, and she ducked below a budding branch as she watched the rider dismount. With a heavily beating heart, she drew into the shade of a willow trunk. Had he seen her? Obviously not, because he was dragging off his tunic. He glanced left and right, and peeled off his trews. The muscles in his thighs tautened as he waded into the water. He washed himself in the river, moisture glistening in his hair, darkening its fairness and causing it to curl riotously.

She wondered why she stayed to watch him, but only when the cold penetrated afresh and she heard her mare shifting did she realise that now was her opportunity to regain her property. Stealthily she pulled herself up the bank, wishing that it had been summer and the willows in full leaf.

She dried herself sketchily on his mantle, her eyes never leaving his naked back, which she could still glimpse through the branches when he stood up. She stripped off the wet shift beneath the mantle and pulled on her cote-hardie with trembling fingers, before dragging his mantle more securely about her and fastening it with the brooch. Her bare feet made no sound as she made her way to where her mare cropped the sparse grass. When Maeve lifted her head, and whinnied, Constance's heart seemed to calm its beating as the man slowly turned in the water.

His eyes narrowed, holding her gaze in a frozen trance. 'By all that's holy,' he murmured, 'how did you get here?'

She stirred, and her hand reached for the bridle. 'I walked, barbarian, following your tracks. Unlike you, horse-thief!'

'You were sleeping, so I—I only borrowed her.' He began to wade towards her.

'You took advantage of my defencelessness!' she accused him, her cheeks flushing.

He stilled in the water, and his eyes, which had never left her face, sharpened their gaze. 'So far, you have punched me on the jaw; tried to knock me senseless with a rock; slapped my face...'

'You slapped me first,' she cried indignantly.

'You punched my face!'

'What did you expect me to do—to lie back and let you have your way with me?'

'There was no danger of that then. I wanted you for a hostage, but we have your kinsman now.' His eyes gleamed with unexpected amusement. 'See, had you not fought me—and your kinsman knocked me senseless for a moment, you would have spent the night differently.'

Heat flooded her body at the look in his eyes, and her hands curled into fists. 'You are despicable! You forced me against my will! You are all that I hate and despise in a man!'

His smile vanished. 'I exerted no force—but *you* don't want to believe that.' He began to move again towards her. 'This morning, I went early to make certain your kinsman was safe and well so that I could reassure you, and I was on my way back to you with that news—but I ought not to have bothered. I should have let you worry and fret about him.'

'I have only your word for that! More likely, you hoped, I would wander in the bog and be swallowed up by that—that *fomor* you spoke about.' Her eyes flashed dark fire. 'If you were in such haste to reassure me, why stop here to bathe?' He was silent. 'You have no answer,' she mocked triumphantly. 'Ha! You must think me a fool!'

'You are, if you would make an enemy of me, Mistress de Wensley,' he snapped. 'Why have you been in the river? I see that your hair is wet.'

'To wash. I,' she paused, 'reeked—of the bog.'

'Ay,' he said grimly. 'And I did not let that prevent me from keeping you warm.'

'Oh!' She stamped her foot, and felt like screaming. 'That is your excuse for what you did?'

'What *we* did,' he said, emphasising the 'we'.

'No!' she screamed. He was almost at the bank, and panic seized her. Swiftly she picked up his clothes and dropped them in the water. Turning on her heel, she pulled herself up on Maeve's back, shutting out the noise of his curses and the splashing. She pressed her knees into her flanks, and left him clutching his wet garments to his chest as he waded out of the river.

Constance rode towards the mound, but when she reached it, she could not remember whether it was left or right she had come, so she chose left, and came out into a different place. She was in a narrow valley where cattle grazed, and there were signs of cultivation. Horses stood in a meadow not far from a small settlement. Near the centre of the valley, on her side, was clustered a group of buildings, some small and conical, but the largest was rectangular. Something about the scene reminded her of her Yorkshire home, and she swallowed a sudden tightness in her throat as a wave of homesickness swept over her. Then she squared her shoulders and started to ride towards the houses.

As Constance neared the buildings, two huge hounds came bounding towards her, followed by a girl. Her hands tightened on the reins, but when the girl called the dogs, they came to an abrupt halt. She approached swiftly, stopping a yard or so in front of her. When she spoke, it was in lilting Irish, which nevertheless did not conceal the warm welcome in her voice. Her braids were fair and her face dusted with freckles. The wide blue eyes fringed with thick gold lashes smiled at her.

Relief flooded through Constance. She felt as if she had found a friend, although the girl could not have been more than seventeen, and she seemed to speak no English.

'I don't understand,' said Constance, smiling.

The girl's heavy brows drew together and she moved closer, and spoke in French. 'What are you doing here? We do not have many visitors, so you are more than welcome.'

'Thank you,' murmured Constance, dismounting. 'I am seeking help. I was lost by the bog last night and had to spend the night there. I need to find the nearest town. Perhaps you can help me?'

The girl sucked in her cheeks and nodded. 'Of course, but you must come in. My elder sister and I were about to break our fast. If you have spent the night in the open, you must be hungry.' She seemed to look beyond Constance, and she turned round swiftly, thinking that perhaps the barbarian had already caught up with her, but there was nobody there.

'You are alone?' asked the girl in surprise.

'Last night—last evening,' she amended quickly, 'I wasn't. I was with a group of travellers, among whom was my kinsman. We were attacked, and they escaped—but he was captured. In the mist, I lost my way.'

Sympathy filled the girl's face. 'You must be cold and hungry. There is a fire lit inside—come and warm yourself.'

Constance's eyes filled with tears at her kind words, and she followed her in, leaving Maeve tearing at the grass in front of the house. A fire burned in the centre of a long narrow hall. Over it, with a spoon in her hand, stood a girl, her dark thick braids dangling either side of her rosy cheeks. She stared with suspicion at Constance, who was immediately aware of her animosity.

'Perhaps I have come at the wrong time?' she said to the girl at her side.

'Of course you haven't. Brigid is always wary of strangers since our foster-brother went back to the hills.' She spoke swiftly to her sister, who answered her sharply before beckoning Constance forward. A stool was placed for her in front of the fire.

'You will have some porridge?' Already Brigid was ladling it into bowls set upon a plank on the floor.

'Thank you.' Constance lowered herself on the stool. Her body was aching, and she was glad to stretch her legs towards the warmth of the fire. She listened as the fair girl told her sister how she had got lost in the mist and that her kinsman had been taken.

'You saw the men who took your kinsman?' asked Brigid.

'Only one of them.' Constance hesitated, before adding, 'He rescued me when I fell in the bog.' She lowered her eyes to the bowl of porridge as Brigid handed it to her.

'Honey?' asked the younger girl, smiling down at her.

'Yes, please.' Constance held the bowl gingerly on her knee. 'What is your name?'

'Kathleen,' she said, spooning a generous dollop onto Constance's porridge. 'And yours?'

'Constance.' She looked up. 'Your sister is Brigid, you say? My dead husband's father spoke of Saint Brigid, telling me of her generous spirit. I do thank both of you for your kindness.'

'You are a widow?' Brigid paused in the act of taking the jar of honey from Kathleen. 'That is sad. You have children?'

'No.' Constance bent over her bowl. Her childlessness had been a bone of contention between Milo and herself. According to him, the fault had lain with her.

'That is also sad,' whispered Kathleen. 'Your husband was English?'

'Anglo-Irish.' Constance dipped her spoon into the porridge and supped the oats. They tasted slightly toasted, and she recalled hearing of the Irish custom of burning the oats in the straw to separate the grain from the chaff. 'My husband had land over here; now it is mine.' Her brow clouded. 'I must not forget Robin, my kinsman. I must go to the nearest town to seek help.' She stood abruptly. 'I don't know what I'm thinking of, sitting here and eating, when Robin's life could be in danger,' she whispered in a strangled voice. 'I must go.'

'Surely you have time to eat,' soothed Kathleen, patting her arm. 'And if your kinsman has been captured, it is likely that his life is in no danger. They will hold him as a hostage.'

'That is true.' Constance sat down again. 'That barbarian who rescued me told me that was so.' She took a spoonful of porridge, although she suddenly had little appetite for it.

'This—this man, he told you that?' said Brigid. 'And he allowed you to go free?'

Constance was suddenly still, her cheeks flushed. 'I escaped him.'

'Escaped?' The two girls gazed at her, noting her embarrassment.

'He did not hurt you?' enquired Kathleen in a gentle voice.

'No, he did not hurt me,' she replied quietly, toying with her spoon.

'If he did not hurt you, then all is well,' said Brigid. 'Where was it you were going?'

Constance lifted her head from her contemplation. 'Naas.'

'It is not so far,' said Kathleen, her face brightening. 'I could show you the way.'

'Would you?' Constance's voice was eager. 'I would appreciate that kindness.'

Kathleen nodded. 'But you must eat your porridge first, for it will do you good.'

As Constance obeyed, her eyes roamed the hall. If only, last night, she had known this place was here, she might have been able to reach it. It was a nice hall, although in need of refurbishment. The walls must have once been whitewashed, but now they were blackened with the smoke of winter fires. Against the wall opposite stood a large wide wooden bed. There was a chest, and crowded on the floor were wooden and earthenware vessels. In a far corner she could see a hand-loom and what she thought was a distaff. Beyond that it was difficult to be certain about anything, because the two small windows were at the front of the house.

Had the barbarian known it was here? It was probable, if he knew the area. Perhaps he might be seeking the help of his companions in the hills, although the wetness of his clothing and the lack of a horse might make that difficult. A slight smile curved her mouth. Even so, later in the day, it was possible that he could come here to seek her. She put the empty bowl on the floor.

'I think I should go now.' There was an air of determination about her. 'That man might come here, and I would not like you to be placed in an awkward position because of me. Your parents...'

'Our parents are dead,' said Kathleen. 'Mother died several years ago, and our father fell from a horse and was killed last autumn. If Niall were here, he might be able to help you because he spends more time in the hills now. Niall is our foster-brother.'

'Even so, I think I should go.' Constance straightened her girdle, which she had fastened about the mantle.

Brigid watched her, a frown on her face. 'You say your husband was Anglo-Irish, yet you speak like an Englishwoman—and not one accustomed to this part of Ireland.'

'I'm newly come from England—and I'm thinking that perhaps I should have stayed there,' she added with a touch of humour.

'Perhaps you should,' said Brigid coolly, picking up her bowl from the floor.

Although Constance was a little taken aback, she did not allow her discomfiture to show on her face, but held out her hand to Brigid. 'I am grateful for the food and shelter. I only pray that I shall be able to obtain help from the authorities in Naas, and that I am quickly reunited with Robin—my kinsman.'

'Let us hope so.' Brigid, ignoring Constance's proffered hand, walked away with the bowls.

Kathleen touched Constance's arm, and smiled. 'Come. I must pick a horse that will be a match for that beautiful creature you have outside.'

The embarrassed flush faded from Constance's face. At least this sister was friendly and did not seem to mind her being English. Quickly she went with her outside.

After a few minutes, they were followed by Brigid, but it was not until the two girls were mounted that she spoke. 'This man—how was it that you managed to escape him and your kinsman did not?'

He lost me in the mist,' Constance lied in a cool voice, before nodding her head in farewell and turning her horse's head.

Kathleen kicked her horse into motion, an expression of suppressed excitement on her face. 'Let's be on our way before my sister can think of an excuse to stop me from helping you,' she whispered.

'Why should she? Perhaps she would have liked to come with us?' murmured Constance.

Kathleen shook her head. 'She hates the English and their towns!' She waved vigorously to Brigid, and then the horses moved away swiftly.

Brigid stood, watching them grow smaller and smaller. Suddenly a hand dropped hard on her shoulder, and she whirled round and stared up at her foster-brother.

'Who was that?' he demanded harshly.

Brigid stared at him in astonishment. 'Kathleen, and an Englishwoman who came here for help. Why are your clothes so wet?'

'Never mind that now,' he rasped, a pulse beating rapidly near the thin white scar next to his eye. 'Is she dark-haired and brown-eyed—and beautiful?'

She thought. 'If you are a man, I suppose she might appear beautiful, but I did not consider her so.'

'Her name is de Wensley,' he said in carefully controlled tones. 'De Wensley, sister. And when I catch up with her, she'll rue the day she tried to get the better of Niall O'More.'

'De Wensley!' exclaimed Brigid in an incredulous voice. 'What is she doing here?'

'She's looking for her estate,' he replied brusquely. 'Where has she gone with Kathleen?'

'To Naas. To seek help to regain her kinsman.' Brigid folded her arms and stared at him. 'How do you know she's a de Wensley?' She paused. 'It wasn't you who....'

Faint colour tinged Niall's high cheekbones. 'What did she tell you?'

'That a man rescued her from a bog—then lost her in the mist.' She eyed him suspiciously. 'It's not like *you* to lose anyone! And what is this about her kinsman being taken as a hostage?'

'We needed someone to exchange for Dermot,' he murmured, pushing away the wolfhound attempting to lick his face. 'And wasn't it right that I should rescue the woman?'

'It would be the kind of chivalrous act you would perform—but I presume that was before you knew who she was.' Her expression darkened. 'We don't want her here, Niall, interfering and changing everything. We had plans...' She wrapped her hands round his arm.

'*You* had plans.' He pulled his arm out of her grasp. 'You'll just have to change them.'

'But couldn't you get rid of her?' Her rosy face was sulky.

Niall loosed an impatient breath. 'And how do you suggest I do that?'

She smiled slyly. 'You could always drop her in another bog!'

His expression was suddenly still. 'You sound like Sil. You haven't been seeing him again?'

A peculiar expression flashed in her eyes. 'Of course not! He—he frightens me. But he—he won't be pleased about your having a hostage to exchange for Dermot.'

'No?' Niall's mouth took on a mutinous twist and he tossed back his wet hair. 'Haven't you realised yet that I'll never be cowered by my cousin's dark powers, despite this?' He touched his scar. 'Dermot is the man who will be the leader after his father dies—and he is the one to stand up to Sil.'

'What are you going to do then?' asked Brigid irritably.

His pale grey eyes were suddenly bright. 'Go after her.'

'Why?' There was suspicion in her face again. 'How was it that she escaped you? I would have thought...'

'Don't think, sister,' he said softly. 'Mistress de Wensley is a resourceful woman, and not to be underestimated.' He squeezed her shoulder. 'Now I must find some dry clothes.' Turning, he went into the house, praying that some of his old clothes were still in the chest.

Now that the walls of Naas could be seen rising ahead, Constance began to wonder if she would be stopped at the gate. She knew that it was illegal to ride without stirrups in the Irish manner; just as it was forbidden to speak the Irish tongue and to wear their style of dress, although she had heard that many among the English occupants of the English-held towns defied the law. As it was, the guards at the gate paid her scant attention, being involved in a heated argument with a couple of men with a cart. Kathleen called a greeting, and one of them waved, and they passed through into the town.

Constance looked about her curiously, and the younger girl leaned towards her. 'Once this was the centre of the Irish kingdom of the Ui Dunlainge and their successors—long before the coming of the Normans—or even the Norsemen. Now it is a frontier fortress town for the English.'

'It looks like it,' murmured Constance, gazing up at the castle. There were men-at-arms going about their affairs, and officials and priests hurrying hither and thither. Her heart lifted. Maybe Master Upton, the man appointed by her father's agent to guide them from Dublin, would still be here.

'Niall could tell you much about our past. It is a pity he is not with us,' Kathleen said regretfully.

'You are fond of your foster-brother?' Constance asked with the barest hint of curiosity.

'I love him,' answered Kathleen simply, 'as if he were my blood brother.' Her eyes shone. 'When Niall is around, life is never dull! Lately, he is not home often, but in the hills guarding his captain's borders since his cousin Dermot was taken. He lives by hunting and warfare now.' She added in a conspiratorial whisper, 'Although he sometimes puts his freedom in danger by daring to do what many men would not, entering the towns of the English to discover what King Richard and his lords are about. He has been to Dublin, and was captured once, but he escaped.'

'I see,' murmured Constance drily. Really, Kathleen was taking a chance telling her all this about her re-sourceful foster-brother! 'How was it that he came to live with your family?'

Kathleen wrinkled her nose. 'His mother was a cousin of my mother. They were both O'Tooles. I do not know the whole story, only that Niall's mother took the veil after his father died, and he and his brother Dougal came to live with my family. I was not born then. My father was Anglo-Irish, serving as—what would you say?—a steward to an English milord, who left Ireland years ago, even before Brigid was born. Father had plans for Niall to take his place, as he had no son, not only as steward but also with the horses.'

'Horses?'

'Horses were my father's first love. He bred and reared them, and even went to the great fairs in England and Italy to sell them, when he could. It is a great pity that Niall went to the hills not long after Father was killed, because, like the Fiann of old, he has a rare gift when it comes to handling animals.'

'Perhaps he will return.'

'Brigid hopes so. She has plans for them both, although I do not think that Niall feels for her the way she does for him. He looks upon her as he does upon me—as a sister.'

'Well, I pray that Brigid gets what she wants,' said Constance, losing interest in the foster-brother. 'Where should I go first? To the castle—or in search of the party I travelled with yesterday?'

'I could direct you to the finest lodging-house,' replied Kathleen happily.

'Then do so.' She was a little surprised that Kathleen was no stranger to the town, having thought that there would not be such familiarity with the English, but it seemed that English and Irish mixed quite well, when they wanted to.

It was as she looked along the crowded streets that she saw a man she recognised. She uttered a cry, and was glad when he turned and came towards them.

CHAPTER THREE

'MASTER BRANDON, how glad I am to see you!' Relieved to see a familiar face, Constance employed more warmth in her tones than she would normally use to address a man she had met only three days before.

The man's green eyes gleamed as he took her extended hand, to hold it between his own. 'No more glad than I am to see you, Mistress Constance! I considered you to be in the clutches of the native Irish, and lost to us.'

'Fortunately I escaped, sir.' Her brow clouded. 'But my kinsman was taken. I fear they hold him to exchange for a hostage in English hands.'

'That is unfortunate, indeed!' He pressed her hand gently. 'They told you that much before you escaped?'

She gave a brief shake of her head. 'The barbarian who first captured me did so, but I escaped from him to a family who showed me great kindness. Now I am uncertain what to do next.'

'Surely there is little you can do but wait for them to contact those who have charge of the hostages? But I know little of these matters.' He released her hand to ease the high curled neck of the scarlet houppelande he wore. Its bagpipe sleeve brushed her knee.

'There must be something I can do?' She bit her lip, and her eyes were suddenly moist with tears. 'A—A way of discovering just where they hold him? Surely there must be some way of contacting the tribesmen that hold Robin a prisoner?'

He stared hard at her, seeming to hesitate before saying, 'Perhaps. But you must be hungry—and your apparel...' His eyes ran swiftly over her. 'You will surely wish to change it?'

She grimaced. 'I wandered into a bog! I had hopes of finding Master Upton and my baggage here.'

He reassured her quickly. 'Master Upton is here.'

She smiled in delight. 'Well, that's a relief! But you said "perhaps". Does that mean that there is something I can do?'

'It is possible. But first let us adjourn this conversation until we have had food and drink, and you can take possession of your baggage.' Lowering his voice, he added, 'Who is this girl?'

Constance clapped a hand to her cheek. 'It is Kathleen, who has been of great help to me. She speaks no English, only French and Irish, but she has been a true friend.'

'Here, girl,' he called in French, tossing Kathleen a coin, which she caught deftly. 'You may go.' He turned to Constance, placing his hands about her waist and smiling up at her. 'You will come down? Because really, Mistress Constance, I cannot continue to converse with you in such a manner.'

'Of course I understand that, Master Brandon, but allow me first to thank Kathleen.' She gasped as he swung her down, not certain whether she liked his presumption.

'You have but a moment, my dear Mistress Constance.' His searching stare was bold. 'I must travel on today, and if you desire my help, we must talk while we eat.'

With some reluctance she turned to Kathleen to thank her, before bidding her farewell.

'It was a pleasure,' responded the girl in a cheery voice. She raised a hand, and soon had disappeared in the crowds that mingled in the street.

Constance stared after her until she was roused by Master Brandon's hand on her sleeve. 'Come, I cannot delay much longer.' He already had Maeve's reins in his grasp. She nodded, and went with him.

On reaching the lodging house, Master Brandon called sharply to an ostler lounging against a wall, who slowly came over. 'You will take good care of this horse, and see if you can find the lady a saddle.'

He nodded, his gaze ranging over Maeve, and the expression on his thin face brightened. 'From Connemara is she, mistress?' addressing Constance.

'I believe her sire was.' She smiled. 'You will see that she is fed and watered, and clean the mud off her?'

'Surely, 'twould be an honour.' He gave her a wide grin.

'Half Irish,' said Master Brandon disparagingly, as he led the way through an open doorway. 'They're mad about horseflesh, as you'll discover if you still intend settling over here.'

They entered a small low-pitched room, which was unoccupied except for the maid sweeping the floor with a besom, and a man of enormous girth sitting on a bench against a wooden wall. He looked up at their entering, and his jowls quivered as he chomped his jaws before speaking. 'Mistress de Wensley, you are here!' His voice expressed his astonishment.

'Master Upton.' She inclined her head, coming to a halt in front of him. 'I trust you have my baggage safe?'

He bumbled to his feet. 'Of course, of course. And Master Milburn, where is he?' His gaze reached beyond her to the doorway.

'He is a prisoner of the native Irish,' Master Brandon answered before she could answer. 'But you may fetch Mistress de Wensley's baggage, for she has need of it, Upton.'

The man bowed and nodded. 'Right away. I will fetch it right away.' His small round eyes went from his face to hers, and back again. 'You want it down here?'

'Of course, man, damn you!' exclaimed Master Brandon in vexed tones. 'She wishes to ascertain that it is all there.'

Constance saw the man flush, and she stayed him with her hand. 'It is upstairs, Master Upton?'

'Ay, mistress. In the tiny chamber Master Brandon and I had to share,' he said hurriedly. 'I will fetch it, and you shall see that not even a riband is missing.'

'There is no need.' She faced Brandon. 'If you will excuse me, I shall take this opportunity to change my clothes.'

There was a brief pause before he nodded, and his thin mouth lengthened. 'Of course. I shall order us some food and wine. You will not delay?'

She forced a smile. 'I shall make all speed.' She turned to Master Upton. 'You will show me the way?'

He chomped his jaws, nodded several times, and lumbered across the room with amazing speed for one of his girth. She followed swiftly, having to slow down only when they reached the stairs to give him time to hoist himself up the steep ascent.

The chamber turned out to be as tiny as Master Upton had hinted, being only a small space behind a partition in a larger room. In a corner was what she supposed was Master Brandon's baggage. Beneath the window stood hers and Robin's. She hurried over to it, making room for Master Upton's bulk.

'There it is, mistress, and not a riband or a pin missing,' he wheezed.

'I do not doubt your honesty, Master Upton.' She removed her pallet from on top, setting it down on the floor.

'That Master Brandon,' he declared indignantly, 'giving himself airs and graces! He might be a messenger for the Earl of March, but he's only a servant like me.'

'That is true,' she said gravely, seeing beyond his irate manner to the hurt beneath. 'I'm sure he did not intend to offend you.'

'That he did,' he said indignantly. 'Him and his peculiar shoes! A man in his position shouldn't be wearing the like. Fancies his chances, he does.'

Constance sought to hide a smile. 'They are out of the ordinary, but very fashionable at court—so my father says.'

'That's as maybe, but Master Brandon's no lord, for all he'd like to be. You be careful of him, Mistress de Wensley. I wouldn't be doing my duty by your father's agent in Dublin if I didn't warn you that he has some strange friends.'

Constance's smile faded. 'I think you have said enough, Master Upton. Master Brandon's friends are his own affair. All this, because he wears pointed shoes!'

'Extremely long, pointed shoes,' muttered Upton, his jowls wobbling.

She suddenly lost patience, feeling inexpressibly weary. 'What does that matter?' she snapped. 'You will leave me now, for I wish to change my gown.'

He nodded, opened his mouth tentatively, then shut it again and left her alone. She frowned as she watched him go. He really was an unusual type to have as a guide, but he had come recommended as trustworthy by her father's agent. What had he meant about Master Brandon's friends? She stared unseeingly out of the window before shaking herself and beginning to undress as she moved away.

She chose a green gown of fustian and, to wear over it, an old favourite cote-hardie of scarlet—the elbow-length wider sleeves of which showed the green of the tight-fitting sleeves of the gown. It was with relief that she found some shoes of soft red leather with pointed toes—but which were not as pointed or long as Master Brandon's. His were so long that they had to be tied to bands about his calves to prevent them from tripping him up!

She sat on her baggage, a comb in her hand, pondering on Master Upton's words, and remembering the first time she had seen Master Brandon. He had worn a blue houppelande cut extremely short so that it barely covered his buttocks. Since it was tight fitting and padded with a high curled-over neck, which came just below his bobbed reddish hair, one could not help noticing him. His slender legs had been clad in scarlet hose—his shoes had also been red. He was nice-looking rather than handsome, with well defined features. His nose was a trifle long and thin.

She caught herself up, realising how carefully she had detailed so much about him. How different he was from the man who had rescued her from the bog after chasing her! How different from the man she had watched sporting in the river! She found herself remembering how intense his grey eyes were, and the fullness of his mouth—the feel of it as it had claimed her lips—the way his hair curled about his head, and the strength in his legs and the broadness of his shoulders. She shook herself. This would not do: he was a rogue, and—worse than a rogue—a man who would not accept responsibility for his actions. Her cheeks burned. Cast him out of your mind, Constance, with all that he accused you of! She slotted him and Master Brandon neatly into the back of her mind, before bundling her discarded clothing in a corner. Only the barbarian's mantle did she set apart. She sat on her baggage and began to undo her untidy braids.

Her fingers worked quickly, and it was not long before she had combed and rebraided her hair. It was as she was fastening their ends with scarlet ribands that she glanced out of the window. Her hand stilled, and she drew back swiftly, her heart seeming to leap into her throat. Cautiously she peered out of the window, feeling the slightest breeze cooling her hot cheeks. It was he! She would recognise that stance anywhere. There was arrogance in every line of him—from the tilt of his tawny head to the way his feet firmly trod the ground. But who was that he was talking to? Ah, the ostler who had taken change of Maeve. She heard another voice joining the conversation: a girl's voice. She leaned a little further, trying to see who it was, and as she did so, the riband slipped from her fingers and fluttered to the ground.

The movement caught Niall's eye, and his head slewed round. They stared at one another in a moment of awareness that seemed to last an age. Then she leaned back swiftly, wondering, with a heavily beating heart, how he had found her and what she feared he could do to her here in an English-occupied town. It was not as though she were alone or defenceless.

'Mistress de Wensley, may I speak with you?' His dulcet tones caused her to flatten herself against the wall. 'Mistress de Wensley, let us not play games! We have seen each other, and I only wish to speak to you. Come to the window, if you please.'

Slowly she did as he requested, looking down on his upturned face. He smiled, so that the creases at the corners of his grey eyes deepened and the scar zig-zagged into the laughter lines. Unexpectedly, her knees trembled and she had to grip the window-ledge tightly.

'Kathleen told me that you are still anxious about your kinsman. I come to reassure you that nothing will happen to harm him. Once my cousin is freed, so will your kinsman be.'

'Kathleen?' she said in a low voice, and instantly she realised who he must be. 'You are her foster-brother?'

'Ay! Niall O'More, at your service.' He bowed.

'I don't consider myself in need of your services, Master—O'More,' she said coolly. 'Did Kathleen guide you to me.'

The girl, recognising her name, came forward. She beamed up at Constance as she put her hand through Niall's arm. 'He was concerned for you.'

'You surprise me,' she said drily. 'Concern for me, Master O'More—or for your own safety? I should leave this town, if I were you.' She brushed back her braids, which had fallen forward. 'But tell me, how are you after your sojourn in the river?'

His eyes sparkled, and his smile set rigidly. 'I should have left you in the bog for the *fomor* to delight in,' he said harshly.

She smiled sweetly. 'I told you, Master—O'More, that I don't believe in them, but there are other devils about ready to prey on a defenceless woman.'

'If you are referring to me,' he countered hotly, 'I would add that you are not defenceless, but more like a wild beast. A cat with claws unsheathed, ready to attack.'

'A cat doesn't attack unless—unless,' she was floundering, lost for words to parry his insult, 'unless it has to defend itself.'

'Nonsense!' A bark of laughter escaped him. 'Cats prey on creatures smaller than themselves, mauling them for pleasure before consuming them.'

Her eyebrows lifted. 'You are hardly smaller than me, sir. And if we are speaking of mauling...' She stopped abruptly, aware of Kathleen's upturned, puzzled face, and was glad that the girl could not understand English. What was she thinking of to bandy words with this Irishman?

'You were speaking of mauling, mistress,' he prompted, folding his arms across his chest, his eyes gleaming. 'Last night you were glad of my holding you, snuggling against me like a kitten does against its mother.'

She gasped indignantly. 'I was frozen—and, besides, I had little choice, if you remember!'

'I make no complaint, mistress.' His voice was suddenly as gentle and soothing as a caress. 'It was a night I'll never forget.' His gaze caught and held hers.

Constance was suddenly aware of the beating of her heart, and she remembered how he had whispered words of love. She swallowed. 'It was a night I would rather forget,' she replied acidly. 'Good day to you, Master O'More. And to you, Kathleen.' Withdrawing her head, she closed the shutters firmly.

She listened for a moment to the indistinct murmur of their voices, before finding another riband. Then she hurried downstairs, still agitated over what had occurred between Master O'More and herself.

Master Brandon, sitting on a bench alone, had already begun his meal. His eyes gazed at her over the rim of his cup, and she saw the admiration leap into them. It pleased her, remembering how she must have appeared earlier.

'You have been a long time,' he murmured, making room for her beside him. 'But it has been worth the wait.'

'I am gratified that you consider it so,' she said demurely, lowering her eyes to watch the manservant pour red wine into her cup.

'I consider you a beautiful woman.' He picked up a knife to carve a chunk of beef from the haunch on the table.

'You flatter me, sir.' She took a sip from her cup. 'That looks appetising.'

'Burnt on the outside, but raw within—just how I like it.' He placed the meat on a trencher in front of her. The juices ran on to the thick bread. 'You misjudge your own charms, and my honesty, if you consider that I speak insincerely. You are a woman that any man would be proud to have by his side.'

'Thank you.' She put down her cup, feeling the colour rise in her face. She was unaccustomed to such fulsome praise.

'It is the truth.' His hand rested on hers. 'I have been considering what is best to be done about your kinsman—and have come to a decision.'

'You have?' She withdrew her hand hurriedly, and taking up her knife, she spiked a chunk of meat adroitly. Was now the time to mention that Master O'More was close? But Master Brandon was speaking again.

'As you know, I am in the Earl of March's employment, and am even now on my way to Kilkenny to give into the king's hands a message from his heir. I also have a message for the Earl of Kildare, so will be stopping at Kilkea Castle. It is possible that the Earl of Desmond is staying there. You might have heard of both these noblemen?'

She nodded. 'They are members of the Gerald family.'

'You have them.' He sounded pleased. 'The Geralds, of course, are one of the oldest of the Anglo-Norman families over here, possessing much land and influence. Desmond has allies among the native Irish. It is possible that he might be able to help you.'

Constance dropped her knife, and her face brightened. 'But that is wonderful! Do you mean that he might be able to arrange matters so that an exchange could be achieved more swiftly?'

'It is possible. Do you have any notion which tribe holds Master Milburn?'

Her brow creased. 'It will be either the O'Tooles or the O'Mores. He said that his kinsmen held Robin.'

'He?' Master Brandon toyed with his cup, a sudden tenseness about his mouth.

'The man who captured me. His mother was an O'Toole, I believe. His father must be an O'More, because that is his name.'

He smiled, and she sensed that he was relieved. 'That should prove useful, knowing his name. You will come with me, then, to Kilkea Castle?'

She hesitated before saying, 'I would like to, only...'

'Only you fear that I might take advantage of my being of assistance to you?' His mouth formed a moue.

'I—I did not say that,' she murmured hurriedly. 'But we are barely acquainted, Master Brandon.'

'I would be better acquainted. Believe me when I say that my intentions are honourable,' he told her stiffly.

A man grunted behind her, and Constance was aware that the conversation was being listened to by the other occupants of the room because of the silence that now occurred. She did not know what to say.

'I—I offer my services with no other intention but to serve you—an Englishwoman in a foreign land.' Master Brandon's low voice filled the silence.

'I understand that,' she said carefully. 'I did not intend offending you. Of course I shall go with you. It is the wiser course, for what can I gain by staying here?'

His mouth lengthened, and picking up his cup, he held it high. 'You have made a wise choice, Mistress Constance. One that I'm sure you will not regret. To the future—and to our hopes—that they may come to fruition.'

She echoed his words, wondering as she did so just what it was exactly that he hoped for, and whether it concerned herself. The idea worried her slightly, but she had committed herself now. She would tell Master Upton to stay on here and take care of the baggage, and also ask him to set about the task of visiting her manor to prepare them for her coming. Had it not been he who had collected the dues on her husband's behalf after his father had died? For now, she must put such ponderings aside and concentrate on what to take with her.

Niall did not give Constance and Master Brandon a second glance, as they rose from the bench and weaved their way through the room. His curiosity was roused, having seen Brandon before in Dublin in company with Sil O'Toole. He fingered the scar on his face. It had been when Art, King of Leinster, and several of the other kings of Ireland had been honoured by the king of

England, and they had become English knights. Even then, Niall had puzzled over Sil keeping company with Brandon, when it was well known that he hated everything English. He would like to find out more about Brandon—and he would rather Mistress de Wensley was kept away from the Geralds, especially Desmond. One never knew with the earl, a generous man, who might take her part and help her. He must do something to prevent her leaving. He rose, and went outside.

As Constance entered the rear yard in company with Master Brandon, she was relieved to see that there was no sign of Niall or Kathleen. They entered the stable, and it was then she realised that Maeve was missing. She went over and checked each individual horse except for the one Master Brandon was saddling up, and then shouted, 'My horse has been stolen!'

'What are you talking about?' Master Brandon came over to her.

'My Maeve!' She punched the partition near to her. 'What a fool I was to believe that anything I possess is safe from him!'

'My dear Mistress Constance, whom are we talking about?'

'I saw him from the window,' she replied in a seething voice. 'We spoke. He reassured me that Robin would come to no harm, so I did not alert the authorities to his presence in this town. He is a common horse-thief—a scoundrel! He should be excommunicated.'

'Do we talk of the ostler?' he asked in a bewildered manner.

'No!' She folded her arms and leaned against the partition, her face stormy. 'We talk of Niall O'More, who would have held me captive.'

'You mean that he was here, and you never told me?' Master Brandon's hand went to her shoulder, gripping it tightly.

'That is exactly what I mean,' she said crossly. 'I thought that by the time I did so, he would be gone.' She shrugged off his hand.

He drew in a hissing breath. 'We could have alerted them at the gates, and prevented him from leaving the town.'

'Well, I am paying for my foolishness. We'll never catch him now.'

He shook his head. 'The ostler was in league with him perhaps?'

'Perhaps. It means that I cannot come with you now.'

He stroked his chin as he stared at her. 'How could he have known you came here, unless he followed you? Mark my words, you were lucky to escape him. He has an eye to your virtue.'

Constance remained silent, her hands tightly clasped in front of her. Only briefly had she sketched in the bones of the story of what had happened to her, and nothing of spending the night in Niall O'More's company.

'You cannot stay here,' Brandon went on. 'It is not safe. It were best you take Upton's horse. He can use the pony for his needs, and thus you can still come with me.'

'All right! I shall go with you,' she said impatiently, and wondered if she was making a mistake in not telling him of the connection between Kathleen and Niall O'More. But if she did, he might suggest going to the sheriff, who would call out whatever forces he held to badger the two sisters. She doubted that they could arrive unseen—and the horse-thief would be gone into the hills before they reached the house.

Brandon gripped her hand, and smiled. 'You have made a wise decision. In this way you'll thwart any plans he might have.'

'I pray so.' Her brow furrowed. 'I only hope Robin will not suffer for any of my mistakes.'

'Why should he?' He pressed her arm. 'If he is their hostage, they will not harm him.'

'I hope you are right. And I thank you for your concern.' She took a deep breath to steady herself. 'Which horse is Master Upton's?' she said brightly.

'Now you will do that for me, Master Upton?' Constance handed him some money.

'Ay, mistress.' He stared at her dubiously. 'But are you sure about the wisdom of going with this man?' He glanced furtively in Master Brandon's direction. 'You are barely acquainted with him.'

'I hardly know *you*, Master Upton,' she replied in icy tones as she pulled on her gloves. 'Yet, I am trusting you.'

'But I have been recommended.' He pocketed the money, his doleful eyes expressing his distress at her words. 'I wouldn't be doing right by your father if I didn't show concern.'

'I am not a child, Master Upton. For four years was I mistress of my own household,' she said with dignity. 'Now, if you do not mind, I will bid you farewell. If you are so concerned for me, pray that all my endeavours on Master Milburn's behalf will be successful.'

'That I shall—and I shall pray for your safety, too.' He stepped away from the horse. 'I'll have a mind, also, to keep my eyes open for that rogue who stole your mount.' He nodded his head vigorously, setting his jowls wobbling.

She could not help smiling wryly, wondering what he would have said if she told him who the rogue was—for surely he must know Kathleen's foster-brother? 'If you can do that, Master Upton,' she said at last, 'I shall be eternally grateful.' She settled herself as comfortably as she could in the saddle, fleetingly mourning the loss— not only of Maeve, but of her own saddle that Niall had unbuckled. 'But I don't doubt that he is miles away from here by now.' She lifted a hand, and then she and Master Brandon were gone.

Niall drew in a hissing breath as he watched them disappear down the street. He turned to Kathleen. 'You will tell Brigid that Mistress de Wensley is leaving Naas.' He led Maeve to the other end of the alley.

'You are going to follow them?' Her eyes sparkled. 'I wish I could go with you.'

'Well, you can't,' he muttered, glancing down at her. 'What is wrong with you, girl? Didn't I punish you enough for your last escapade? Promise me now that you will do as I ask.'

She hesitated, then nodded. 'Pat is to ride your horse home with me?'

He nodded. 'That's exactly right. And don't tell Brigid everything!'

'No, of course not!' She bit her lip guiltily. 'She would be vexed with you, and I can't abide her sulking. But why do you take Mistress Constance's horse?'

'I want to see the lady's face when we meet.' He grinned, and she smiled back.

'She will be vexed, and might have you clapped in gaol!'

'She'll be vexed, all right, but I doubt she has the power to have me put in gaol if it is only Desmond I have to contend with. Kildare is another matter, but he doesn't know my face.' He vaulted into the saddle. 'You go now and tell Pat.' He fished in his pouch, bringing out a coin which he handed to her. 'Go and treat yourself to whatever takes your fancy, but don't forget to do what I've told you.'

'I won't.' She clutched the coin tightly.

'You can also tell Pat, when he returns from escorting you home, that it should be safe for him to return to the inn.'

She nodded, and blew him a kiss, which he caught and blew back to her. As she vanished into the throng of passers-by, he shook his head slowly, before heading up the street towards the gateway. Already Brandon and Mistress de Wensley were out of sight, but because he knew their destination, he did not let that worry him. Perhaps he could get ahead by ways not know to them. He did not doubt that he would be able to gain entry to Kilkea Castle, and he was sure that Brandon and Mistress de Wensley could not reach there before nightfall.

He passed through the gates, and saw a group of riders a little way ahead. Probably among them would be Master Brandon and Mistress de Wensley. It was interesting that Desmond had been mentioned, because where Desmond was, one often found the native Irish gathering. If Sil O'Toole arrived there also...? Altogether, life was going to prove far from dull over the next few days. Perhaps it would never be tedious again, should Mistress de Wensley decide to stay in Ireland.

CHAPTER FOUR

As Constance gazed at the rolling expanse of fertile grassland, she experienced relief that she and Master Brandon were not travelling alone. Not because she feared attack from the natives—the Wicklow Hills were now well to the east, and they were heading south-west across the Curragh—but because, despite her words to Master Upton, what he had said had gone home. What she did know of Master Brandon was that he was English, he had a taste for flamboyant clothes, and that he was in the service of the Earl of March, heir to the king of England.

Her eyes wandered to his back, and as if conscious of that stare Master Brandon broke off his conversation with the man next to him and turned to her. 'You are weary, Mistress de Wensley?'

'Not at all,' she lied, of necessity causing the horse to increase its speed so that they drew closer. 'I was considering how well this country would suit horses.'

'You have an interest there?' His voice expressed surprise. 'I would have thought sheep...'

'Sheep are my father's business,' she broke in swiftly, 'and cloth is Robin's. I have lived and breathed sheep since I was born, and I have had enough of them. No, I would breed horses.'

'But if you wed again, surely it will be your husband's decision whether you use your land for horses or sheep?' His brows arched. 'Sheep are much more profitable.'

'I do not intend to wed again yet, Master Brandon,' she replied stiffly. 'It is not a year since my husband was killed.'

'I understand.' He spoke with feeling. 'But later—this is not the place for a woman alone. So much can be achieved by choosing the right husband or wife. Judicious marriages have helped many a family to become powerful. We have talked of the Gerald family, but there are also the Butlers. The Duke of Ormonde is descended from a hereditary butler of Ireland, and it is with Ormonde that the king stays in Kilkenny.' He paused, and she noticed how brightly his green eyes shone—like a cat's. 'My lord March is a great landowner—lord of Meath, Earl of Ulster and lord of Connacht who is now heir to Richard's throne. When the king leaves this country, he will be Lieutenant of Ireland, but if Richard were to die tomorrow, he would be king of all England.' He paused to draw breath. 'It is an awesome thought,' he added unevenly, 'to consider that one day I could be a member of the king of England's household.'

'Then you would not be staying in Ireland, Master Brandon,' she said forcibly, somewhat taken aback by the blast of his words. 'You would be best then to look for a wife in England.'

'But if one's heart were touched...' He stared at her boldly. 'You would not wish to live here permanently, Mistress Constance? What about a life at court—and with rents and dues coming in from your lands over here?'

She was at a loss how to reply. It was obvious that he was serious in his pursuit, but how to put him off without offending him? She could hardly turn back now. Soon it would be dark, and it was planned that they spend the night at a monastery. 'The king is only a young man. In his prime, one might say, and very much alive. He could have a son of his own yet,' she said lightly.

'We might wait a long time to see it,' he replied good-humouredly. 'If he weds his child bride, the Princess Isabelle of France, she is what—nine or ten years old? Besides, the match might never take place.'

Constance did not like the way the conversation was going. 'Perhaps not,' she murmured in bored tones, determined to change the subject. Somehow all this talk of power and property, thrones and heirs, made her uneasy. 'Tell me, Master Brandon, have you heard the tale of Saint Brigid and this country we are passing through? When she asked the king who owned it to give it to her, and he refused, she requested just the area then that her mantle would cover. It is said that the holy mantle grew and grew to cover the whole of the Curragh. Here she built a church and a convent, and a sacred fire was kept burning there, always guarded by twenty nuns. It was at a time, you understand, when much of Ireland was being opened to the gospel by Saint Patrick, and there was still much paganism.' He opened his mouth to speak, but she hurried on. 'She was never a woman of narrow interests, neither did she avoid the company of men. She asked a bishop to take up residence with her, and under his aegis a monastery grew whose monks excelled in the making of chalices and shrines and beautiful religious objects. She was his co-equal—is that not wonderful? It is just how our Lord Jesus said it should be. Man and woman, Greek and Jew—one could say English and Irish—all are equal in Christ.'

'Where did you hear such nonsense?' he said with a touch of irritability. 'Men and women being equal—you don't want to believe it!'

'My father has read the Scriptures, and he has told me that in Christ men and women are equal.' She flushed with annoyance.

'Is he a Lollard?' His tones were uneasy.

She nodded. 'Even now he is in London in hope of reform of the Church.'

'It won't happen,' he said firmly. 'He would be wiser not to involve himself in such matters. It is heresy.'

'All change is heresy until it is accepted by the majority.' She stared at him defiantly. 'I would have you know, Master Brandon, that I have been reared to accept the teachings of Wycliffe.'

'It could be dangerous in the future to profess such beliefs,' he muttered, controlling his horse as it veered too close to Constance's mount. 'I should not boast of it, if I were you.'

'Why should I not? The king's mother favoured Wycliffe, as did his uncle, John of Gaunt.' Her brow furrowed.

'But the king doesn't,' he retorted swiftly. 'Within a few days, it is likely that he will be travelling to Waterford to take ship for home. He has been requested to return about the very matter you speak of. You would be wiser forgetting such beliefs and instead fixing your mind on gaining your kinsman's freedom.' Master Brandon urged his horse on to catch up with the man he had been conversing with earlier. She was left alone, and was thankful when the monastery came into sight. She retired early, tired out by the events of the last twenty-four hours.

They left again shortly after sunrise, and she could not help noticing that Master Brandon's manner towards her was warm again; neither of them made mention of the subject they had almost quarrelled over the day before. Instead, he amused her with stories of people he had met and places he had visited, so that she soon felt at ease in his company, but she could not help wondering whether he was all that he seemed. His clothes, his manners, the people of note he mentioned in such a knowing manner, all seemed at variance with his role of simple messenger.

At Athy, they left the rest of the company to travel the remaining few miles alone. A castle came into sight, just as the note of a horn sounded. Into view rode several horsemen and a pack of hounds. Two men, walking, carried a deer bound by its feet to a pole laid across their shoulders.

'The one in the fur-trimmed surcote is Desmond,' commented Master Brandon in a pleased voice. 'But Kildare is not with them.'

Constance's eyes followed his, and instantly she realised why he had pointed the earl out in such a way. The rest of the party were clad in tunics and plaid trews. She stiffened suddenly.

'Let us go and make ourselves known.' He spurred his palfrey into action.

Constance followed more slowly. Her incredulity was fighting for dominance with her sudden rage. There among the riders, astride her own Maeve, was Niall O'More! She met his eyes, which were brimful of amusement, and her mouth tightened as he inclined his head. How had he come here? Surely it could not be coincidence? The sheer audacity of the man to be riding her mare, and not to seem to be in the least put out by meeting her! Was he a friend of the Earl of Desmond? If that were so, what chance had she of obtaining help from that quarter? She was on the point of despairing of gaining Robin's freedom through that channel, when at that moment Master Brandon signalled to her. With a great deal of reluctance she went forward.

'Your Grace, this is Mistress Constance de Wensley,' Brandon introduced her, his manner slightly nervous.

'De Wensley,' murmured the Earl of Desmond, smiling at her encouragingly. 'I have surely heard that name recently.' He turned to Niall. 'Was it not you, O'More, that mentioned it?'

'Ay, my lord.' He caused Maeve to move closer to the earl. 'This is the woman I spoke to you about. The one I rescued from the bog.' His grey eyes surveyed Constance.

A hot tide of angry scarlet coloured her cheeks. 'Rescued! I would not have been in the bog had you not pursued me! And then you took my mare, and left me alone in a foreign land.'

'You missed me, perhaps?' he teased.

She snorted. 'I missed my mare! Just as I did yesterday. Your Grace,' she turned to him, 'ask Master O'More whether that mare he is riding is not mine.'

The earl turned his head to Niall. 'O'More, what say you to that?'

'It is true—but she has something of mine,' he said, seemingly unperturbed.

Constance gasped. 'I have taken nothing belonging to you!'

'Surely you have.' He stilled Maeve's sudden skittishness with a skilfulness that caused her a sudden pang of jealousy, and part of her dream was suddenly vivid in her mind. He had long slender fingers that could coax pleasure, however unwilling the recipient, and she *must* have been unwilling!

'It is not true,' she muttered, lowering her eyes. She would not put it past him to be able to read her mind.

'Hush now, children,' commanded the earl. 'I would know more of this that is between you—but later.' The lines about his eyes and mouth deepened as his glance took in both of them. 'You shall eat with us at the high table, and after we have eaten, you may both say what you have to.' He gave a brief nod and rode on towards the castle. The rest of the hunting party, with Niall in their midst, swept past Constance and Brandon, leaving them staring.

'Well, would you have expected your enemy to turn up here?' grunted Brandon with obvious annoyance. 'And Kildare isn't here, after all. He was called away on an urgent matter. Still,' he smiled, 'there's no good in worrying about that. Tomorrow I shall have to go on to Kilkenny, come what may. O'More seems friendly with the earl, which might prove in his favour. What did you take from him? You never mentioned it.'

'I took nothing,' she snapped. 'He is lying!'

'He seemed pretty confident.' Brandon flicked the reins, and cantered ahead without waiting for her.

Constance gave serious contemplation at that moment to turning round and going back the way she had come. If there had not been Robin to consider, and Maeve—she wanted her horse back!—she might have done so. She sighed, and pressing the horse's flanks with her thighs, she headed towards the castle.

With Master Upton's horse stabled, Constance walked sedately across the courtyard. To her ears came the tap-tap of a mason's hammer as he worked to repair a wall. Brandon waited for her at the entrance to the hall, slapping his gloves against his thigh. 'You have taken a long time. Could you not have allowed one of the grooms to see to your horse?'

'I did,' she replied calmly. 'It was Maeve that delayed me. I wanted to be sure that the man had not damaged her in any way.'

'And had he?' he said impatiently.

She gave a reluctant shake of her head, then felt guilty. She had not wanted Maeve to be injured or badly treated, but she had wanted another reason not to like the man. 'Shall we go in?'

Brandon nodded. 'You do realise what an honour it is to be asked to sit at the high table?' he said, somewhat pompously.

'Ay, but I have also heard that the Irish do not care for such things. That they have different ways from ours. And many of the earl's party were dressed in the Irish manner—so I presume that they are Irish.'

'Not necessarily,' he muttered, following her into the hall. 'Some of the Anglo-Normans like their barbaric costume.'

'I see.' Constance shivered slightly as she looked about the hall. The sun had been warm, but it could not penetrate the walls of the building, which was gloomy, little daylight managing to pierce the openings in the walls.

All was noise and chatter, hustle and bustle. Serving men and women scurried everywhere, carrying salvers and pitchers. The odour of cooking meat was strong. The strains of a harp being tuned mingled with snatches of song, as a baritone voice sought the right key. Most of the tables were already filled, but a few spaces remained at the high table, which stood on a dais at the top of the hall.

The Earl of Desmond was already seated, and next to him sat the harpist, his head tilted a little to one side as he listened to the notes he was plucking. There were several women of mixed ages, all dressed in bright colours, scarlets, greens and blues. Some wore tunics, while others were glad in gowns similar to that worn by Constance. There was the dull gleam of gold and silver on mantles, and about throats and on fluttering hands. Two young men were vigorously arguing, and for a moment she thought that a fight would break out, but the earl broke off his conversation with the harpist and they drew apart. Then she saw Niall, his tawny head close to one of the girls, and she heard him laugh. At that moment he looked up, and their gazes held before he turned back to the girl at his side and spoke to her.

As they came to a halt in front of the earl, Constance's hands curled into fists. What had Niall O'More said to him about her? Had he already prejudiced her case by fabricating a tale different from hers? Was he speaking to that girl about her? She was pretty, and she seemed taken with him.

The earl looked up at them, not seeming at all angry that they were late. 'Ah, you have found your way here, both of you. Find yourselves places. Sorcha, make room for Master Brandon and Mistress de Wensley beside you,' he called down the table, and the girl to whom Niall had been speaking smiled at them both, and moved closer to him. He murmured something, and she giggled. Constance experienced a spurt of irritation, wishing herself anywhere but where she was. It was likely that he *was* talking about her, and she hated him for doing so! She was glad when Brandon sat on the other side of the girl so that there were two persons between her and Master O'More.

A page came forward, a silver bowl in his hands and a towel laid across his arm. He offered the bowl to her, and she dipped her fingers in the warm scented water before wiping them on the towel. Presumably the rest of the table had already washed their hands. A trumpet blared, and the hall marshal entered, carrying a silver platter bearing what looked like—and smelled like— mutton. Behind him followed several other servants bearing dishes.

Constance thrust all thought of Niall out of her mind, and waited to be served. One dish was set between Brandon and herself, and another between Niall and Sorcha, and so on up the table. It was mutton served with a spicy sauce. It was good manners to see to your neighbour's need first, so she served Brandon. He thanked her, and fell on the food, his eyes not on her but on the scene about him. More dishes were brought and set before them: a pike stuffed with herbs, a capon, baked custards in pastry. There were rabbits and eels cooked in pies. All were washed down with wine, not the ale served at the lower tables.

She ate and drank, and like Brandon's her eyes roamed the hall, occasionally coming back to glance along the table to where Niall O'More sat. Several times she heard the girl's light bubbling laughter, and a pang, almost painful in its intensity, shot through her. It seemed a long time since she had laughed like that.

Suddenly there came a hammering, and a hush slowly settled over the gathering. The harpist rose to his feet and spoke slowly in Irish and English. 'Our most illustrious Lord Desmond will now delight us with his latest tale. Pray silence, friends.' There was a cheer, which was quickly quelled as the harpist plucked several notes. The earl rose to his feet.

'I forgot to tell you,' whispered Brandon, who had turned to her as soon as the harpist spoke, 'they call him Gerald the Poet. I doubt we shall understand a word of it, because it will be in Irish. You know of their way of handing down their history and legends in such a manner?'

She nodded. Had not Milo's father told her such tales? Niall O'More, as she had first seen him running alongside her mare, was suddenly vivid in her mind. And as she listened to the earl's voice lifting and soaring, falling and deepening, without understanding a word, pictures were painted in her head. Spellbound, she closed her eyes, oblivious of those about her.

Niall, a few feet away, watched her. He rubbed at his scar, wondering whose side Gerald would take, or whether he would choose to interfere in this affair. One never knew with Gerald. It was well known that he was a man of wonderful bounty, cheerful in conversation, easy of access, and charitable in his deeds. He was also a man of wit and ingenuity. But what was Constance to Brandon? A De Wensley widow with land in the offing. Did he have her in mind for a wife? If that was so, he himself would definitely have to consider a way of preventing such an event!

He glanced at the earl, wondering if he knew what business Brandon was about. They were to speak privately later. He had overheard as much when Gerald had spoken to Brandon outside. A frown creased his forehead as he toyed with the stem of his cup. There was something here that puzzled him. Did Mistress de Wensley have any part in it? His eyes rested on her face again, and he watched her as the earl finished speaking. He saw her stir and her eyelids lift. She seemed dazed as she looked about her, and she appeared suddenly vulnerable. There was a peculiar tightness about his chest as she noticed him, followed by a soaring of his spirit because there was no antagonism in her eyes. Then Brandon leaned forward and cut her off from his vision.

There was movement all over the hall now. The pages came with their bowls, and any grease that had not been wiped on the diners' bread was washed away in the scented water. Those at the lower tables began to file out. There was plenty to be done out of doors at this time of year, and Constance almost wished she was going with them. Her mood of relaxation had not dispersed yet, and she had no mind for animosity, but she must regain her mare and strive for Robin's freedom.

Master Brandon rose, as did the majority of those at the high table, and quickly she stood also. Perhaps the earl had forgotten about her being there, and her dispute with Master O'More? But even as she thought that, he spoke, commanding her to come in front of him, along with Master O'More. 'The rest of you may go. All but you, Brandon. I presume that you know something of this matter?' His humorous eyes rested on him. 'After all, it was you who brought the lady to me. An unexpected guest, but quite delightful.' He turned his gaze to Constance. 'You are welcome to stay the night. Tomorrow I shall be leaving for Munster.'

'Then you do not believe me to be the thief that Master O'More called me, Your Grace?' she asked boldly, smiling at him.

'Even if you were, child, I would forgive you. If you stole something from Master O'More, I am sure you must have had a good reason.' His eyes lingered on the bare graceful neck revealed by the cut of her gown.

'My Lord!' 'Your Grace!' Niall and Brandon spoke in unison, and then glared at each other.

Constance spoke quickly. 'Your Grace, I did not steal anything from this man.' She rested one hand on the high table as she half turned towards Niall. 'But he has used me disgracefully! Deny, if you can, that you chased me and caught me with evil intent in your heart.'

'I do deny it,' he said vigorously. 'I would not have kissed you if you had not tried to kill me and put our lives at risk.' His grey eyes mocked her. 'Deny *that* if you can!'

'I had no intention of killing you,' she countered, her hands curling into fists. 'Only of knocking you senseless.'

'And you would not call that evil intent, I suppose?' His voice lilted.

'I would call it prevention, Master O'More. You had every intention of making me your captive,' she responded icily.

'Of course I did. That's why I ran after you. You had a fair chance of escaping, and I wager if you had ridden in a sensible manner, not side-saddle, you might have done so.' He smiled, before adding, 'Fair's fair now. I caught you, and if it hadn't been for your kinsman taking an unfair advantage, we would not be having this argument, would we?'

She gasped, staring at him unbelievingly, before turning to the earl. She gripped the table with both hands. 'Your Grace, you heard him admit to planning to take me captive. He should be detained and placed in gaol.'

'You know that's right, O'More,' he declared in a serious voice, his eyes going from one to the other. 'Child, is that what you would like me to do with him?'

'It is what he deserves,' put in Brandon, folding his arms across his chest.

'But to be sure, my Lord, I did not plan it,' said Niall unemotionally, staring at Constance. 'It was a spur-of-the-moment deed. You know how it is—you see something you fancy, and you go after it.' His eyes rested on the earl's face. 'It can involve a man in all sorts of trouble.'

'That is true,' replied the earl, with a touch of regret. 'Perhaps it would be simpler if you returned Mistress de Wensley's horse to her, and she returns whatever it is of yours she has.'

'Much simpler,' murmured Niall.

Constance made a strangled sound. 'I don't believe this! I haven't stolen anything of his. He holds my kinsman captive, Your Grace! If it were only a simple matter of a mare—much as I love Maeve—I would not have come here. I knew this could happen as soon as I set eyes on him, and he accused me. You knew my name because he had spoken of me to you.'

'He spoke only of Master Brandon, asking whether I had met him, and if I had known your late husband.' The earl leaned forward, his eyes intent. 'I had no thought to it earlier, but I have been thinking since. Kildare once mentioned your late husband's father.'

'He fled with my husband over twenty years ago, but he was born in Ireland. Did you know him, Your Grace?' Constance pushed back her braids, which had fallen forward.

The earl tapped his fingers on the table, not seeming to have heard her question.

A great weariness washed over her, and she was aware that Niall was standing extremely still. She tried again. 'My father has business contacts in Dublin. He could lose all or most of what he has built up over here, if my kinsman is kept prisoner for long. There are men he has to see,' she said urgently. 'Please, Master O'More must know where he is.'

'Ahh! I have it now,' cried the earl, lifting his head, gratification written on his face. 'Milo de Wensley. Wife dead. He abducted some Irishman's wife. She was alone while the husband was on a raid with the rest of the men. The two of them spent only a short time together— I doubt it was a week. Perhaps they thought that the husband might not return, but he did. De Wensley barely escaped with his life, and the wife returned to her husband. Don't remember what happened to her afterwards.'

He smiled at the three of them. 'You say that your husband is dead, Mistress de Wensley?'

'I think you already know that. Master O'More, perhaps, told you?' she said through stiff lips.

He nodded. 'Is his father dead, too?'

'Ay,' she whispered. 'He was a gentle man, a dreamer, who never stopped talking about this country, which he loved. I often wondered why he never came back, but now I realise that he was frightened to return.'

There was a silence, and she was conscious of Niall's eyes upon her face. Brandon had moved away, and was leaning against the table's end.

'Why have you come here, Mistress de Wensley?' asked the earl gently.

'The manor he possessed is now mine. We had no children.' Her fingers pleated a fold of her skirt. 'The way he talked about it made me want to see it—to live here, if I could.'

'I doubt there is much land. He was not a rich man.' The earl toyed with the cup in front of him, a sympathetic expression on his face.

'The way *he* spoke of it—but then...' She was remembering Robin's words. Distance lends enchantment. Had the old man imagined the past to be far brighter and bigger and better than it actually had been? A laboured sigh escaped her.

'Does this land mean so much to you?' Niall's question made her lift her head. His grey gaze was sombre. 'I thought a woman like you... your clothes... you said your father was rich.'

'My father is rich, but my husband was not. This land is the only property left to me,' she said quietly. 'All my clothes were provided by my father, as was the money to bring me here. But, now, Robin is my main concern.'

'You couldn't hold it alone, you know,' he murmured. 'You need a husband.' His throat moved, and his voice was harsh when he added, 'You could become a prey to the hawks on both sides—who would ruin you before they led you to the church door.'

'Hush, O'More,' rebuked the earl, as Constance's cheeks flushed. 'What kind of impression of us are you giving Mistress de Wensley?'

'I am not a fool, Master O'More,' interposed Constance, deliberately holding his gaze. 'I know the kinds of beasts men can be.'

The earl stood up. 'Then you will realise the wisdom of returning to your father, child. This is not the place for a woman alone.' He smiled kindly on her before turning away and going over to Brandon. Some words were exchanged between them, and then they crossed the hall and went outside.

Constance and Niall were left staring after them, then she stirred as if waking from a trance. 'It seems that my journey was wasted.' The words were barely audible, but Niall heard them.

'You misjudged the earl. He will not become involved in this matter, knowing how important it is that my cousin is freed as soon as possible.' His voice was carefully controlled.

'Just as it is important to me that my kinsman is freed as soon as possible. Well, I shall not be going back to England, Master O'More, if you think you would be rid of me in that way.' Her face hardened.

'I do not wish to be rid of you, Mistress de Wensley,' he said quietly.

'No?' she said. 'Why did you follow me here? I presume you knew that I was coming?'

He nodded. 'I was in the inn, and heard you talking. How well do you know Master Brandon?'

'I don't think that is any of your affair, Master O'More.' She began to move towards the door. His presence was really too overpowering.

'He has his eye on you,' he said irritably. 'Do you consider it wise to entrust yourself to his protection?' He caught up with her in two strides.

'You—You dare to say that to me? I don't consider you the right person to show concern about my virtue, Master O'More.' She passed through the door and out into the warmth of the sunshine, wondering what to do next.

'But I am concerned.' He smiled—such a delightfully captivating smile that Constance had to stem the sudden fluttering sensations that it roused.

'There is no need,' she snapped. 'Now may I have my mare back? Desmond said you were to return her to me.'

His smile vanished. 'You are not proposing to go anywhere else today, are you?'

'I have no notion where to go at this moment.' She began to walk swiftly to the stables, wishing that he would go away. His closeness was making her aware of what passed between them during the night spent by the bog.

'Stay till morning. Gerald asked you to.' He strode beside her.

'I don't know if I would be safe while you are around, Master O'More.' It seemed that she was not to be rid of him, and she could not think sensibly when he was near.

'There'll be hawking in the morning before Gerald leaves. Kildare was going to show him a new bird, but the falconer will do so instead. Stay till then, and perhaps you can make up your mind. Maybe I'll be able to help you.' He gave her a sidelong glance, which she met squarely.

'You, Master O'More? You amaze me! The only way you could help me to make up my mind is by staying here, so that I will know that the best thing for me is to leave.'

'I'll be leaving tomorrow, most likely.' He smiled. 'That's if I have a horse. Perhaps you would care to come with me and see how well I've cared for your Maeve? Did you know that her namesake was a queen who broke the hearts of men and caused the death of two of the bravest friends in Irish history?'

She nodded, was about to refuse, changed her mind, and walked swiftly alongside him to the stables.

CHAPTER FIVE

'SHE'S A fine beast.' Niall held out a wrinkled apple on the palm of his hand. 'Pat said you told him her sire was Irish. I've seen horses like her in Connemara. I had a mind to buy one last year before my foster-father died.'

'Pat is the ostler at the inn?' Her hand caressed Maeve's mane.

He nodded. 'He wasn't best pleased when I took your mare.'

'Why did you take her? To annoy me even more?' she suggested unemotionally.

'Partly. And to prevent you from travelling with Brandon. I don't like the man.' He wiped his hands on his trews. 'He dresses too fine for a messenger.'

'You sound just like Master Upton.' Her hand fell to her side.

He shrugged. 'Master Upton is a perceptive man. I wonder whether Brandon really thought that by coming here you would be able to gain your kinsman's freedom?'

'I considered that he did so.' She bristled slightly. 'You said that you wanted Robin to exchange him for your cousin. How long could such an exchange take?'

'It depends. Fortunately Dermot is not one of the more important hostages, like the O'Neill lads who have been held at Trim since 1390. It was their being held that resulted in the O'Neill submitting to Richard. Others soon followed.' His face shadowed as he moved away from the mare.

'Could your cousin not be freed if the king of Leinster and his allies left the mountains, as they promised earlier this year?'

'Where would they go?' He pushed open the door, and went outside. She followed him. 'But why promise, if the vow cannot be kept?'

His eyes narrowed against the sun as he faced her. 'King Art is guaranteed an annual payment of eighty marks to him and his heirs for ever. *And* his wife's inheritance in the barony of Norragh.' He whistled tunelessly.

'Would he not have that, anyway?'

He shook his head. 'Four years ago, her lands were taken into Richard's control because she married the king of Leinster, one of Richard's principal enemies. Art was determined to have what was rightly his. For it, he undertook that all his armed men of war, his household and his nation would leave and go with him at the king of England's wages to make war on other lands occupied by the king's rebels.' He gave a bark of laughter, and kicked a pebble. 'It seems a madness, doesn't it?'

She nodded. 'But understandable. Richard wishes to keep the Pale safe from attacks from the hills.'

'He's fighting to keep it English! And it's a losing battle. There has to be communication between those in the hills and the people of the plains and towns. On both sides there are those who would adhere to the old ways, who wish to pretend that change means subjugation. We could learn from each other, but the English laws often work against our doing so. The English are forbidden to learn our language and to speak it, although many do. Now that French is no longer widely spoken because the new English tongue is taking its place, it makes sense for the English to learn Irish. For why should the Irish learn English?'

'You've learnt it. I—I was surprised when you spoke to me in my own tongue when first we met.' She sought to stem her rising colour, remembering how he had kissed her so enthusiastically.

'I'm not an ignorant barbarian, for all you have called me one,' he responded quickly. 'I learnt it because of necessity, and because my foster-father taught me. But those who live in the hills have their own laws and ways of living. Their history is in the old tongue, written on their hearts. Just as the music in the soil is sung in our blood.' He paused. 'They'll never leave the hills and mountains, and I doubt there's much Richard can do to force them. Besides, why should Irishmen fight other Irishmen on his behalf?'

'It wouldn't be the first time you have fought each other,' she responded impatiently. 'Wasn't it because of such tribal warfare that the kings of England and the Norman overlords came here?'

'Ay,' he said roughly. 'And the man who invited the Normans in was a MacMurrough like Art. But you are mistaken in thinking that many kings of England have set foot here. Their barons, ay.' He frowned. 'Henry's John; and now Richard. Only this century we were invaded by the king of Scotland, Robert the Bruce. In the annals it says that it was a terrible time. There was famine and murder. It's even written that man ate man in those days.'

She shuddered. 'Terrible, indeed!'

He came to a standstill by a bench. 'But such talk isn't suitable for your ears.'

'I am not a child, Master O'More,' she said indignantly, gazing up at him with wide brown eyes. 'I am more than twenty years old.'

'I am aware that you are a woman, Mistress de Wensley.' His gaze washed over her as he placed a foot on the bench, resting his arm across his knee. The too ready colour rushed to her face, and she was lost for words. 'No doubt Brandon is aware of it, too,' he added softly. 'You really should be more careful of the company you keep.'

Her mouth fell open, and then she gave a husky laugh. 'You are warning me about Master Brandon? What about yourself, sir?'

'Oh, I have no fear of Brandon,' he replied, deliberately misunderstanding her. 'But you might be deceived by his fine clothes and polished manner.'

'Oh, you are impossible,' she cried, throwing up her hands. 'It is you that I need to be on my guard against!'

His grey eyes gleamed. 'Are you on your guard now? Because I warn you that if I were to try to kiss you, I doubt that you could prevent me.' He straightened, and she stepped back hurriedly.

'You shouldn't talk to me like that—j—just when we were d—debating how best we can set about freeing our kinsmen.'

'Is *that* what we were doing?' He was smiling that smile again that made her feel quite weak. What was wrong with her? How could this—*barbarian*—have such an effect? 'I'd much rather discuss what you are going to do if you find your manor.'

She looked away. 'Why should it concern you?'

'Maybe it's because I am concerned about you—a lone woman.'

'You worry about the hawks, perhaps?' she said sweetly.

He raised both eyebrows. 'Perhaps.'

'Well, it is none of your affair, Master O'More.' She pushed at the gravel on the path with the toe of her shoe. 'And I doubt that I shall be alone.' She paused, gazing at the toe of her shoe, which was now dusty. 'There is always Master Brandon I could call upon.'

Niall drew in his breath. Was she serious? 'You'd be a fool, then,' he rapped. 'What can he know about running a manor?'

'He doesn't need to know anything,' she murmured, hiding a smile. 'Surely there will be a steward to run everything?'

'And what if there isn't?' He folded his arms across his chest, and leaned back slightly on his heels. 'You'll be lost then. This isn't England.'

'Then I shall run it,' she replied calmly, determined to wipe the smile off his face. 'I am not the fool you think me. My father and stepmother saw to it that I knew something about such matters when they thought they were not going to have any sons. I would like to breed and sell horses also, so I would find myself a man who was well experienced where horses are concerned. I believe you know a little about horses, Master O'More?' she declared with an air of innocence.

'A little!' He moved closer, and she stepped back hurriedly, felt the bench against the backs of her knees and sat down abruptly. 'I wager Kathleen or Brigid didn't tell you I knew a little!' He bent over her. 'I've lived and breathed horses since I was born!'

'Surely you exaggerate?' she retorted, a mite breathlessly. 'Next you'll be saying that you were born in the saddle.'

'Not quite.' The corner of his mouth quivered. 'We don't use saddles.'

Laughter caught in her throat and warmed her eyes. He placed a hand on her shoulder, and leaned closer.

From round the hedge came Master Brandon, startling them apart. His eyes searched Constance's face before sliding to Niall's. 'You have not been pressing your attentions on Mistress de Wensley, I hope, O'More?' he said angrily.

'I do not consider that any of your business, Brandon,' responded Niall brusquely.

A flush raced along Brandon's cheekbones. 'I brought Mistress de Wensley here. I have an interest in her welfare, and so feel responsible for her.'

'Is that right now?' he said in a rich Irish brogue. 'Is it that maybe you've realised that, when an earl calls an inheritance small, maybe he's comparing it with the size of his own possessions?'

Brandon's mouth thinned. 'I thought nothing of the kind! I am merely concerned for Mistress de Wensley. And I do not consider you to be the right company for her to keep.'

'And you are, I suppose?' sneered Niall, his gaze ruthlessly raking Brandon.

'Master Brandon! Master O'More!' Constance rose swiftly. 'I beg you to stop this quarrelling.'

'Why?' demanded Niall, his eyes suddenly alight with mischief. 'You should find it exciting to have two men fighting over you.'

'Well, I don't!' she countered crossly. 'And I am not staying here to listen.'

'Well, go away, and come back later. We can finish our conversation then.' Niall turned her round and gave her a slight push.

She gasped indignantly, but instead of turning round, she marched swiftly to the end of the hedge and round it. There she stopped to peer round the corner, and to listen.

'You stink of the stables, O'More!' Brandon was stepping away, as Niall advanced on him.

'You smell as sweet and cloying as a whorehouse, man!' snapped Niall. 'No surprise that you and Sil O'Toole like each other's company.'

'Sil O'Toole!' Brandon's expression changed abruptly. 'Why do you mention him?'

Niall could have kicked himself. He had not meant to mention Sil, but he would have had to be blind not to see that the name had a powerful effect on the Englishman. 'My mother was an O'Toole. Sil and I are kinsmen.' He smiled blandly.

'He has perhaps spoken of me?' asked Brandon eagerly.

'He hasn't told me everything. He's ten years older than me, and always full of secrets that he's unwilling to share,' he parried.

'He maybe has given you a message for me?'

Niall stepped back a little and folded his arms. 'You were expecting one?'

Brandon shook his head. 'He said that I would see him here, but he hasn't appeared. And you're the kind of man I would expect him to use.'

'You flatter me, Brandon.' Niall's voice was expressionless. 'But if Sil arranged to meet you, he'll be here.'

'That's all right, then.' Brandon sat on the bench. 'I wish I'd known before that you were his kinsman. He's told you about this affair?' He shot him a glance that could not quite conceal a sudden excitement.

Niall smiled enigmatically. 'Your secret's safe with me.'

'He's going to use you?' He sounded animated.

'Sil uses everybody. He's a glutton for power.'

'I can believe that.' Brandon smiled up at him, and his green eyes shone. 'I admire him. He has a manner that is quite frighteningly ruthless.'

'Oh, Sil's ruthless. I could tell you tales that would make your blood get quite heated.' His fingers wandered to his scar.

'Another time, O'More.' Brandon stood, and patted his arm, almost caressing it. 'I didn't really wish to fight over Mistress de Wensley. Her father's quite sickeningly rich, but she does have two half-brothers. There's not much there really in the way of power and money—and she's a self-willed creature.' He lifted a handkerchief and sniffed it. 'But one has to keep up appearances. She has strange ideas of equality, and her father's a Lollard. That could be dangerous for a man on his way to the top.' He replaced the scrap of linen in his sleeve. 'You are welcome to her, O'More, if you really want her.'

'You're too kind, Brandon,' said Niall drily. He could not bear being close to the man any longer. 'I must go. The earl wanted to speak to me. Good day to you.' He strode swiftly away.

Constance darted back behind the hedge, her heart beating fast. Neither of the men had bothered to lower his voice, and she had overheard every word. She was angry for allowing herself to be deceived in the first place by Master Brandon, but at least she now knew the full measure of the man. As for Master O'More! Who was this Sil O'Toole, and why should he be meeting Brandon here? And Niall O'More, was he involved in whatever it was? It was a mystery.

She waited till Brandon and Niall had vanished in the other direction, and then wandered back to the bench and sat on it. The sun was warm on her face, like a caress, and she pondered over what might have happened if Master Brandon had not come round the corner when he had. Would Niall O'More have kissed her? How dared Master Brandon say that he was welcome to her if he wanted her! As if she had no choice in the matter! The arrogance of men was enough to make any woman of spirit rebel. And he had answered, 'You're too kind, Brandon,' with a peculiar note in his voice. Had he been thinking, as she had at that moment, of the night spent by the bog? Had he found her to his taste? He had said that he would never forget that night! Agitated by the thought, she rose hurriedly. She was dwelling too much on what had happened—on *that* man who had been at the centre of it. She ought to be considering what she was going to do about Robin. Her brow puckered as her mind searched for inspiration. Perhaps she should broach the subject again with the earl. She began to walk towards the castle, hoping she might find him.

Niall strode along, his thoughts on his conversation with Brandon, but was surprised out of his reverie by the Earl of Desmond calling his name. He lifted his head, and saw the two pages who had brought the finger-bowls to them at dinner wielding shields and light swords on the green. They were most likely the sons of noble families placed with the Earl of Kildare to learn fighting skills, and to observe how noblemen should behave at table and towards others.

'Come on, lads, don't give up yet,' called the earl, as the two panting boys drew apart. 'What do you think of them, O'More?'

'They have plenty of fight in them. But I doubt you called me to discuss them, my lord,' he murmured unemotionally.

Amusement deepened the lines on the earl's face. 'Shall we walk?'

Niall fell in step beside him. 'You wish to discuss Mistress de Wensley's kinsman?'

'Not at all!' Desmond sounded disconcerted. 'Should I? That is your affair, O'More, and I understand your reasons for taking him captive. You and your cousin Dermot are close, I believe.'

'We spent some time together as boys before I left the hills with my brother.' Niall's voice had softened. 'The friendship forged then held good, although we did not see so much of each other.'

'Ahh! Your brother! I had almost forgotten you had a brother.' He pressed two fingers lightly against his forehead. 'Now I understand your interest in Mistress de Wensley.'

'My interest has little to do with my brother. I did not know who she was when first we met,' he said warily. 'Afterwards—ay, it made some difference.'

'She is an attractive woman, who will need an eye kept on her if she does not return to England.'

'I have something in mind.'

'You plan to take her under your wing? You're the right man to do so.'

'I think so,' replied Niall, with a flicker of a smile. 'Is that all?'

The earl shook his head. 'Sil O'Toole is coming here later. A rare occasion, and a surprising one. I know he hasn't much liking for my kind of Irishness. My family have lived here for nigh on two hundred years, and he still considers us intruders.'

'My cousin Sil is a proud and intolerant man.'

'He has a gift—so much can be forgiven him. He can hold a gathering mesmerised.' He hesitated. 'You will forgive what I say next, O'More, if it sounds inhospitable.'

'You would like me to leave? You have heard of our quarrel and fear that I will pick a fight with him?' He stared intently at the earl.

'No! No!' exclaimed the earl, sounding distressed. 'I don't ask that.' He clasped his hands behind his back. 'I tell you, O'More, that there is much about Sil that I cannot like. Even so...'

'...he is to be the guest of honour,' finished Niall. 'What do you wish me to do?'

Desmond sighed. 'Just do not make yourself conspicuous. Sit somewhere else, if you can.'

'That is agreeable to me. I have no desire to eat at the same table as Sil. You do me no discourtesy.'

'I am glad. Now let us talk about some other matter.' He put his arm about Niall's shoulders. 'Tell me more of Mistress de Wensley. What are your plans concerning her? I pray that they are honourable.'

Niall nodded. They began to walk and talk. Yet even as they did so, interesting and important as the subject was, part of his mind was searching for a way to discover what was bringing Sil to meet Brandon in Kilkea Castle.

Constance was wondering where Niall was... Perhaps he had departed, for she could not see him anywhere at the high table. If he had gone, it must be for the best. She rinsed her fingers in the bowl as the pages silently moved along the line of people; her eyes wandered slowly about the hall. There seemed to be even more men and women this evening, their chatter filling the place with babble.

Then she saw Niall sitting at one of the lower tables, and her nerves gave a funny little dance. Had he chosen to sit there to save any embarrassment, thinking that she might bring up the subject of Robin again? Suddenly she saw him stiffen, and an expression of such distaste crossed his face that her eyes were immediately drawn like those of the rest of the company to the doorway.

A man had entered. He presented an awesome spectacle as he paused there to survey the company. He was extremely tall, and wore a full-length tunic that billowed in the slight movement of air. His hair was black and long, and he possessed a beak of a nose that gave his face a predatory cast. He strode to the high table, and a murmur rippled through the company. As he approached, Constance felt a shiver pass down her spine. His eyes looked almost black. They shone brilliantly and with great concentration on those sitting in front of him. Almost, she thought, as though he expected them to rise at his coming and to bow.

The Earl of Desmond did rise, to welcome him in Irish. He answered in a surprisingly melodious voice. Brandon stirred at her side, and gave a tiny excited gasp. Constance looked at him, to see what she was convinced was almost adoration on his face. In a flash she realised who it was, and would have cast Sil another look except that he had sat down at the earl's right hand, and supper was served. When the meal ended, Sil rose with the earl. Several times Constance's eyes had been drawn to where Niall was sitting and she looked at him now, but again he was not looking towards her. What was it about this man that he did not like?

A hush now settled on the hall, and Sil proceeded to speak. It was magic—she realised that almost immediately. His voice could create visions and stir the blood in a way that the earl's had not. There was an entreaty in its tones that at times caused tears to start in her eyes, but then it would alter, and she felt angry, dissatisfied, even though she could not understand a word. When he finished speaking, there was no movement or sound. It was as though a spell had been woven.

Then a man moved. She looked up quickly, to see Niall. For a moment she was aware of a vibrancy in the air, and of the two men staring at each other, then Niall walked out. It was as though a stopper had been pulled on a flask, and talk immediately filled the hall. She would have liked to leave herself, to breathe in some fresh air, but Sorcha began to ask in French her opinion of Sil, who was a bard. It was some time before she was able to get away, and by then most people were moving. The tables were being cleared, and the bard had disappeared.

As she crossed the lawn, she was wondering if Sil had left already, or whether he had gone to meet Brandon. The remembrance of that earlier conversation between Niall and Brandon was clear in her mind. She was walking along the hedge when she heard voices. One she recognised as Brandon's.

'You have arranged it all, then?' he asked excitedly. 'There is no problem about the money?'

'None at all,' replied the bard's voice in French. 'If you knew me better, you would not have to ask. They will take what I give them and find pleasure in the deed. To kill the king of England will cause songs to be sung about us for ever more.' The deep tones held a note of exultation.

'Shh!' whispered Brandon. 'Do you have to say those words so loud!'

Constance could almost see him glancing about, and she clapped a hand over her mouth to silence her breathing.

'You are like a rabbit, Brandon, always fearful of being snared,' said Sil, with a hint of contempt in his voice.

'It's all right for you,' muttered the Englishman. 'You can flee to the hills. I must go to Kilkenny and see Richard, to make certain his plans have not changed.'

'You will let us know the day of his departure from Kilkenny? I have told you where to meet my messenger.'

'Of course.' Brandon's voice took on a nervous note. 'But what do you intend doing about your kinsman? I had no idea of the situation between you.'

'You can leave Niall O'More to me.' There was menace in the words. 'You are certain you told him nothing?'

Brandon must have nodded his head, because after that there was a silence and only the sound of retreating footsteps, and an indistinct murmur of voices as they must have reached the end of the hedge.

Constance's blood was racing so fast that she felt quite dizzy. What was she to do? She could not think straight. She pressed herself against the hedge as she caught sight of the men from the corner of her eye. They were not coming this way, but were heading towards the castle, seeming deep in conversation. Brandon lifted his head and glanced behind him. She again pressed herself deeper into the hedge, praying that he would not see her. It gave way, and she fell, breaking some newly burgeoning twigs.

Her hair was caught on a twig; then her sleeve caught as she attempted to free herself. She squirmed and tugged, wishing that she had never come out into this part of the garden. It seemed created for intrigue, and she wanted to free herself before anything else happened. Tears welled in her eyes as, gritting her teeth, she forced her way up, leaving wisps of hair clinging to the thorns. Her cheek received a scratch as she erupted on to the path.

When an arm shot out and seized her shoulder, a scream was forced out of her. Then she realised it was Niall. 'O, sweet Jesu! What a fright you gave me,' she gasped.

'I gave you a fright?' The grey eyes narrowed as he stared down at her intently. 'What were you doing lurking in there?'

'I wasn't lurking.' Her voice was brittle, as her hand searched for bits of twig caught in her hair.

'You weren't meeting Brandon here, were you?'

She started. 'Brandon! Why should I meet Brandon? Besides, he's with that—that bard!'

'You have seen them together?' His hand moved from her shoulder to pick a leaf from her hair. 'Which way did they go?'

'Towards the castle.' She lowered her eyes, suddenly unsure of him, and whether he could have any part at all in this whole matter. Her fingers smoothed a snag in her scarlet sleeve. 'Why do you ask?'

'Because I take an interest in what my kinsman does.' He brought his face closer to hers. 'You've got blood on your cheek.'

She made a noise in her throat and would have rubbed her cheek, only he shocked her by licking at the scratch. 'Wh—What are you doing?' A shiver passed through her.

'Haven't you ever seen beasts licking their wounds? Or heard how the Son of Mary used spittle to bring sight to a blind beggar?' His eyes were level with hers, and suddenly she found it difficult to swallow. His tongue caressed her cheek again before his mouth came slowly down over hers.

It was their only point of contact, and if she had considered, she could have pulled away, but the kiss was so gentle that she experienced no threat, only an unsought sensuality. He lifted his head, and she stepped back hurriedly. 'You should not have done that!' Her voice was uneven.

Niall smiled. 'You said Brandon went towards the castle with Sil?'

'Ay, but what do you want with them?'

'Later,' he called, as he began to move away from her. 'Stay away from Brandon.'

'Ohh!' Her fingers curled into the palms of her hands. She was angry with herself and Niall for leaving her without any kind of explanation as to why he was so interested in Brandon and Sil. Perhaps he did have some part in the plot she had just overheard? Although it had not sounded like it, from the way his kinsman had spoken.

Her hands went to her cheeks. The king's life was in danger, but what could she do about it? The earl—could he be trusted? He had welcomed the bard so warmly, and favoured the Irish. He had been unwilling to help her to gain Robin's freedom. Was he involved? She paced the lawn, her thoughts in a turmoil, not knowing which way to turn. Why had she not pulled away when Niall O'More kissed her? She touched her lips, and without more ado, made her way towards the castle. It was getting dark.

When she had almost reached the entrance to the hall, the tall figure of a man came towards her. He did not move out of her path, and was almost on top of her before she swerved. As she passed him by, he caught hold of her sleeve. He spoke in Irish, and she recognised the deep melodious voice. Anger surged inside her.

'Would you please release me?' Ice dripped from her tongue.

He peered into her face, and gave a mirthless laugh. 'You are the English widow who came with Brandon.' The brilliant eyes seemed to bore into hers. She experienced a sudden lethargy, and her head began to swim. His head came closer to hers, and she tried to fight the unexpected weakness—she was struggling as his arms went round her. Then there came the sound of feet on the other side of the door. He released her abruptly, so that she almost fell. He swept her aside before striding off into the night, his light-coloured tunic flowing behind him.

Constance clutched at the stone wall, as the door opened to reveal Niall in the entrance. 'Have you seen Sil?' he rasped.

She nodded. 'He went—that way.' Her hand half rose, then fell. He touched her shoulder lightly, and was gone in the wake of Sil.

Straightening slowly, she gazed after him. He was just a pale shadow in the descending gloom. On an impulse, she followed. She had almost reached the stables when Sil, on horseback, clattered past her. She spun round to see where he would go. Surely the gates would be closed at this time of night? He urged his horse on, scattering the guards, and set the horse to jump the gap in the wall where the mason had been working earlier that day. She ran the rest of the way to the stables, glad that the moon was abroad to give some light.

As she entered, she saw Niall pulling himself up from the ground. 'What has he done to you?'

'Almost rode me down.' He rubbed his head, before staggering over to the horses.

'Where do you think you're going in that state?' she demanded, following him over.

'Got to go after Sil,' he muttered, swaying slightly as his hand reached for a bridle on the wall.

'You're in no fit state,' she said impatiently. 'I'll go.'

He stared at her. 'You...damn well won't! It's dangerous!'

Her expression was scornful as she snatched the bridle from his fingers and dragged it over Maeve's head. She was up in minutes. Niall's mouth compressed tightly and he shook his head to clear it, and as she would have gone past him, he suddenly seized hold of her and somehow managed to drag himself up behind. They almost fell off, but she clung to Maeve's mane, and he clung to her. The door was already open, so all the mare had to do was to move off into the moonlight.

CHAPTER SIX

THIS IS pure madness, thought Constance, as she set
Maeve to jump the gap. She shut her eyes, and hung on.
The moon reflected light back from the white flanks;
muscles bunched as the mare from Connemara leapt and
soared into the air like some mythical creature from olden
days. The guards, who had already fallen back to stare
in astonishment after Sil, murmured in admiration.

Constance's whispered words in the mare's ear contained a jubilant note as she came down to earth again.

'One day,' muttered Niall, 'I shall go to Connemara
to find a stallion—a worthy mate—for this mare of
yours—and we shall breed such horses the like of which
will be the talk of all Ireland—and England, as well.'

'We, Master O'More?' she questioned coolly. 'You
are presumptuous!'

'And if I am, Mistress de Wensley, what is wrong with
that?' He placed his arm more firmly about her and
rested his head against her back. 'If you are to breed
horses, you will need a man of my experience. And Pat—
he would be another worth recruiting.'

'So, I am to employ a horse-thief and his accom-
plice?' she retorted in a mocking voice. 'You must consider me a fool.'

'You would be a fool not to consider hiring me, because—you—will not—find a better man.' The words
were slightly slurred.

'Not only are you presumptuous, but you are conceited!' She experienced a moment's anxiety as she felt
his hands loosen before tightening again and lacing about
her waist.

'I know my worth.' He forced himself upright, and peered over her shoulder at the moonlit scene before them. He could only just make out the rider ahead.

'You are quite impossible—and you would have been better staying behind.' She paused. 'Have you any notion where Sil is going?'

'Hmm! I'm a man who knows what he wants,' he murmured, 'and I thought you a woman who possessed a similar ambition.'

'Because I wish to breed horses?' she asked impatiently, straightening her back as his head rested against it again. He was much too close for her to be able to relax.

'Because you wish to live in *Ireland* and breed horses. You own land and a horse—I have talent and a few horses of my own. To be sure, Mistress de Wensley, we were fated to meet,' he said derisively.

'Ha! If that were so, I consider that fate has played a cruel trick on me,' she responded vigorously. 'Now, it is Sil's destination that I am concerned about.'

'I have some idea where he is going,' murmured Niall.

'Where?' She felt his hands slipping again, and instinctively one of her own grabbed hold of one of his. 'Do you wish to fall off this horse, Master O'More?' she asked in a brisk voice. 'If you do, I shall have to leave you and follow Sil.'

'I believe you would, an' all.' He gave a laugh. 'You are a hard woman, Mistress de Wensley.' The fingers of his hand laced through hers. 'But I have no intentions of falling off. The dizziness will pass.'

'Did you bang your head when Sil almost ran you down?' She wanted to pull her hand away—the way he held her fingers caused her nerves to behave erratically, and that was not good for her concentration; the ground was uneven in places and the moonlight cast shadows. It was dangerous to ride in such a way.

'Ay, on the wall of the stable.' His finger stroked the palm of her hand, and she would have snatched her hand away, but he held it firmly. 'Don't worry about losing Sil. I'm almost certain I know where he's going. It might be best if we do lose sight of him for a while. We don't want him to suspect he's being followed.' He paused. 'Why *did* you want to follow him, as a matter of interest?'

For a moment Constance was at a loss for words. Should she tell him what she had overheard? Yet surely this man would have no love for Richard of England? Most likely he would favour such a plot.

'I don't like the man,' she said at last. 'And I think he's up to some mischief—and, besides, you wanted to follow him, and it was an impetuous decision I made to go in your place.' She shrugged casually. 'My mistake, I think.'

'If we are caught, ay.' His voice suddenly sounded grim. 'I'm almost sure he's heading for a cave in the hills not far from Athy.'

'A cave! For what purpose?'

'It's a spot where all the outcasts gather; those who have broken either English or Irish law. After Dermot was captured, I kept a watch on Sil, because I believed he might have betrayed our cousin. He knew that Dermot had the strength and position to foil his ambitions to lead our clan back into the past. Not that some of the laws and customs were not wise and good—they were, and we adhere to some still—but the old religion with its human sacrifice—no!' he declared vehemently.

Constance felt ice trickle down her spine. 'Surely such rites do not still take place?' she asked huskily.

'One would like to think that they didn't, but in the dense oak groves and the mountains, who can tell? I've seen bones...' His voice tailed off.

'How—How did you know they weren't animal bones?'

'I've seen bones like those in a barrow. There's one only a short distance from... where my foster-sisters dwell.'

Constance experienced a fearful unreality—it seemed terrible to have a pagan burial site so near to a home. 'Why did you go inside? Surely spirits must haunt such a place?'

'A dare, it was.' His voice sank deliberately. 'And once inside, I wished I hadn't gone—so dark and cold—not the chill of a misty night but that of death's breath. I felt as though icy hands were laid on the back of my neck.' The shiver that raced through Constance made Niall smile, and his fingers tightened about hers. 'But then I said to myself: Why should I fear the spirits of my ancestors? The gospel had not been brought to them, so they died in ignorance, not deliberate sin—and most likely their souls rest in some other place—uneasy though they may be—even so, I shot out of there as soon as I could because I thought I heard a keening noise.'

'Don't—tell me any more,' she whispered, her fingers twisting convulsively about his, before she realised what she was doing and pulled her hand away.

'I won't, if it frightens you,' he said meekly.

'I'm not frightened,' she replied sharply. 'But—but sound carries at night. And, besides, you should be telling me which way to go, because I think we've lost Sil.'

Niall gave her instructions and Maeve cantered on, fresh after a day's rest. She bore her double burden well. Constance wondered what they would do when they came to the cave. Would they be able to get close enough to discover if Sil went there because it had some connection with the plot to kill the king? Why was Brandon involved in such a plot? Could it just be that he was a pawn in the hands of his master, the Earl of March? That Richard was unpopular with many, she knew. In the past, he had been known to behave unreasonably,

committing men to the block without trial, then re-
canting and pardoning them, yet she had always had
some sympathy and admiration for him.

King at ten, Richard's seat on the throne had always
been precarious while behind it stood his uncles,
Lancaster, York and Gloucester. In the years that had
seen him struggling to manhood, it had been Gloucester,
the youngest of the uncles, who had proved the greatest
threat in his attempt to gain the reins of power for
himself. It was rumoured that there had been a time when
Gloucester had sought to depose Richard, and only the
opposition of Derby, Lancaster's son, and a couple of
others, had circumvented so crude an usurpation.

If Richard were to be killed here in Ireland, would
Gloucester, Derby and Lancaster be prepared to sit back
and allow the Earl of March to mount the throne? What
of Richard's plans for a marriage that would extend the
truce with France? What of England? What about her
own family? Civil war could tear her country apart, and
England could become an easy target for the Scots on
her northern borders and the ships that harried her
southern coast. She would have to do something to warn
the king—go to Kilkenny, if necessary. But first, the more
she could learn about Sil's plot, the more reason the
king would have to believe her.

Niall's voice interrupted her thoughts. 'Not far now,
and you'll stay with Maeve while I venture closer.'

'But I want to see what is going on,' she whispered,
doubting that he would tell her what he overheard—that
was, if he managed to get close enough to hear anything.

'Well, you can't,' he said firmly. 'Stop here.'
Constance brought Maeve to a halt, prepared to argue.
'You'll stay in the trees, and if there's any sign or sound
of trouble, you mount Maeve and gallop back to
Desmond.'

'That's foolish! I'd lose myself,' she whispered
impatiently.

'Lose yourself then.' Niall dismounted. 'Just as long as you don't allow Sil or any of his cut-throats to find you.' He frowned, as he looked up at her.

'But what if they catch you?' she demanded, ignoring his hand, and sliding to the ground herself.

He stroked his moustache. His face was shadowed by the trees, and she could not read his expression. 'You worry about yourself. If you have to run, it will be too late for me; and you could tell Kathleen and Brigid about my fate. I'm sure you'd find pleasure in telling them that I was dead!'

'I don't know why you should think *that*, Master O'More,' she said, 'but if it is so dangerous—perhaps you should not go any closer. Let us forget about discovering what Sil is about, and go back. We'll still be in time for the hawking tomorrow.'

'Go back—just because there's a risk? I've escaped from more dangerous places than this.'

Before she could say any more, he melted into the shadows, his mantle swirling about his ankles. 'Fool,' she said in a low voice, 'if you think that I'm going to wait here meekly for your return.' Even so, she did wait for a short time before following in his wake up the hill. She kept to the shadows cast by boulders and trees until she could see the mouth of the cave lit by flickering flames. She could hear the rumble of voices and the occasional laugh, but there was no sign of Niall or any other human being.

Carefully she crept closer, crouching low. The last few yards she travelled on her stomach, until she was over a lip of rock and inside the entrance. She stayed there a moment, conscious of the racing of her heart. The way down into the cave was beneath her. Fear kept her motionless as she strained to hear what was being said. She caught the melodious tones of Sil's voice, and even from that distance she experienced the power of the spell he wove. Then she realised that he was speaking in Irish, and her spirits sank. What a fool *she* was not to have thought of that!

Suddenly there was a shout in the cave below, and a babble of voices sent her scrambling into a dark corner. The next moment a man came running up a narrow slope, his mantle flying behind him like a giant bat. He was out and over the lip of rock within seconds, the moonlight glinting on his tawny hair. Relieved, Constance rose, ready to follow, just as another man burst into the open. He was huge! At first he did not see her, then some flicker of movement on her part caused him to whirl, and he gave a roar as he came towards her.

Constance's mouth went dry, and the cry for help came out as a croak. Even so, it made Niall brake on the hill and turn. He could see her, and the unshaven hairy mountain of a man reaching for her. He cursed under his breath, and raced up the hill, dragging the axe from his girdle. One throw he would have, if he was lucky, and no other men appeared. He leaped the lip of rock, landing on both feet. His eyes lined up his target, and he prayed that Constance would not move. The axe went flying from his hand.

Constance's arms attempted to ward off the crumpling figure, but his weight proved too much and she toppled backwards with his body on top of her. Niall was there in a trice, to roll the man away. The axe had bitten deep into his neck, and without wiping the blade, he thrust it into his girdle. Then he pulled her to her feet and pushed her over the rocky lip and down the hill.

Shouts sounded as they entered the trees. He bundled her on to the mare before dragging himself up behind. Constance wanted to thank him, but the words would not come, and, besides, she could feel his fury as a tangible beast between them.

Because she did not speak, Niall kept silent, his anger fermenting inside him. The fear he had experienced when he had seen her struggling with the man was still with him, and he did not like feeling in such a way about any woman. Its hold almost suffocated him.

They still had not spoken when the walls of Kilkea Castle came in sight. Then Niall told Constance to stop before the gap in the wall. She thought it was because the mare was tired, and he did not wish to burden Maeve with his weight during the jump. She would have dismounted herself, but he stilled her with a rough hand.

'No!' he rapped. 'You go on.' The lines about his nose and mouth were taut. 'A woman who can't obey is nothing but trouble! Good night to you, Mistress de Wensley.' He turned on his heel before she could speak, and strode off into the night.

For a moment, Constance was too stunned to move or think, then her temper rose. How dared he speak to her like that! He was not her husband or master to expect her to do everything he said! So what did she care if she never saw the man again! All the better! Aware of the guards on the other side of the wall, she turned Maeve away from the sight of Niall O'More, determined to banish all thought of him from her mind. She had more important matters to concern her; her king had to be warned, and only she could do the warning! Tomorrow morning she would go to Kilkenny. She set her horse to the gap, and cleared it with inches to spare.

A couple of guards ran after her. They were not those who had watched her and Niall depart, but fortunately, on close inspection, one of them remembering seeing her earlier in the day. Or was it now yesterday? She yawned, as one escorted her to the stables. 'You can leave me here,' she said in French. 'I shall not disturb the people in the castle, but sleep here.'

The guard shrugged. There was no accounting for the way women behaved, especially where affairs of the heart were concerned. Lovers' tiff, no doubt about it, the way Niall O'More had marched off like that! High born or low born, the women all seemed to like him. Now where could he have been with this one? Away from the prying eyes of the Englishman she had come with, most probably; for had he not been asking about her, and been in a fury when told she had gone with Niall O'More? He shook his head and went back to his post.

Constance had thought she would have to lie awake as she curled up in some straw, but she was so tired that no sooner had she closed her eyes, than she fell asleep. She was woken by some grooms entering the stables, who stared at her in astonishment.

She smiled brightly. 'Good morning.' She brushed away some wisps of straw as she scrambled to her feet, seeing no need to explain why she was there. 'Are they up and about inside the castle now?'

One, who had a wart on his nose, nodded dumbly, while another said, 'Ay, mistress, and wondering where you've been.'

'Oh, there was no need for them to worry about me. I'll go and change my clothes.' Again she smiled. 'Good day to you.' With a wave of the hand, she sauntered out into a sunny day that held no promise of seeing Niall O'More again, and almost into the arms of Master Brandon.

He seized hold of her, and his face held an ugly expression, the tip of his long nose seeming to quiver. 'One of the guards said that you went with O'More. Are you a fool? Where did he take you?'

'I beg your pardon?' She stared at him disdainfully. 'Will you be so good as to stop hurting my arm?'

He released her reluctantly. 'I—did not mean to hurt you.' His smile was forced. 'But I have been worried about you, and hearing that you left with O'More, I feared you had come to some harm.'

She raised dark eyebrows. 'You really had no need to worry. Master O'More wished to explain to me in more detail his reasons for holding my kinsman hostage, and to reassure me as to his safety.'

'So you went alone with him at night outside the castle?' Brandon responded sarcastically.

Constance lowered her eyes and toyed with her fingers. 'I have always had a yearning to ride in the moonlight—and Master O'More can be very persuasive.'

'You disappoint me, Mistress Constance. It is obvious that you need the guidance of a good man. He is a rogue.'

'Oh, no doubt about it, Master Brandon.' She lifted her head and smiled guilelessly at him. 'But I so much wanted someone to speed Robin's release that I allowed myself to be persuaded. But it appears that not even the earl can do anything, so I have decided to return to Naas and await news of Robin there. That is, if His Grace would be so kind as to provide me with an escort. After the hawking, I shall ask him about it. You, I believe, are going on to Kilkenny?'

He grunted approval, and ventured to take her hand. 'Maybe, after my business in Kilkenny is finished, I can come and see you in Naas?' His green eyes were sharp as he raised her hand to his lips.

She concealed her distaste behind another smile. 'It will be a pleasure to see you again, but now, if you don't mind——' she withdrew her hand, '—I really must change my clothes.'

He bowed, and she inclined her head before walking quickly away. As soon as she had changed, her intention was to keep a sharp watch on Master Brandon, and to follow him all the way to Kilkenny.

The falcon soared skywards, and all heads turned to follow its flight, hands quickly shielding eyes from the sun. For a second, Constance admired the bird's graceful flight before tugging on the reins and moving out of the shadow of the trees. If she delayed any longer, Master Brandon would be lost to her. Still she lingered, part of her reluctant to leave the security of the gathering, while another little part wondered about Niall O'More's whereabouts.

The Earl of Desmond had appeared to find it not at all surprising that he should leave in the way he had, and to consider it possible that he would return in a like manner. He asked no questions about her reasons for having gone with Niall outside his castle walls, and she had supplied none, still uncertain where the earl's loyalties lay. She had only herself to rely on, and somehow she had to convince King Richard that there was a plot against his life. She could not live with herself if she did nothing.

She came to the road, and went in the reverse direction to that she had come with Brandon the day before. Was it only yesterday? It seemed an age. Already he was almost out of sight, and she urged her mare on, determined not to dwell on what had happened last night, but rather on what might lie ahead when she met the king. She could not dare to suggest that the Earl of March might be involved in the plot against his life, but surely he would draw his own conclusions. The money to pay his assassins must have come from someone with more possessions than Master Brandon.

Clouds were banking on the horizon. Would it rain later? Sorcha had told her that Kilkenny was but about fifteen miles or so away. The road had taken a twist, and Brandon was lost to sight. An anxious frown knitted her brow, and she urged Maeve on. Suddenly she became aware of the sound of hoofbeats, and saw a rider approaching her across the fields. So far she had seen few people, and the sight of the lone horseman unnerved her. Already she was apprehensive because she was alone. She gave Maeve her head, hoping to outride him. For a while it seemed she would keep her lead, until she realised that he was coming towards the road at an angle and would reach it a little ahead of her, unless she quickened her pace even more. She whispered into her mare's ear and dug in her heels. Maeve's stride lengthened.

Constance forgot everything but the rush of the wind and the rhythm of her body in harmony with that of the mare, until she heard her name being called. She spared a glance over her shoulder, and saw that the rider was closer than she had dreamed possible, and that it was Niall O'More. Her nerves danced.

'You'll break your neck if you don't slow down!' he shouted.

'I don't intend to fall!' she called back, even as she wondered how he had known where to find her.

Maeve passed the place where Constance had estimated he would come on to the road. Some perverse spirit caused her a sudden heady joy at the thought of battling with him, and winning. Then she glanced behind again, and he was not far away. His face was set in grim lines that suddenly scared her. After that, she knew suddenly that he would catch up. Her whole body was beginning to ache unbearably, and slowly, inexorably, he was beginning to overtake her. Now he was alongside, inching past, and then she realised that to continue was pointless.

He came to a halt a short distance ahead by the time she had slowed Maeve to a walk. He dismounted and came over, and without speaking, seized hold of her and dragged her down.

'Let me go!' She struggled, attempting to free her wrist from his constricting hold.

'By all the saints, I won't,' he said in a seething voice. 'Look at Maeve! You should never have ridden her so hard.' He shook her violently.

'It's none of your business what I choose to do,' she declared angrily. 'She's my mare!'

'It is my business when you speak about breeding horses. You need a lesson on how to treat animals.'

'No, I don't!' She glared at him.

He drew in a harsh breath and swung her round.

'What are you doing?' Her voice rose, and she fought him as he forced her down and across his knee. A scream escaped her as his hand came down over her squirming buttocks. The second time, it hurt!

'You devil!' she yelled, trying to push herself up off his leg. His hand descended again, and she screamed again, then pinched his thigh hard, and he pushed her off his knee.

For a second she lay spread-eagled on the ground, so furious that she could not move. Then she hoisted herself up and turned to face him. He still knelt, rubbing his thigh. She flew at him and pushed him, catching him off balance. He sprawled on the earth, anger still in his expression.

'How dare you hit me!' she raged. 'How dare you even touch me! I swore after my husband was killed that never again would I suffer as I did at his hands. Never! Never!' Tears started in her eyes, and swiftly she strode past him to her mare.

As she looked at Maeve, the tears ran down her cheeks. Damn him! Damn him! He was right. She should never have ridden her so hard. She began to unbutton her cote-hardie with the intention of casting it over the sweating mare, when two hands came round her waist, seizing her tightly. Niall rammed her back hard against his body.

'Mistress High-and-Mighty-de-Wensley, are you looking at her? See how laboured her breathing is still?'

'I am not speaking to you,' she responded ve-hemently, seeking to prise his hands apart.

Instead, he trapped them. 'You are stubborn! Stubborn as only a woman can be!' His teeth caught the lobe of her ear and teased it roughly.

She shook her head violently. 'You are a brute! A monster! And I told you not to touch me!'

'You are tempting me to do more than touch you.' His hands moved with hers still trapped inside, to her thighs, and spread out there.

Her heart began to beat violently, half through fear, half in unexpected excitement. She screamed, attempting to free herself as his fingers pinched up her skirts at the sides. 'You brute,' she said in a trembling voice. 'Let me go.'

'I haven't done anything to you—yet.' He dropped his head on her hair.

'Don't—do anything—please!' Tears of frustration rolled down her cheeks. 'Why do you do this to me?'

'Because it pleases me,' he said softly, 'and because you tell me not to.' His mouth brushed her cheek. 'Face me.'

'I'll do nothing of the kind!' She sniffed in an attempt to stem her tears. 'You are a swine.'

'I'm not behaving so badly. I could be worse.'

She was suddenly still. 'Ohh!' She closed her eyes tightly as his teeth tugged at her earlobe again. 'You are a...!'

'I know—a barbarian, to be sure.' He allowed her skirts to fall before twirling her to face him. Briefly his eyes searched her face, tear-stained and flushed.

She twisted her head this way and that, not prepared for the chaos his touch now caused. He seized her chin and forced it round, and kissed her with a complete disregard for her need to carry on breathing. Weakly she hammered on his chest. A couple of deep breaths was all he allowed her before imprisoning her hands in one of his and kissing her again. She was unable to resist when he forced her head back and down until her knees gave way.

She lay on the ground staring up at him, as he flicked her skirts above her knees. 'Not all women have shapely legs,' he murmured conversationally, 'but yours are pretty.'

'It's not for you to say that,' she said in a low voice, struggling to sit up.

He quirked a brow, and tugged her skirts down. 'I pay you a compliment, and you complain! Nothing I do seems to please my lady.'

'I'm *not* your lady—and that's the reason for my not wishing for your attentions. I don't desire the advances of *any* man!'

'I don't believe you!' His eyes looked into hers, and she moistened her mouth. 'What about Brandon?' His voice had hardened.

'Why do you ask about Brandon?' she said, puzzled.

'You're following him,' he replied tersely. 'I've been keeping a watch on the castle since we parted last night. I had to run and borrow a horse to follow you.'

'Horse-stealing again, Master O'More?' she mocked. 'And you talked about my employing you.'

'It's your other horse that I've taken,' he said softly, kneeling on the grass beside her. 'Now, if you don't tell me why you're following Brandon, I'll...' His hand rested on her covered thigh.

She stared at him intently from beneath long lashes. 'I'm sure you would,' she said huskily. 'But I ask myself why you stop to ask me questions?'

He shrugged. 'I ask myself the same question—but why don't you just answer mine?'

She hesitated. 'It's not for the reason you believe. And I tell you only because then you might go away and stop chasing me.'

He grinned. 'Why should I? But don't you think you should stop chasing after Brandon.' His hand caressed her thigh, and suddenly she had difficulty breathing again.

'I told you I'm not chasing him! I'm following him.'

'There's a difference?' The grey eyes probed hers, and he moved closer.

'Of course there is. But,' she paused to slap the hand that stroked her thigh, 'tell me whether you learned anything in the cave? I...' He stopped the words with a kiss, so gentle, yet so thorough that it caused her lips to part, and she instantly forgot her question.

When they drew apart, they stayed staring at each other. A muscle moved in Niall's cheek, and he had to clear his throat. 'What did you ask?'

Constance had to search her mind. 'Last night, when we followed Sil, did you learn anything about his plans? It could be a matter of life and death! Could you tell me—please?'

CHAPTER SEVEN

'YOUR DEATH and my life, Mistress de Wensley!' Niall declared harshly, his face darkening as he sat back on his heels. 'That's what the information almost cost us!'

'I'm sorry.' Constance knelt up, her expression downcast, one hand smoothing her skirts. 'But, I, too, wanted to hear what Sil had to say.'

'And did you?' A slight smile lifted a corner of his mouth.

She sighed, and pulled at the grass. 'You know that he spoke in Irish.'

He made a noise in his throat. 'So you almost got us killed for nothing!'

She tossed her head. 'It was you who went down into the cave and had to flee! What happened? Did Sil recognise you?'

He shrugged. 'I doubt if it was visual recognition—but Sil sometimes seems to know when I'm around—just as I have unpleasant sensations whenever he appears, without having to set eyes on him.'

'A kind of magic?' A cold shiver passed through her.

'Perhaps,' he murmured, toying with his moustache. 'But why are you so interested in Sil's doings?'

She hesitated, still unsure how far to trust him. 'He and Brandon are plotting something.'

'What?' Niall leaned over her. She lowered her head and tore at the grass, indecision clear on her face.

He hissed in exasperation. 'You are the most irritating woman!'

'I could return the compliment.' She scowled.

'Unless you tell me what they're plotting, I won't tell you what I overheard.'

'Ohh!' She tore at a clump of grass and threw it at him. 'You make me so angry!'

His hands brushed at the blades of grass on his tunic. 'Losing your temper won't make me tell you,' he said softly. 'I am going to put out of my mind whatever mischief Sil and his band of cut-throats are plotting.'

'You did hear what Sil was planning to do?' she asked quickly.

He smiled. 'Perhaps it's something to do with your following Brandon to Kilkenny?'

'Maybe.' She scrambled to her feet, suddenly remembering the urgency of her mission.

'Then could it be something to do with the king of England?' Constance sent him a glance before hurrying over to her horse. He followed. 'You're planning to go to Kilkenny alone?' She nodded, not looking at him. 'Can you find the way?'

'It can't be too difficult, and if I stay on the road, I'm bound to come to it sooner or later.'

'It could be later rather than sooner.' He watched her pull herself up on the mare. 'Really, Mistress de Wensley, you cannot go charging about the country alone. It could lead you into all kinds of trouble.'

Her expression told him how she felt about that remark, and if he was in any doubt, she told him. 'If you had not taken my kinsman from me, I would not be careering about the country alone.'

He raised his brows to that. 'That is true—and the reason why I feel obliged to help you. I'll come with you to Kilkenny.'

'You'll come? Why?' She watched him mount.

He drew alongside. 'I have just explained. I feel responsible for you and, besides, I want to see what you're going to do about this plot of Sil's and Brandon's.'

'You know what it is?' she said quickly, feeling a kind of relief.

He smiled. 'I can guess, if it involves Sil and the king of England.'

'Then you will tell me what you overheard?' Now her relief coloured her voice.

Niall pursed his mouth in thought. 'What would you do with the information if I gave it to you?'

'I'd take it to King Richard, of course!' Constance eased her shoulders, taking a deep breath of air laden with the scent of meadow flowers and newly growing grass, and she wished that there was naught else to consider but the pure satisfaction of being out of doors on such a day. 'As soon as I overheard Brandon and Sil plotting against his life, I decided that I would have to go and warn him.'

'When and where was this?' His hand rested on hers a moment. 'Is that the reason why you decided to follow Sil last night?'

'Of course.'

There was a silence. Then, ''Why didn't you tell me?'

She smiled without answering his question, but did say, 'I didn't go to the Earl of Desmond and tell him, either. I wasn't sure that I could trust him.'

'And you didn't trust me.' He took his hand away.

She made no answer. 'It was just before we met in the garden. Sil was overjoyed about the plan. How or when it is to be, I don't know, but he spoke of men singing songs about the deed. I suppose they would,' she added unhappily.

He nodded. 'So you ventured out alone to warn the king?'

'Of course! He must be warned. You can't comprehend what his murder could mean! It could cause a civil war. I understand that you cannot care that England is bedevilled on all sides by enemies who would take advantage of such an event, but I do!' She tilted her chin. 'That is why I must go to Kilkenny.'

He grunted. 'You might have been better off staying in England, if your heart is still there. Why did you come to Ireland, if you feel like this?'

'You know why I came to Ireland!' Why did he sound so vexed? 'And I still intend living here, if I can. But, at the moment, what I want to do is not important— saving Richard's life is. I understand if you want no part of it, but I pray that you will not prevent my doing my uttermost to put him on his guard.' She heeled Maeve into a gallop.

Niall muttered a curse under his breath, and started after her. When he caught up, he asked, 'Why do you presume that I desire Richard's death? He is leaving Ireland; that is good enough for me! His death would not rid us of the Anglo-Norman presence, or of the English in Dublin. I doubt that anything could—they have been here too long. Sil might consider it would, but I don't. As for Brandon, I can only believe that this is a plot to place another on Richard's throne. Maybe the Earl of March, if Brandon really is his messenger.'

'That is what I believe.' She turned her head quickly, glad that he was there beside her. 'How do you think they will kill him?'

'I know how they *plan* to kill him,' he replied positively. 'An ambush. Richard won't be expecting that. Some of the men from the Leinster counties and Waterford are making the effort to cut passes in the woods. Sil's henchmen plan to infiltrate the area and kill the men.' He paused. 'I didn't hear any mention of Richard last night, only of this plan to kill the men cutting down trees. I considered it just a senseless slaughter against those who would support Richard. The kind of pointless destruction that Sil likes to indulge in.'

'My thoughts were of a dagger in some dark passage.' She gave a reluctant laugh.

He shook his head. 'It is not so easy to enter Kilkenny Castle and depart. The town is an English stronghold, and there will be many men-at-arms because Richard is staying there. They would not choose that way. How do you think to gain entry to the castle and Richard's presence?'

'It should not prove too difficult.' Her brows furrowed. 'They will surely not regard me as a threat to the king?'

'It might not be as easy as you consider it to be. I'd best go with you.'

'You?' She stared at him. 'Will it not be dangerous for you?'

'No more dangerous than entering Dublin Castle, and I escaped from there.' He smiled diabolically.

She said nothing. If he wanted to live dangerously, she could not prevent him. Only a tiny part of her would admit that she was glad of some company.

The clouds that had been banked on the horizon had swiftly covered the whole sky, and the first few tentative drops of rain began to fall as Constance caught her first sighting of Kilkenny. A tall single rounded tower drew her attention. 'What is that?'

'St Canice's Cathedral. It's worth seeing, but we aren't here as pilgrims. Another time, perhaps.'

She wondered what he meant by that; he was no longer looking at her, but at the bulk of the castle at the far end of the High Street. Her eyes lifted to the standard fluttering damply from one of the towers and she could just make out the White Hart of Richard Plantagenet. Suddenly it seemed incredible that she was here, considering approaching the castle. How would she get in? It seemed mad to think that all she had to say to the guards was that the king's life was in danger and she wished to see him.

'What do you wish to do first?' Niall's casually-spoken words caused her to jump. 'Chance your fortune at the castle immediately or have some food and drink while considering how best to approach the task of reaching the king of England?'

She experienced panic. It seemed unbelievable to think that she could gain entry. Still she eyed the castle. 'I'll chance my luck. How do I get in?'

'The main gate is in the south wall. It's strongly fortified with bastions, a drawbridge and a portcullis, but I don't consider that the guards will see you as any kind of threat.' There was a glint deep within his grey eyes. 'Do you wish for my company?'

She took in his appearance, especially the drooping moustache and the scar. 'Alone, I might stand a chance of getting in.'

'I have served my purpose? Do our paths part, now?'

'You should be relieved that I don't plan to embroil you any further in this matter.' Her fingers toyed with the reins.

'I am.' His expression was solemn. 'But perhaps I'll wait awhile.'

She stared at him suspiciously. 'You won't do anything foolish? It isn't safe for you to loiter here, I shouldn't wonder.'

'If I were concerned for my safety, Mistress de Wensley,' he chided, 'would I have come with you?'

There seemed no answer to that, so she turned from him and went towards the castle. As she approached, she began to wonder if Brandon had arrived in Kilkenny. What could she say to him if she met him face to face? Should she pretend that it was something he had said that had brought her to Kilkenny? He had mentioned the Duke of Ormonde—was he not the justiciar? If she told him she thought it possible that he might be able to help her to obtain Robin's quick release, that might suffice, but what was the point of worrying? She might not come across him at all.

She brought her horse to an abrupt halt in front of the guards, who were standing, pike in hand. They looked at her and then at each other. They crossed their pikes to form a barrier.

'Now what is it you're wanting, mistress?'

'I would like to see King Richard, if you please?' she said in a firm voice.

The one on the right eyed her tolerantly. 'You have papers—a pass?'

'A—A pass? No. Do I need one?' Her glance passed over him, before fixing rigidly at a point just above his head.

'Of course you do,' said the other man. 'Else why would we be bothering asking for one?' His unoccupied hand rested on Maeve's mane.

'What I have to say to the king is of the uttermost importance—a matter of life and death! You must let me through.' She made to move forward, but the man seized the bridle.

'Now, mistress, none of that. No pass, no entry. You'd be amazed at how many want to see the king of England, but he doesn't have time to see everybody. You can come back when you have a pass.'

'But, please, you must let me in! It's vital! Am I not one of his loyal subjects? Do I not speak English as well as you do?'

'Better,' said the man frankly, 'but that's not to say you couldn't be out to knife him.'

'Do I look the sort of woman who could do such a deed?' She could feel her temper rising.

'Can't tell by looks.' He scrubbed at his nose. 'Why don't you go away and forget about whatever's bothering you?'

'I can't!' she cried angrily. 'Oh, why won't you listen?'

'What's going on here?' Another guard, with a leather breastplate and spiky reddish hair bristling from beneath his steel helmet, sauntered up. Both men turned.

'Oh, 'tis you, Captain,' said the younger of the two men. 'This wench refuses to move on.'

Constance and the captain surveyed each other. She forced a smile. 'If you please, Captain, I can't get these men to understand that this is a matter of life and death. It is vital that I see the king.'

'Can't see the king without a pass,' he replied unsmilingly. 'Move on.'

'Ohh!' She exploded into anger. 'I have a warning of a plot against his life, you dolt! If any of you had a farthing's worth of sense, you would take me to him immediately!'

The captain reddened. 'Now don't you take that tone with me, wench, or I'll have you clapped in irons quicker than you can turn round and ride off! Away with you.'

She glared at him, realising that he was not going to give way, and without another word, pulled on the reins and turned away. What was she going to do? One thing was certain: she could not give up her attempt to see the king. Somehow she would get inside the castle. She would not be beaten!

'So they didn't believe you,' reiterated Niall solemnly, putting down his knife to fill their horn cups again.

'You've said that twice already,' Constance muttered irritably before taking a gulp of ale. 'I think you're glad that they didn't.'

'Why should I be glad? What benefit is it to me?' He half smiled. Constance made no answer, only staring at him moodily. He bent his head and continued with his meal, knowing that sooner or later she would have to ask for his help, or give up. He wanted her to be dependent on him, but he was prepared to wait, knowing that it would be difficult for her. They had had an unfortunate beginning, but he had never encountered a woman like her, and she roused in him emotions that he was not prepared to admit to anyone, least of all to her.

Not yet, anyway! It would not be easy to master her. Some women liked it, but she needed gentle persuasive handling. He *would* be master to her, one day, and not the hired servant that she might envisage! He heard her clear her throat, and lifted his head, cramming the last piece of bread into his mouth.

'How would *you* have attempted to gain entry?' she blurted out, her fingers tightening about the bowl. He chewed with great deliberation, aware of her impatience. 'Well?' Her eyes darkened. Great brown eyes they were—liquidly expressive and thickly lashed. He wiped his mouth on the back of his hand.

'There's only one way, and that's to have a legitimate reason for entering the castle. If Brandon is inside, how will he have got there?' He put his bowl and the platter on the floor.

'He's a messenger—or so he says. I've no doubt he will have a proper pass.'

He nodded. 'Or papers from the Earl of March. Has he come here to discover exactly when Richard's leaving? It's no fun lying in the bracken in the rain—or beneath dripping trees, waiting in ambush.'

'You should know,' she said sweetly, adding hastily as he quirked a brow. 'That *is* the reason. I remember their saying so—and he's to pass the message on to another man in Kilkenny. But how does this help *me*? I'm no messenger.'

'There are plenty of comings and goings. Pages and squires going about their business, some people delivering messages. I got into conversation with a man delivering wine. It seems there's some kind of feast tonight.' He paused to down the remains of his ale. 'The livery worn by certain nobles and religious orders will pass through without question.'

Her face wore an interested expression as she leaned forward. 'Are you suggesting that I dress up as a page?'

'I'm suggesting nothing of the sort,' he retorted, startled. 'You're a woman!'

Her eyes were cool. 'I—could make a perfect page. You are too tall, and, besides, you have that barbarous moustache.' His brow darkened and he caressed the hair on his upper lip. 'In the old days,' she continued, 'women fought alongside their menfolk in battle. I don't see the harm in my dressing up as a page.' He still did not answer, and she was starting to become exasperated. 'It wouldn't be as dangerous as going into battle.'

'No,' he said shortly.

She stared hard at him. 'How do we obtain livery?'

'We?' He groaned.

'You aren't going to help me, then? I tell you, Master O'More, I am quite capable of doing this myself—of dressing up in a boy's clothes and entering the castle. It—it's simply a matter of knowing where to find the clothes. I thought you might know.' She lowered her voice. 'Kathleen told me you were a spy.'

'Hush!' He held up a hand. 'To be sure now, you've convinced me that it would downright foolish of me not to help you. But where Kathleen has the notion that I'm a spy... Well!' He shrugged.

'It's not true?' A small smile played about her mouth.

'Would I be helping you now if I were a spy?' His hand reached for the jug of ale. 'That would be a foolishness.'

She hummed a snatch of a tune, watching him fill his cup, her face expressionless, not believing him at all. If he was a spy as Kathleen said, then entering the castle on her behalf could present him with a perfect opportunity to do whatever spies do.

He put down the jug and looked at her. 'You do accept that you can't do this dressing up? It wouldn't be right.' He took a gulp of his drink.

'I don't accept it at all. As for its being right, who is to know that it's me in disguise? Besides, nobody here knows me, so what does it matter?' she said impatiently. 'Where do we get the livery?'

He was silent a long time, keeping her in suspense as he downed all of the ale. Placing the cup on the floor, he laced his hands in his lap. 'You'll have to play the part of a boy convincingly.'

'Of course.' A muscle in her throat twitched. 'What do I have to do? How shall we...?'

'This is the plan.' His head drew close to hers as he unfolded their next step.

Constance, watching the rain drizzling down as she loitered near the entrance to the alley that Niall had pointed out, wondered if she had been slightly deranged when she agreed to the plan. Ever since she had come to Ireland, she had experienced a feeling of having strayed into a different world, one in which it was possible to believe in one-eyed monsters with great claws from the dawn of time dwelling in a bog, in heroes drawn from legend being reincarnated in a man, of an enemy becoming an ally—and of a fellow countryman being an enemy.

She suddenly realised that Niall was coming as he had said he would, strolling beside a dark-haired youth in livery, who had his head lowered to keep the rain from his face. When they were almost level with her, she sallied forth just as Niall elbowed the youth with some force, making him collide into her. She gave a cry, and clutched at the young man's arm.

'I beg your pardon,' stammered the youth, staring into her face, 'but someone pushed me.' He glanced about him wildly, but Niall had already disappeared.

'I've hurt my ankle,' moaned Constance, pulling at his arm. 'Could you assist me, sir?'

He presented her with a nonplussed expression as he turned. 'I would, mistress, if I weren't in such haste. A

message I have for the Earl of Ormonde from the bishop
of...'

'You would leave me in such difficulty?' She groaned
as she put her foot to the ground. 'How am I to get
home? If only you could lend me your arm. It isn't far.'

He hesitated before doing as she asked, but within a
matter of seconds they were walking up the alley. They
had not gone far when she heard footsteps behind. The
next moment, a hand covered the boy's mouth, and an
arm went about his waist. She pulled her hand from his
arm as he was dragged backwards. He stared at her with
astonished, furious eyes before beginning to struggle, but
he was no match for Niall, who half carried him to the
far end of the alley, that opened on to a small area where
rubbish was piled high.

'Off with your livery, my lad,' ordered Niall.

'My—my livery?' He gazed fearfully, as Niall drew
out his knife.

Constance spoke reassuringly. 'You will not be harmed
if you do as you're told.'

The boy hesitated no longer and soon had stripped
off his tunic, hose, cap and cloak. Niall handed them
to Constance. 'It's a pity about the rain now,' he said
quite cheerfully, pulling a rope from about his waist.

She made no reply, only turning her back on him. She
undressed hurriedly down to her shift. Now was not the
time to be concerned about modesty. On with the boy's
clothes as speedily as possible. The only difficulty was
that of hiding her hair within the cap, but she managed
to wind her braids round and squash them beneath it.
Then she bundled up her discarded clothing and gave it
to Niall.

He scrutinised her carefully. 'You'll have to watch how
you walk—and talk.'

'I know.' She picked up the boy's damp scroll from
where it had fallen when Niall had given her the clothes,

and brushed specks of dirt from it. Her heart had begun to beat uncomfortably fast.

'Will you walk now,' Niall ordered curtly. 'I wish to see that you do it well.'

'And why should I not?' Her eyes sparked. 'It can't be difficult.'

'Just do it,' he snapped impatiently.

'I'm doing it!' She glared at him over her shoulders as she began rather self-consciously to stride about the square, skirting the refuge that gave off a distasteful odour.

'Not too bad,' he said grudgingly. 'But remember that you're not wearing skirts, so you can stride out better than that.'

She nodded, coming to a halt a foot or so from him. 'Shall I go now?'

'You can go when you like.' He shrugged, and turned towards the boy. 'Where have you come from, lad?' The boy told him, staring at Constance with an air of fascinated resignation. 'Well, you can say you have a message for the earl. It should suffice to get you into the castle, but whether it will get you to Ormonde, I don't know.' He shrugged. 'It's fortunate that your voice is deep for a woman.' He faced the boy again. 'Are you cold, lad?' He nodded, and Niall took his mantle from his shoulders and wrapped it about him.

Constance watched, waiting for him to turn and wish her luck, but he did not. After a few minutes she walked away, forgetting about the part she played. There was an uncomfortable tightness in her chest.

'For the sake of the Virgin, woman, remember you're a lad!' he roared.

She jumped, not turning round, but instead fled up the alley, not stopping until she reached the far end. Without her skirts flapping about her ankles, she experienced a sense of freedom. She strode along with all the semblance of not having a care in the world, despite the wind which had risen so that the rain was dashed into her face. At least she had an excuse to hold the cap firmly on her head. The weight of her hair was causing her some anxiety.

At last she reached the entrance to the castle, where different guards were on duty, and for that she was relieved. Taking a deep breath, she marched up to them, ready to state whence she had come and whom she wished to see. But neither of them asked, and only a hand was lifted to wave her through. Her spirits rose as she entered the courtyard.

Despite the weather, there was much bustle. She stood indecisively, the wind buffeting her, wondering which way to go, when she received a blow in the back. She clutched frantically at her cap as she whirled round.

'Make way, lad! Don't be standing like a stock in the rain getting in the way! About your business, or you'll be for it!' The hooded figure carrying a barrel on his shoulder brushed by her and headed towards the shelter of the castle. Slowly she followed, but he disappeared round a corner, and she presumed he was going to the buttery. A girl ran past her, and as she entered the building, Constance heard the sounds of activity within and hurried quickly in her wake.

The great hall hummed with noise and was alive with colour and movement. Jugglers were practising with balls. Scullions hurried hither and thither, almost colliding at times, so that there was a danger of the silver dishes crashing to the floor. A man filled the air with lilting dance music, and a bear on a chain lumbered about on its hind legs.

With a quick darting look at the high table, Constance saw that it was unoccupied, although the side tables were almost filled. Her eyes searched for a sign of Brandon, but she could not see him. Without further delay, she caught the arm of a passing maid servant. 'Tell me, please, where I will find His Grace, the Earl of Ormonde?'

'Here, let me go,' cried the girl. 'I have no time now.'

'It's a matter of life or death. Tell me swiftly!' demanded Constance in a gruff voice.

The girl squinted at her. 'I've heard that before, and it's *my* life that's going to be the matter if I don't get on!'

'Never mind that now, just tell me,' urged Constance.

'He could be anywhere. Crowded with folk this place is today, and it's like the inside of a rabbit-warren at this time. And dark what with the rain and all.

'Where am I likely to find him? Is he with the king?'

'Most likely.' The girl looked at her strangely, then about her. She pulled her arm away. 'If you're quick—that man in the blue and green, who is just about to leave the hall, is probably on his way to tell the earl that all is almost ready.'

'My thanks!' Constance darted away in the direction that the girl had indicated, dodging folk as she saw the man vanish, and breaking into a run. She was just in time to see the end of his cloak as he went up some steps, but was unable to catch him until he stopped in front of a door.

Her calves were aching, and she was panting as she came to a halt. One hand held on to the cap, while the other still clutched the scroll. 'Please, sir, is the king within? Or His Grace?'

The man turned and stared at her. 'Now what's this, lad? His Grace has finished with business for the night. Have you not heard that there's a feast, and it's about to begin? Why don't you go downstairs and join in?'

'I can't do that. I must speak to the earl or the king,' she gasped, her heart thudding in her breast.

'Nonsense, lad! If you wish to deliver that scroll, give it to me.' He held out his hand.

'You may take it and welcome, but I did not come for that. Indeed it isn't even my task to deliver it. But I must speak to His Grace or to the king. It's a matter of life or death!'

His fingers curled about the scroll, and as he took it, he peered closely at her. 'What's this, lad?'

She drew in a shaky breath. 'I've told you: it's a matter of life or death. The king's life. It is in danger!' As she spoke, the door was suddenly flung open and several men were visible in a group near the entrance. It was the man at the centre who drew Constance's attention.

Gracefully built and clad in a fur-trimmed purple velvet houppelande, stood Richard of England. A gold circlet studded with rubies surmounted the fair hair curling about his ears. His nose was straight and narrow, and he favoured a neat moustache and a small curling beard. His heavy-lidded eyes showed a brightness—as if he had just shared a jest with his companions.

'Your Majesty!' Constance, forgetting her guise, sank to the floor in an awkward curtsy, her cloak billowing.

'Why, who is this?' asked Richard of the man clutching the scroll.

'The lad claims that your life is in danger, sire,' said the man, attempting to force a note of amusement in his voice.

A wariness replaced the brightness in Richard's face. 'What's this, boy? I pray that it's not some kind of jest.' He prodded Constance with the tapering point of his purple velvet shoe. 'Rise, boy, and explain yourself.

She stood, straightening her cap as she did so. Suddenly recognition flashed in her face as she saw the man standing just a little to the left of the king. Stepping back a little, she kept both the king and Master Brandon in her eye, realising that so far he had not recognised her. She moistened her mouth. 'It is no jest, sire. I overheard a plot. Two men who planned to have you killed before leaving Ireland.'

A murmur broke out behind the purple-clad figure standing rigidly in front of her. Only he and Brandon kept silence. Then a shudder seemed to pass through the king. 'You have the names of these men?' he yelled, his fists clenching tightly.

She hesitated. 'One stands next to you,' she got out after several long seconds. 'His name is Brandon. He and an Irish...' Then suddenly Brandon shouldered Richard aside and sent the man with the scroll flying by elbowing him viciously in the stomach, as he himself took to his heels.

CHAPTER EIGHT

'AFTER HIM!' screamed the king, recovering himself by
clutching at the arm of the man on his other side.

Without pausing to consider, Constance fled in
Brandon's wake, with other men in pursuit. The cap,
always precariously placed, began to slip. She made a
grab, too late, and it fell to the ground. Only briefly did
she slow down on the steps before she realised that there
was little point in picking it up. She ran on down. It was
as Brandon reached the foot of the steps that she saw a
figure in the doorway. She cried out, and Brandon
turned, recognition dawning on his face. He pulled a
knife from his girdle and flung it at her.

She reached up slowly as a painful stinging tore
through her upper arm. Blood slowly welled up between
her fingers. She leaned against the wall, watching as
Brandon struggled with Niall. The next moment, both
of them went tumbling through the doorway. Her head
was spinning and she felt sick. Her knees gave way so
that she sank to the ground. As she did so, the others
in pursuit clattered down the steps past her. When at
last she opened her eyes, it was on a semicircle of men.

'Here's a surprise!' said one of them, kneeling on the
step beside her. 'What's your name, mistress?'

'Constance—de Wensley,' she whispered, attempting
to sit straighter. She winced.

'Easy now, young lady.' His arm went about her
shoulders, and his face was on a level with hers. It was
a pleasant face, if slightly anxious. 'It was you who
warned the king?'

'Ay, and what I said was true! They plan to ambush—or at least that's what Master O'More told me.' She forced her drooping eyelids up, wondering whether she had imagined that the man struggling with Brandon had been Niall.

'O'More?' Surprise flashed in the man's eyes. 'This man was with you?'

She shook her head. 'He was not supposed to be here—but I am certain that he was the man fighting with Master Brandon. Then, I think I must have swooned.'

'Do you know where this ambush is to take place?'

Again she shook her head. 'I'm sorry, not exactly. But I believe there are men clearing the forests in Leinster and Waterford. They will be attacked and replaced by Sil the Bard's cut-throats.'

'That is good enough for me,' he said firmly. 'You have warned us, so action can be taken. Unfortunately, as far as we can discover, Master Brandon has escaped from the castle. A search is being made of the town, but he could be away by now. Is there any more you can tell us?'

'We followed Sil O'Toole to a cave not far from Athy—that is where these men gather who will ambush the king.'

'It is known to us. And I have heard of Sil O'Toole,' he said with a grimness about his mouth. 'This has been a great shock to his Majesty, and it is possible that he will wish to talk to you later. Now, I shall arrange for you to be removed to a chamber where my physician can tend your wound. I shall see you again, but now my guests await me.'

'*You* are the Earl of Ormonde?'

He nodded, patting her hand before getting up.

The rest soon departed, except for the man to whom she had handed the scroll. 'If you can walk, I shall show you where you may await the physician,' he said with the slightest hint of disapproval.

'I can certainly walk,' she replied with dignity, 'if you could help me up.'

He bent over and awkwardly hauled her to her feet. She decided not to admit to an overpowering weakness in her knees and a mugginess in her head. Her right hand covered her wound, which still bled sluggishly. Slowly she followed him down the stairs and through a doorway. It was a small ante-chamber to which he led her, that contained a narrow bed and a wooden chest. She lowered herself on to the bed.

'I shall fetch the physician.' He gave a stiff bow, and departed.

She stared dumbly after him, before kicking off her shoes and easing herself on the bed. Her shoulder ached and her arm throbbed. She did not feel like moving for a long time, as her eyes closed and her mind drifted into a pale void.

The physician roused her. He was grey-haired, with a cadaverous face that looked as if he never smiled. He showed no emotion, despite her being still clad in boys' clothes. Perhaps he had been warned what to expect. He was accompanied by an elderly plumpish woman carrying a bowl and linen.

Constance attempted to sit up, but he stayed her with a hand, settling himself sideways on the bed. For a while she concentrated on anything but the pain of having her wound cleaned and dressed. She wondered where Niall was, and whether he had followed Brandon. When it was over, the physician lowered her arm gently on to the coverlet, and the woman loomed at his shoulder. 'Thank you.' Constance smiled weakly. 'Shall I be able to get up now?'

'I would advise you to rest,' he murmured, collecting his implements together, 'although the pain might keep you awake. His Grace suggested that you sleep here. It is doubtful whether the king will be able to see you tonight—or His Grace, for that matter. The feasting is likely to go on into the early hours. If there is anything you need, you could make it known to Mistress Dorothy here.'

The woman beamed at her. 'You would like some food, my chick, and a cup of spiced wine, perhaps?'

'Thank you.' Constance was warmed by her smile.

Mistress Dorothy picked up the bowl and the blood-stained cloth. 'Now you rest, and I won't be long with your food.' On those words, she and the physician left the room.

Constance lay staring into the shadows cast by the flickering lamp on the wall behind the bed, wishing that she had not been so foolish as to call out to Brandon. She had had no reason for doing so, unless it was because in that moment she had caught sight of Niall—she was certain it had been he—and wished him to be aware of whom she was chasing. It had been foolish!

Where was Niall now? What had he been doing? Had he not trusted her to deal with the matter herself? Just like a man! She turned on her side, wishing she could sleep for a while, but the wound in her arm was throbbing, and there was too much on her mind.

After a short while Mistress Dorothy brought her some capon and bread, accompanied by a pewter cup of tawny-coloured wine, which steamed gently. She helped her to sit up, then watched her eat and drink, before helping her out of her borrowed clothes. 'Now you rest, my chick,' she said, 'and I'll be back in the morning to see how you are. Maybe your pain will have eased. Women weren't meant to embroil themselves in men's affairs! You be glad now that it's no worse.' With that, she departed, chuckling to herself.

The wine had warmed and soothed Constance's nerves. She lay back, cushioned slightly from the pain, and was just drifting into sleep when she heard the door open. Struggling against the lethargy that held her, she forced her eyelids open to see a shadowy figure looming over her. Her mouth opened to scream, but a hand quickly stopped the sound.

'Hush, now, 'tis only me.' Slowly the hand was removed. 'Are you badly hurt?'

'What are you doing here?' She blinked sleepily at him. He looked pale in the lamplight. 'You gave me a fright—but you are always doing so!'

'Always?' Niall smiled grimly. 'That's a fine welcome you give me after the trouble I've had getting back in here and finding where they put you!'

Immediately she was fully awake. 'You shouldn't have come back! What if they catch you?'

He scowled. 'You think so little of me that you didn't expect me to show concern about your being wounded?' He sat on the bed.

Surprised at his vehemence, she was at a loss to respond, so she changed the subject. 'Never mind that!' She shifted her legs slightly to give him more room, and then wondered if that was wise. 'Did you catch Brandon?'

'Almost, but in the end he escaped,' he said regretfully. 'He's a slippery customer.'

'You let him escape?' She winced as she sat up. 'But I saw you struggling—you nearly had him.'

'I never thought he possessed such strength.' He scowled. 'Perhaps it was being so desperate. He bit me!'

'Bit you? This is not a fortunate day for you, is it, Master O'More?' she said unsteadily.

He sighed heavily. 'That it isn't! I might have caught him had it not been raining as though the heavens had burst asunder, but he gave me the slip up some lane.'

'It might be that he went to the house of the man Sil said he was to meet. He could have passed on a warning.'

'Most likely,' he said shortly, 'but I couldn't force entry into every house in that area.'

'No, I suppose you couldn't,' she murmured, surprising herself by feeling sorry for him. 'It will be useless for the earl to arrange any sort of surprise attack on the men near Athy now.'

He nodded. 'You told him?'

'Ay.' There was a silence.

'You haven't said how badly you are hurt.' Niall's hand rested lightly on her covered leg. 'Yet I presume, from the way you speak, that there isn't much wrong?'

'A flesh wound, that is all.' She touched her arm, conscious of his hand resting on her leg. 'Although there seemed a terrible lot of blood. I fainted with the loss of it.'

'That bad, was it?' he drawled, not looking at her. 'What caused you to draw attention to yourself like that? It was foolish! I could have dealt with him easily enough.'

'So it seems,' she said drily. 'I'm wounded—and you lost him.'

'Well, there's nothing more we can do now.' He got up abruptly. 'How did it happen that you were chasing Brandon?' His face was in shadow so that she could not read his expression, but he sounded irritable.

'The most foolish of reasons,' she murmured. 'My king said, "After him!", so I—went after him.'

A reluctant laugh sounded in the chamber as Niall sat on the bed again. 'Such an obedient subject . . . You surprise me! But then you are always doing that in the short time I have known you. And Ormonde?'

'He must have been there then, but I didn't know him to recognise him. Later he spoke to me—he was kind—and he called his own physician to tend me. I have been fed well, also.'

'You didn't mention my name, I hope?'' His eyes were on her face.

She bent her head, toying with her fingers. 'Why should I mention your name?'

'That's not an answer; and by the tone of your voice, you did.' He leaned towards her until his face was only inches away.

'He—He sounded surprised.' She pleated the coverlet between her fingers.

'That doesn't amaze me,' he said sarcastically, resting his arm on the pillow behind her head.

'But you can't be the only O'More in Ireland?' She hitched the covers a little higher so that they covered her shoulders.

'It was Ormonde who had me imprisoned in Dublin Castle,' he murmured.

'Oh!' She could not think of anything else to say. His closeness was having its effect on her. 'If—If you are concerned for your safety, perhaps you should go now?'

'You want to be rid of me?' He sounded amused.

She turned her head slowly, and their noses bumped. She drew back hurriedly. 'You really should go!' There was a hint of panic in her voice.

'Do you fear me still, mistress?' There was mockery in his tone.

She averted her face. 'I have cause to fear you,' she replied in a low voice.

'But I don't believe you are scared of me! From the way you conduct yourself, I doubt that much frightens you.' His finger traced a path down her cheek, and she closed her eyes briefly.

'Then you are mistaken.' Now she faced him. 'There is much that I fear. My father said that I was foolhardy even to contemplate coming to Ireland, and now I know he was right.'

'Because of me?' he asked harshly, his fingers tightening about her chin. He tilted her face so that they gazed into each other's eyes.

'In part,' she responded in a strained voice. 'Robin warned me also of the foolishness of my wishing to stay here, but I would not listen, because I thought it would be different from what it has been, so far.'

'Normally, life is not the way it has been for both of us in the last few days,' he said quietly. 'Give Ireland a chance—give *me* a chance to prove to you that that plan you had to breed horses could work.' He seized her shoulders with both hands. 'Don't go back to England— not yet! Not before you decide whether your estates are a place you can reject—or the place of your dreams!'

She was silenced by the blaze of excitement that his words conjured up. Then she looked up into his scarred face, and doubted. 'But...there's Robin!' She sighed. 'How can I trust you, when so much has happened between us?'

'Trust me!' He shook her slightly. 'I shall not fail you. As for your kinsman, when you speak to Ormonde again, tell him about his being held hostage. It is possible that he might be able to help with the negotiations, so that both men are freed more swiftly.'

'I had thought of it.' Her excitement rekindled. 'Have I not risked my life to bring a warning to Richard? That surely is a strong reason for Ormonde to comply with my request.'

Niall nodded. 'If you don't try, what hope is there of having what you desire.' He released her abruptly. 'I must go.'

Her body jerked upright. 'You are leaving *now*?'

His expression was suddenly inscrutable. 'Isn't that what you wanted? Or would you like to see me captured?' His hand was on the door.

'No,' she replied baldly.

'Good.' His voice was soft, almost a caress. 'When you speak to Ormonde, ask him about Henry Christade—and you'll understand why I dare not stay any longer.' He opened the door and was half-way through it, when she spoke.

'How will you find me?'

'I'll find you,' he answered, 'even if it was necessary to scour the whole of Wicklow.' Quietly the door closed behind him

Constance flopped back on the bed, staring into the shadows. Uncertainty immediately assailed her. Was she mad? Fancy contemplating linking her life with a man like Niall O'More! Were they not enemies? Yet how many times had he saved her from being hurt? If they had not spent that night together by the bog, how would she feel about him now? She had no way of answering that question—because it could not be blotted out. He had said he would never forget it—and she wanted to forget it, but could not. Why could she not be sensible and cast the man completely from her thoughts? Perhaps it was as he had said—that they were fated to meet. But for what purpose and to what end? Maybe it would end here in this castle? It could be that they had been drawn together to save the king's life—and that after tonight she would never see him again. She snuggled down in the bed, attempting to banish all thought of Niall's talk about giving him a chance, and of his scouring Wicklow to find her. If he did find her, perhaps she *might* give him that chance he had asked for.

When she woke the next morning, she lay luxuriating in the comfort of having a bed. But it was not long before she was disturbed by the entry of Mistress Dorothy bringing ale, bread and smoked bacon. The news, she declared, was that His Grace would see her in the hall as soon as possible—if she was feeling well enough.

'Of course I'm well enough,' Constance replied, before eating her breakfast.

Afterwards she submitted to the woman's ministrations in re-dressing her arm and anointing it with salve. There was some explaining to do when Mistress Dorothy discovered her clothes on the chest. Constance realised that Niall must have placed them there before waking her last night, yet he had not said a word. The woman could hardly credit that a man could get in and out with all the guard alerted. It was a matter that had made

Constance wonder, and she could only surmise that he might have swum the river or the moat to escape. At last she was ready, and without more ado she went in search of the Earl of Ormonde.

He was sitting at a table, reading a scroll, and did not look up until she was in front of him. Then he scrutinised her carefully. 'You look quite different, Mistress de Wensley. Please be seated. I pray that your wound is not causing you too much discomfort?' he asked with grave courtesy.

'No, Your Grace.' Her expression composed, she sat on a stool.

There was a short silence before he spoke. 'Perhaps you can explain, first, how you came in a boy's livery into my castle?'

'I could not enter by any other means.' She proceeded to tell him most of what had happened, omitting how she had obtained the livery.

He toyed with the quill on the table. 'You do not have to shield O'More, mistress. A boy has been here with your baggage and your mare.' She was silent, intertwining her fingers. 'I know from the boy's description that it was Niall O'More, but I cannot understand how he came to help you—unless it was to serve his own ends.'

Her face showed conflicting emotions. 'I did question his motives myself, but I cannot see what he could gain by putting his life in danger. Please tell me, Your Grace, who is Henry Christade?'

He seemed taken aback. 'Henry Christade is a squire in the king's service, acting as an interpreter. He speaks Irish. Surely he has nothing to do with this plot to kill the king?'

Her dark brows knitted. 'There is nothing else?'

'What do you wish to know?' He moved the quill aside.

She leaned forward. 'Master O'More told me to ask you about him. He said that I might understand why he

had to leave so hurriedly. He had no mind to meet you,
I believe.'

'That young man and I have words to say to each
other,' said the earl grimly. 'He once borrowed my
favourite horse. He has yet to return it to me. How is
it that you met this man?'

After the barest hesitation she told him of Robin's
capture.

'Ah! I think I understand.' He leaned back in his chair.
'I will tell you a little more about Christade. He was in
my service a long time ago, and was captured by the
native Irish. For seven years he lived with them, until
his captor was in turn taken by the Duke of Clarence.
An exchange was arranged, although Christade was reluctant to leave, having married the daughter of his
captor. He had two daughters of his own, by then. He
and his wife went with one daughter to live in Bristol,
the other stayed behind to comfort her grandfather. It
is likely that O'More feared being captured and exchanged for your kinsman.' Absently the earl smoothed
the parchment on the table. 'I understand O'More's
concern for Dermot O'Toole, having heard of the
friendship between them. Now Sil O'Toole——' he
picked up the quill, turning it between his fingers, '—is
another matter altogether. It's rumoured that it was he
who struck the blow that resulted in the scar on O'More's
face, so ensuring that there was no chance of his ever
gaining the chieftaincy of his tribe. Although I doubt
whether he had such ambitions; his loyalty would be to
Dermot, who has a greater claim.'

Constance was confounded—the horse-thief a chief
of a tribe! 'But surely that would mean that he was a
member of the Irish nobility?'

The earl smiled. 'If you asked half the men in Ireland,
they would claim to be descended from the old kings of
Ireland—and most likely it would be true! There are
some who would claim that the old ways were the better

ways. Sil O'Toole, for instance!' He frowned. 'The
reason, perhaps, for O'More's face being spoilt. His
mother is some kind of cousin to the chief, and so many
of their young bloods get killed. If not in fighting us,
they fight among themselves. In the old days, a man had
to be perfect in face and form to rule—and if Sil had
his way...' He shrugged.

'But of what concern can it be of Sil's? He's a bard.'

'Their bards exert some influence—but I would say
that Sil is more than a bard—he is a *filidh*.'

Her brow wrinkled. 'What is a *filidh*? I have heard
the word, but I cannot remember.'

'They are much more than poets—they are also seers
and teachers. They can advise the ruler and witness con-
tracts. They also use their power of satire to undermine
a leader's confidence, and that can destroy a chief and
make him look unworthy in the eyes of the tribe. Maybe
he feared that O'More, if he gained the leadership, would
not be so easily influenced by him because O'More was
reared outside the tribal influence, on account of his
mother's actions. It is possible that it was because Sil
was involved that he took a hand in helping you to thwart
this plot against the king's life.' He shrugged his velvet-
clad shoulders. 'But that is enough about O'More. I must
tell you that Sil escaped our net. Brandon must have
reached him in time to warn him. When some of our
men went to the cave, the gang were gone. They could
be lying in wait somewhere on the road to Waterford,
but we shall be ready for an ambush.' He stopped to
gaze at her over his clasped hands. 'I shall do what I
can to ensure the speedy exchange of your kinsman for
Dermot O'Toole. He is not one of the more important
hostages,' he said at last. 'But really we cannot allow
you to wander over Ireland in the way you have, Mistress
de Wensley. Your falling into the hands of O'More is
proof of that. Not to mention Brandon's.' He pressed

his fingertips together. 'This man Upton—you left him at Naas?'

She nodded. 'I would like to return there, if possible.'

'That can be arranged, although it might be wiser for you to return to England. This is not a country for lone women, Mistress de Wensley.' He smiled austerely. 'I doubt that any country is, and if you wished to stay on this manor of yours, I could not possibly provide you with constant protection. Besides, it is beyond my jurisdiction.'

'I do not ask it, Your Grace. However, having come all this way, I would not wish to leave without ever setting foot on my own land.'

'I understand that.' He patted her hand. 'You go, then, and I shall see that you have protection as far as Naas. Also, if there is no arrangement made for you to receive the rents due to you before you leave for England, I can do something about them.'

'Thank you, but I am almost certain that they have been paid.'

'That is all right, then.' He cleared his throat. 'You will take a cup of wine with me?'

'Thank you.' Her heart was a little lighter as she watched a servant coming at his beckoning.

The earl faced her again, his brow clouded. 'I doubt that I need to warn you to be on your guard against O'More. For his own satisfaction, he chose to help you to warn the king—to be revenged against Sil.'

A shadow darkened Constance's momentary gladness. 'I am not a fool, Your Grace,' she said quietly, tilting her chin. 'And I appreciate your concern.'

He nodded, smiled, and pulled a ring from his little finger. 'King Richard, I am afraid, is unable to see you. Following what you told us, we have had to change our plans. But he has bidden me to give this to you as a token of his gratitude.' He handed her the ring. It was of gold, with a small ruby surmounted by tiny diamonds.

'It is a generous gift,' she murmured, lifting her head. 'I did not expect any reward but that of serving my king.'

'He is grateful for your warning, and grieved by your injury. It is not so long ago that he lost his own wife to the ravages of the plague, and he is sensitive to any person's injury, especially a woman's.'

'I remember hearing about her death,' she murmured. 'They said that the king's grief was so great that he burned down the Palace of Sheen, where Queen Anne died.' She pushed the ring on to the middle finger of her right hand. It was slightly too large. 'You will thank him for me?'

'Certainly I will do so.' The earl inclined his head, then leaned back as a servant set a salver between them on the table. 'But you will heed my warning concerning O'More?' He gazed at her intently. 'I have heard that he has a certain charm that women find attractive. It was my god-daughter who told me so.' He gave a wry smile. 'It was she who lent him my horse, so enabling him to escape from Dublin Castle when I was justiciar.' He shook his head. 'Girls, they are so easily deceived!' He picked up the pewter cup. 'To your future, Mistress de Wensley—may it be long and happy.'

'Your health, Your Grace.' She took only a sip of the wine, but he downed his in one gulp.'

'Now I must leave you.' He pushed back his chair. 'I shall arrange an escort for you now—that is, if you are feeling well enough to travel?'

'Ay, Your Grace.' She guessed that she might well be in their way if she stayed. And besides—despite the dull ache in her arm—she wished to be on her way. Would Niall O'More come to seek her out?

'I bid you farewell, Mistress de Wensley, and thank you again.' He smiled down at her.

She rose, putting down the cup. 'I thank you for your kindness.' She hesitated. 'You will—not forget—about Robin Milburn, my kinsman, and Dermot O'Toole?'

'No, child.' He raised a hand and left her standing, then she sat to finish her wine and to consider her next step. She could not help wondering where exactly Niall had gone after he had left. Maybe his desire for revenge against Sil would take him to the mountains. Danger seems to draw the man, she thought vexedly, before chiding herself for even thinking about a scurvy horse-thief, who had used her in this matter for his own ends as he had in others. She stared moodily into the liquid sparkling in the cup before tossing it all back. Now she had to face the journey back to Naas. So much travelling, of late! She would be glad when she could stay put for a while.

Constance stared about her. It seemed incredible that she could have been here and not realised it was the place she sought. Had she not considered it familiar? There were the oaks grouping on a rise. There were the fields with men labouring among the sprouting barley and oats. She turned to Master Upton. 'You say that the girls did not seem surprised to hear of my coming?' she asked. 'You did reassure them that I would not turn them out of the house?'

'Ay.' His jowls wobbled.

'Good, Master Upton.' She smiled at him reassuringly. 'You say that you know the foster-brother?'

He nodded. 'All the years I've been collecting the rents and dues for the de Wensleys.'

'Would you say that he is an honest man—a man that I could trust?' Her fingers curled tightly on the reins as she considered how Niall had withheld from her the information concerning the whereabouts of her estate.

Master Upton rubbed his chin. 'He's a fair man—and his foster-father trusted him implicitly.'

'But was the foster-father to be trusted?' she asked impatiently. This was not the answer she wanted, because she felt she needed another reason for Niall not to stay. She wanted to be rid of him immediately, so that he would not be around, setting her world upside-down and disturbing her emotions.

'I believed him to be.' There was bewilderment in Master Upton's voice. 'Have I done wrong to tell Master Niall that you would have need of his services?'

'That has yet to be seen,' she said coolly. 'When last I was here, I was informed that he lived in the hills.'

'He told me that he was no longer needed to the extent that he was last year.' Master Upton pulled up abruptly, his eyes round with apprehension, as from round the side of the side of the house came the two wolfhounds. The nearest dog snapped at his boot, but desisted at the word of command from the man who came after them.

Niall and Constance gazed at each other. He quirked one brow. 'Good day to you, Mistress de Wensley. To be sure 'tis a fine one that brings you here.'

'Are you so sure about that, Master O'More?' she replied in a chilly voice. The Earl of Ormonde's warning was ringing in her ears. He charmed the women, did he? Well, his smile was not going to work on her!

Some of the light died in his eyes. 'To be sure I'm sure,' he said quietly. 'Now would you be accepting my hand to help you down?'

'Why not?' she replied sweetly, placing her fingers in his hand and sliding from the mare. His other hand steadied her, and for a second their bodies brushed against each other. She experienced a tingling sensation and moved back swiftly, a flush running along her cheekbones. 'It will be the last time I will be needing your help, Master O'More,' she said hastily.

'And why is that?' He took a step towards her. 'Is it that you're upset because I didn't tell you about this being your estate?'

'Of course! Why didn't you tell me?' she demanded, her temper flaring. 'All the talk about scouring Wicklow to find me!'

His expression was instantly as fiery as hers. 'I said, if it were necessary! I thought you would be relieved to find me here waiting for you.'

'Relieved!' She threw up her arms. 'Why should I be relieved to set eyes on a horse-thief and a deceiver? I would be relieved never to see you again, Master O'More.'

'That's easily remedied, Mistress de Wensley. I'll go!' He stared at her stonily. 'But if you change your mind, you'll have to beg me to come back, because I tire of your insults.' He turned on his heel, and walked away.

CHAPTER NINE

'SWEET JESU, mistress, have you taken leave of your senses?' cried Master Upton, dismounting awkwardly, his expression one of distress. 'Who will protect you if Master Niall isn't here?'

'Who protected Kathleen and Brigid when he wasn't here?' she snapped, her fingers curling and uncurling on her horse's neck. 'I don't need the man.' Her eyes were on Niall's retreating figure.

'He was never far away. Folk have only to hear that he's withdrawn his protection from these estates, and they'll come down on you from the hills like a flock of hungry crows.'

'And how will they get to know? Is he going to tell them? What about his foster-sisters? Will he leave them without his protection?'

'They are not here at the moment.' He gnawed his lip anxiously.

'What?' She stared at him in surprise.

'They have gone to the hills. It was the first of May yesterday, and they have taken the cows to their summer pasture. Brigid is expected back at any time—but if Master Niall is not here, she might not stay.'

Constance's face showed her sudden uncertainty, then her expression hardened. 'That is her decision. You heard what Master O'More said—that I would have to beg him to come back. I *never* beg, Master Upton. If you would see to the horses, I'm going inside the house.'

He half-opened his mouth, but before he could speak, she turned and went inside. Nothing seemed changed inside the house, except for the quiet. Silence was suddenly a noiseless echo sounding in her head, one to which she had become accustomed in all the years of her marriage. She would have liked to have become better acquainted with Kathleen, but it seemed that it was not to be.

She wandered about the hall, debating whether to stay. Now that she was here alone, her plans seemed nonsense. How many men had stressed that to her? How many times had the danger of her being alone been emphasised? This place belonged to her, and she wanted to stay—but wanting was not enough if she had no one to help her. Robin had been right, so had her father, and Ormonde, and Desmond. It seemed that she needed a man like Niall O'More if she were to remain.

There was a noise at the door, and she turned eagerly, but it was only Master Upton with her baggage. 'I think we'll be needing water,' he said, sinking wearily on to a stool, and dumping her baggage.

He looked so woebegone that a stir of pity welled inside Constance. It was hot outside, and he was not a thin man! She smiled. 'I shall go and fetch some. I know the way.'

His face eased into a grin. 'That's kind of you, mistress. I'll just stay awhile here out of the sun, if I may?'

'Yes, of course, Master Upton.' She patted his shoulder as she passed.

As she walked to the river, she could not help remembering how she had seen Niall there, and how furious he had been when she dropped his clothes in the water. What had he said when they met again? She bit her lip in thought, the pail swinging from her fingers. Her spirits plummeted. He should have left her in the bog for the *fomor*, that was it. Yet he had not! How many times had he responded to her cry for help? Once—twice—thrice?

Then her heart gave a treacherous leap as she saw Niall sitting on a rock. A small fire crackled a few feet away from him, over which hung several fish on a stick. He looked up at her and then away again, his arms hooked about his legs.

Her throat was suddenly tight, and she had to swallow before she forced words out. 'I—I thought you had gone?'

'Not yet. I'm not sure whether I'm going or staying— yet.' He looked at her, the grey eyes intense.

Constance placed the pail on the ground and clasped her hands tightly behind her back. She could not beg him—she could not! But she wanted to keep him here, so she searched for something to say—anything! She cleared her throat. 'Why are you cooking fish out here?'

'Who wants to spend time indoors on such a day? Besides, it makes the hall less smoky.' His tone was coolly polite as he made a move to remove the fish. 'I caught them just before I had warning that you were coming. The fire was already lit, and I had considered asking you to dinner.'

'Are you asking me now?' A tentative smile tugged at her mouth.

'That depends.' He took up a wooden bowl and quickly placed the hot fish inside it.

'On what—my begging you to stay?' she retorted in a low voice.

'No.' He glanced at her quickly. 'On whether you are considering staying for dinner.'

'The fish smell delicious.' She sat on the rock he had vacated and stared into the water.

'They'll taste just as good.' Niall sat beside her. It was a tight squeeze, but he made no apologies nor asked her permission. His thigh was warm against hers, and she found that disturbing.

'Did Master Upton tell you where the girls have gone?' His eyes were on the task in hand as his fingers busied themselves with the slightly smoked fish.

'To the summer pasture. He said that Brigid would be returning, but she might not stay if you weren't here.' She was silent as she looked across the river towards the Wicklow Hills, not really caring about Brigid staying— she would have preferred Kathleen's company, but she needed him. 'Are you staying?'

'Are you asking me?' His expression was sombre as he met her gaze. He edged the bowl towards her.

'I—I'm asking.' She looked down at the fish and took up a piece. Her cheeks were flushed as a result of his searching glance.

'Why do you want me to stay?' He took a bite of fish, his teeth crunching the crispy pieces.

She lifted her head. 'What is it you want me to say, Master O'More?'

'That you need me here—that you want me to stay.' He smiled unexpectedly. 'Is it so much to ask?'

She moistened her lips. 'It is, when you are asking the mistress to say such things to the—the . . .'

'Servant?' he supplied tersely.

'I did not say that!' she declared, remembering Ormonde's statement that about half the Irishmen in Ireland claimed to be descendants of their kings. He was so proud, this man! She rose abruptly, so that Niall had to move quickly to prevent the bowl from falling. They exchanged looks. 'You ask too much, too soon,' she said.

'Is it not true?' He placed the bowl on the rock and stood behind her.

'Isn't what true—that you are the servant, or—or . . .?' she floundered. How could she say that she wanted him and needed him?

'Don't you need me?' he demanded. 'Most of my life has been spent here. I know the men and their families. I speak their language in more ways than one. I understand horses! I would help you, woman, but you are too proud to see it!' He seized hold of her and spun her round to face him. For several moments he stayed still, holding her, and all she could think of as they stood so close was that she was glad to be wearing the scarlet gown that so suited her colouring. Shock rippled through her at her sudden desire. No, it was almost a hunger in her—for his appreciation of her as a woman.

'Am I so proud?' she whispered. 'Yet it is I who do not wish to offend your pride by saying the word "servant" after knowing that you have helped to oversee the manor for years. You have played the role of master here, and now I come from across the seas—the hated, the despised, English oppressor.'

A slight smile crossed his face, and he flicked her cheek with a finger before realising that she might not like it— and he had vowed to keep his distance! 'Hated—despised? No, Mistress de Wensley,' he murmured, 'you are none of those things. Unforgiving, maybe! Stubborn and courageous, ay! You are those things.' He moved away. 'I want to stay here and work for you because this is the place where I am happiest. I was brought up here. You are a woman alone who cannot stay without protection. So let us decide to stop fighting and work side by side for the future of the estate. And maybe, in time, we shall forget the past.'

She nodded wordlessly, strangely moved by his words, although she had never thought herself so unforgiving— yet there were events in her life that she had never forgotten, things that Milo had done to her that she found hard to forgive.

Niall touched her arm. 'Won't you sit down again?' She did so, and he placed the bowl on her knee. 'I mentioned to you that at some time I would wish to find a stallion for Maeve. There is such a stallion in Connemara that I would like to buy. If you are in agreement, we could do so together. We need strength in a breed; a much more important trait than speed.'

'You would need to go to Connemara to buy this horse?' She forced herself to concentrate on what he was saying, but his arm was against hers and she found his closeness once again distracting.

He nodded. 'I would not go just yet. I have been away from here for some time, and your coming will mean changes. In a month or so, maybe.'

'This horse in Connemara is important to you?' She picked up another piece of fish. She had regained her appetite now that their quarrel seemed over, and, moreover, the journey had made her hungry.

'Ay!' His face took on a dreamy expression. 'He is strong, and could sire many foals that we could sell in England and Italy.'

'Who would go with them?' She licked her fingers, watching his face from the corner of her eye.

'I would have to, of course. My foster-father took me with him to the fair at Lincoln when I was just a lad of maybe ten. And I have been to the fair at Antwerp and to several others with unpronounceable names in France and Italy.' His face was bright with enthusiasm.

'It would be dangerous.' A shadow crossed her countenance.

He looked up at her quickly, and shrugged. 'Life is dangerous. Was it not so for you coming here? But that did not deter you, and you are a woman! The young horses become frightened at sea, and I would have to be there with them.'

'You might not be able to manage several alone. You would need help. In the past, I went across the sea to France with Philippa and my father.'

He cocked an enquiring look at her. 'Philippa?'

'My stepmother,' she supplied. 'Before my step-brothers were born, I went with them to Calais—that was before I was wed.' She fell silent, and Niall remembered again what she had said about her husband when he had caught up with her on the way to Kilkenny. There was a look in her eyes now that made him feel angry towards the dead de Wensley, and protective towards her.

He wanted to rid her of that look. 'Why did you go to Calais?'

She smiled. 'My father, as I told you, is a wool-merchant, although now he takes little part in actually selling the wool.' Her face took on a faraway expression. 'When I was a child we did not have much—a small plot of land in Yorkshire that had been my grandfather's father's. But when Father went to France to fight in the train of John of Gaunt, he stayed in Calais and realised the potential of rearing sheep and selling their wool abroad. When he married my stepmother, she brought him a manor in Kent—that is in the south of England, if you do not know it.'

'I know of it—when I passed through London with my foster-father. But go on.' He was finding her tale interesting, and was relieved that she now seemed relaxed in his company.

'So they put sheep on that manor also. Then they both became interested in weaving their own wool—there were already Flemish weavers in Yorkshire and Kent—so they imported some for their manors, and they taught our own people.' She looked at him fully. 'Cloth brought him to Ireland, and as a consequence Robin and me.'

A shadow darkened her eyes, then her face brightened again. 'But we were talking about horses. Ormonde told me that you borrowed his favourite horse and never returned it.'

'"Borrowed" is the right word,' stated Niall. 'I have the horse still, but it is not so easy to return a horse to an enemy.' He pulled a face. 'What else did Ormonde say about me?'

'That you charmed his god-daughter into helping you to escape,' she said lightly. 'Next time you take such a risk as entering an English castle, there might not be a woman to help you.'

'I don't need a woman to help me.' His eyes lazily surveyed her oval face. 'Women should stay out of such matters. Look what happened to you.'

'That was unfortunate. But we are talking about *you*— you were caught at Dublin Castle.'

He shrugged. '*That* was unfortunate! The English suspect most beggars of not being what they seem.'

Her eyebrows lifted. 'You dressed up as a beggar?'

He winked. ''Tis surprising how much information the men at the gates drop, and I needed to know where Dermot was being taken.' He gave a heavy sigh. 'He's at Trim, one of the most formidable of the English strongholds. If it had been any other, I would have chanced a rescue.'

'Alone?' She wrinkled her nose.

'It is easier to slip through their defences like that then with a horde of armed men,' he said confidently.

'No doubt,' she responded drily.

He grinned. 'You don't believe me, even though I got in and out of Kilkenny Castle without being caught?'

'You weren't rescuing anybody, then.' She paused to swallow the last of the fish.

'That's true,' he said solemnly. 'You—You did ask Ormonde about your kinsman and Dermot?'

She nodded. 'He said he would do all he could. He also mentioned that Sil and his men had gone from the cave near Athy.'

He nodded. 'What else did he say?' She hesitated. 'Well?' His eyes narrowed.

'He spoke of Sil. He suggested that you might have helped me simply to have your revenge on Sil for scarring you deliberately.'

He rose slowly. 'Go on.'

Constance looked away. 'In the old days, the tribes would not accept a leader who was not perfect in face and form, so that's why Sil did that to you, he said.'

The colour drained from Niall's face. 'Do *you* find me ugly—marred in perfection?'

'No!' she exclaimed starkly, turning from him to contemplate the river. It disturbed her to see him thus affected.

'It's partly true,' he said in a tight voice. 'Sil would have blinded me because my brother defied him. He called our mother names...' He stopped abruptly, before continuing in a weary voice. '*If* Dermot had not come along—but that was a long time ago. You understand now why he hates Dermot, and why I love Dermot. Sil would let him remain in captivity, so that he can gain more time to sap away confidence in the leadership. He blames Dermot's father for giving his support to Art MacMurrough. He whispers and schemes, drawing in this man and that. Only Dermot is strong enough to turn the tide.'

'You're strong enough,' she whispered, whirling round. 'You could withstand him.'

'Maybe for a while, with the support of some friends in the tribe, but all would not follow me.' He ran a finger down his scar. 'This does exclude me—as well as my upbringing outside the tribe. There is also a strong possibility that Sil knows what part you and I had in spoiling his plans for the murder. He will come one day seeking us out, but I have my spies to watch him, and when I receive warning, Constance, you will run—all the way back to England, if necessary.'

She looked at him, aghast. 'How can you talk so— how can you decide what I am to do? I am mistress here, and I have no intentions of fleeing from the likes of Sil O'Toole! When you have warning, we shall inform the English authorities, and they will deal with Sil and his cut-throats.'

Niall seized her by the shoulders. 'You will do as you are told! What do you know about this country or its people, except what you have heard from an old man who fled years ago and dreamed of the past in his old age? You saw and heard Sil at Desmond's feast. He has powers that even I fear, although I can withstand them—perhaps because we are kin, and maybe...maybe I have inherited a share of those powers, but, God willing, I would never use them for evil as he does.' His eyes scanned her face. 'I could tell you of black deeds perpetrated by Sil that would make your blood run chill and give you dark dreams that would cause you to wake screaming.' He held her a little away from him, and his voice softened. 'Don't be deceived by Sil's flowing robes; he is no weakling, and being a woman would not save you from ending up on the hill with his knife or sickle to your throat, breast or stomach—and that after he had cast you beneath his spell and used you to his satisfaction.'

She moistened her lips. 'I—I believe you are trying to frighten me, Niall.' she said, with a reluctant laugh. 'Well, you have succeeded!'

'Good,' he said emphatically. 'You will run when you are told?'

'I shall run—but what will you do?'

'I shall fight.' There was a silence while each tried to read the other's expression.

'Of course,' she murmured, twisting out of his hold and looking away from him. 'I should have realised that without asking.'

'Stop worrying.' He touched her shoulder reassuringly before bending to take a jug from the river. 'What I have scared you with, will not happen to you.'

'You have a hundred pairs of eyes that can see everywhere?' She turned to face him, her olive-skinned face shadowed by anxiety.

'Something near that number.' He took a drink of ale before handing the jug to her.

'Am I to believe that—and trust your word not to worry?' She held the jug firmly between both hands.

'Trust me,' he said quietly. 'And drink up.'

She took a gulp of ale, and felt in her mind an image without pictures but with sensations, of this man lying with her—caressing her—loving her—taking her. Hurriedly she gave her attention to the river, swirling, babbling round rocks, rushing on to its goal. Was she a fool to trust this man—or had she allowed her pity and a pair of grey eyes to sway her judgement?

He was suddenly behind her, and she jumped when he spoke. 'You are not missing your family too much?'

'I am used to my own company,' she replied, rather breathlessly. 'Milo was often away. As for my close family, I miss them a good deal at times. I have longed, since coming to Ireland, for the particular sound of a voice. And London—strangely I have missed smelly old London.' Her voice strengthened. 'I found Dublin to be strangely homelike. I liked the river and the sea. In some ways, it reminded me of Liverpool, where Robin's family lives and I spent some part of my childhood after my mother died. You go up from the river steeply there, too.' She halted abruptly, her heart beating heavily just because he was standing so close. She wanted to turn round, to see what would happen if she did so. Would he kiss her? If that happened, it would be because she had allowed it, and then she could not guarantee that he would keep his distance. He *must* keep his distance! She felt there was danger if he did not. The fault lay in that first meeting—and all the subsequent meetings which had got them off on to a wrong footing.

'Go on,' said Niall softly, interupting her racing thoughts. 'What about this manor—do you feel at home here?'

'Not yet, but it does remind me of Yorkshire in some ways. And I love Yorkshire.' She turned to face him, and her next words were mundane. 'I've just remembered that I came for water! Poor Master Upton was sweating copiously with the heat.'

'You should not be fetching water,' he said with a frown. 'But perhaps we should not have eaten all the fish.'

'I doubt there would have been enough for Master Upton!'

'He's a big man who would take some feeding!' He grinned. 'I pray that he's not staying? There isn't much left to eat in the storeroom. I would be constantly hunting while Brigid baked bread.'

'Is there enough flour for bread?' She watched him fill the pail.

'Brigid will know that—ask her when she returns.' He began to walk, and she fell in step beside him.

They were both silent. Constance was suddenly remembering what Kathleen had said about her sister having plans for Niall and herself. Did he know of those plans, or did he feel brotherly towards Brigid, as Kathleen had said? She was suddenly uneasy; having appreciated the girl's kindness to her, she did not want to upset her sister, but perhaps Kathleen had misread her sister's intentions.

The house was in sight, and she could see Master Upton leaning against the wall, his eyes shut against the sun. Niall exchanged glances with her. 'Perhaps Master Upton did not need the water as much as he appeared to?'

'He was vexed with me,' she murmured, her eyes gleaming with sudden understanding. 'He wanted you to stay here.'

'Clever Master Upton! He knew I had gone to the river.' He grinned and quickened his pace.

When he shook the guide by the shoulder, Master Upton's eyes opened to stare blearily at them. A beaming smile split his cherubic countenance. 'You are staying, Master O'More?'

Niall nodded. 'I presume that you will have to be on your way back to Dublin?'

Master Upton nodded. 'With a clear mind, now that I know you will take care of Mistress de Wensley.' He straightened up and stared at Constance. 'I shall fetch my horse, if there is naught else I can do for you, mistress?'

'I think you have done enough, Master Upton.' A twinkle lurked in the brown eyes. 'Would you like a drink of water, perhaps, before you go?'

'That I would, so I'll fetch a cup.' He hurried away into the house, chuckling to himself.

After Master Upton had left, Constance stood in the centre of the hall gazing about her.

'What is wrong?' asked Niall, following her gaze. 'Do you not like the house?' He sounded anxious.

'I like the house well enough,' she responded seriously, 'but another bed is needed, and a screen. There are no trestles—and a chair would be useful. Also the walls...'

'They need washing, I know,' he interrupted, a frown creasing his brow, 'but Brigid has had no opportunity to begin the springtime tasks. Besides, washing walls is really a man's job. I'll see what I can do for you there.' He moved away. 'Also, you might need a girl to help you until Brigid returns. Who knows, she might stay a day longer than she intended? She worries at Kathleen, expecting her to do everything she asks, instead of letting the girl get on with her work.' He paused at the door, his hand on the jamb. 'If you need clean blankets, there are newly woven ones in the chest.' He disappeared out of the door.

For a moment Constance stared after him, wondering where he would sleep, then she picked up her baggage and moved it to the bed. She noticed that the mattress sagged in the middle. When she came, the girl could help her to take it outside, where it could be shaken and left for a while in the fresh air.

She changed swiftly into a grey serge gown and covered her head and neck with a linen coif and a wimple. The door opened just as she was pulling on a pair of old cotton mittens. Just in time, she thought, turning round. 'Brigid!' she exclaimed in surprise. 'Niall thought you would not be back so soon.'

'Did he not?' retorted the girl in an insolent tone. 'Perhaps he hoped that I would delay my return so that he could be alone with you? Maybe you wanted to have him to yourself, also?' Her cold eyes raked Constance's appearance, and her mouth twisted. 'And he considers *you* beautiful.'

'I beg your pardon?' Constance could not believe what she was hearing.

'You perhaps did not hear me, Englishwoman?' Stiff-legged, she moved over to Constance and glared at her. 'You come over here and believe you can not only take our homes, but our men as well.'

Some of the colour drained from Constance's face. 'What are you talking about? Have you taken leave of your senses to address me in such a way?'

'You are the enemy. You are not wanted here, Mistress Constance de Wensley.' Brigid folded her arms. 'So the sooner you return to England, the better it will be for you—for all of us. We don't want your interference in our plans. You will take what is mine, and we can't allow that.'

'We? Who is "we"?' retorted Constance in a low voice, her temper beginning to ignite. 'Is it Kathleen you link your name with? I do not believe that *she* sees me as an enemy. But you—you didn't like me in the first place, did you?'

Uncertainty flickered in Brigid's face, and for a moment she looked lost. Then suddenly it was as if she found herself. 'We Irish don't want you. You English take what belongs to us. You must go back to England.'

'I have no intention of returning to England,' said Constance acidly, walking away from the girl before she gave in to her desire to strike her. 'And if you hate me so much, perhaps it would be best if you returned to the hills where you have left Kathleen, and stay there until you learn some manners.' She began to gather up armfuls of rushes from the floor, deliberately turning her back on the girl.

'But you have to go!' cried Brigid. 'If you don't, I have to—to...' The rest of the words were lost to Constance, as they were much to low to be heard, but the noise of the girl's feet padding swiftly across the floor caused her to whirl round. Brigid was coming at her with a knife! Constance could neither think nor move, then, as the girl raised her arm, she flung the rushes in her face before pushing her over. The knife went flying, and Constance darted after it before Brigid could get there. She had her hand to it, when she caught the sound of the girl stumbling to her feet, and quickly she faced her to see that Brigid's hand was to her head. For a second they stared at each other, then Brigid's eyes went to the knife in Constance's hand—and she fled from the hall.

The knife slid from Constance's trembling fingers as she forced her shaking knees to support her before starting across the hall in Brigid's wake. What had got into the girl that she should behave in such a terrible way? A demon? Perhaps that was the reason? Fear clutched her heart. She had to find Niall and tell him what had happened.

She did not have to search far, for as she went round the side of the house, Niall was coming towards her. He was accompanied by a girl of perhaps fourteen, who was dragging a sledge behind her, upon which was a sack.

'What is wrong?' Niall seized both Constance's hands, scrutinising her wan face. 'You look as though you had seen a ghost!'

'I—I...' she stammered, searching for words. 'Brigid was here! She said things...behaved in such a way!'

'What things? In what way?' He squeezed her hands gently.

'That I wasn't welcome here—that I came to steal what was hers. This land...Her—Her...' She stopped abruptly. Her man, Brigid had said, meaning Niall, perhaps!

'Brigid said that?' he demanded incredulously. 'I told her...I don't believe she could be so foolish!'

'You think I am fabricating this tale?' She snatched her hands out of his hold, and a flush crept over her face.

'No, but...' He ran a hand through his hair, raising it into a curling crest. His face wore a bewildered expression. 'Perhaps you misheard?'

'There is nothing wrong with my hearing!' Constance tilted her chin and folded her arms. 'But if you wish to take her side against me...'

'I'm not taking sides,' he said irascibly, starting to lose control of his temper.

'It sounds as though you are,' she blazed. 'Jealousy can be a terrible sin!'

'Are you saying that Brigid is jealous of you?' Some of the anger went from his face. 'That's understandable. She has been a kind of lady of the manor here for some time.'

'That I could understand,' said Constance, unfolding her arms, 'but she told me to leave—to go back to England. When I refused, she came back at me with a knife.'

He stared at her silently, his expression dumbfounded. 'Then what happened?'

'I flung some rushes at her and pushed her over—then she fled.' She drew a shaky breath. 'It is the truth, believe me!'

'You say it's true, so I have to believe you—but there must be some explanation.' He dropped a hand on the shoulder of the girl by him. 'This is Grannia, who will help you to bake bread and perform other tasks that you want done. I'm going to find Brigid and get to the bottom of this matter.' He lifted a hand in farewell and strode off towards where the dogs lay in a patch of sun.

Constance took a deep breath and turned to face Grannia, relieved that he was going to do something.

CHAPTER TEN

WITH GREAT determination, Constance put Brigid out of her mind. 'There is a bakehouse here?' she asked.

'No bakehouse.' Grannia smiled shyly. 'But, Mistress de Wensley, if you will allow me, I shall show you how to manage without one.' She touched Constance's arm and led the way into the house, pulling the sledge behind her.

Constance watched silently as the fire was lit. Grannia gave her a flashing smile as she brought the broad plank of wood that Brigid had used to put the bowls on for the porridge, on the day that Constance had first come into the house. How could Brigid have tried to kill her? Frowning, she watched Grannia take up a large bowl, and dust it inside. Soon the girl had everything to hand. Constance pulled up a stool to watch her more closely. Later she would sweep the floor and rid it of the dirty rushes, but it would have to wait until the breadmaking was finished. Perhaps Niall would have returned with Brigid by then?

It was a long process making the dough, leaving it to rise and kneading it. In the middle of the waiting, Constance asked Grannia to help her to remove the mattress. They shook it well, and left it spread out on a bush to air.

The dough was formed into round cakes, which were left to rise again while Grannia gathered some forked sticks. She placed them standing up on the hot stones surrounding the fire. When the cakes were risen to her satisfaction, they were stood on their ends against the sticks in front of the fire.

While Grannia tidied up, Constance watched the bread. Her mind wandered, and a sudden loneliness swept over her. She would have liked her stepmother to talk to, to pour out her worries about Niall and Brigid. Did the girl care for her foster-brother? Was she jealous of Constance? Yet surely, when Brigid calmed down, she would realise that you did not get rid of people because you wanted them out of the way. Jealousy was an unenviable emotion. She herself had suffered from it in the past, when her half-brothers had been born. She rued the day that she had responded to that feeling by running away with Milo de Wensley. Was Brigid so jealous that it was driving her mad? Had jealousy not driven a wedge between her own father and his brother because of her mother, who was now only a memory to them all? Jealousy could change a person out of all recognition. What was she to do if Niall returned with Brigid? Was Brigid to stay on in the house?

'Mistress de Wensley! The bread is burning!' Grannia's words caused her to start, and move hurriedly. It was with relief that she saw that only one of the cakes had been singed. They were removed hastily out of the fire, and later moved to a basket and covered with a cloth.

'With Master Niall to feed, we shall be baking every day,' said Grannia, her brown hair falling into her eyes. 'He is always hungry, and loves freshly-baked bread with lashings of butter—but he will have to do without that for a while. Until Mistress Kathleen has had the making of it.'

'That is what she'll be doing while she's away?' Constance took up an armful of rushes, and Grannia followed suit.

'Ay, and there'll be buttermilk and cheese—but not a lot of cheese.' They began the arduous task of cleaning the rushes from the hall, gathering them in a great pile for burning outside. Then they took besoms and began to sweep the floor clear of bones, bits of grass and seedheads, mice-droppings, and any other rubbish that had gathered. A worried frown crossed Constance's face as she wondered whether Niall had found Brigid.

'Something is bothering you?' Grannia's hazel eyes scanned her face. 'Would Master Niall not like you doing this? I can do it by myself, if you wish, for it is too menial a task for you.'

'I don't mind doing it,' murmured Constance, forcing a smile. And that was true! There was a kind of satisfaction in getting rid of filth and dirt and making something tidy and clean again. As she worked, there was a lilt in the sway of her body.

Niall entered suddenly, and stopped to watch her. The dogs bounded over to the pile of rubbish, and eased a bone out. Niall seized Constance's arm and moved her swiftly out of the way. His arm went about her waist, and it was as though a current of light flashed through her. Their eyes met, and his flaxen brows drew together. 'This is no task for you!' he said roughly, snatching the besom from her slackened grasp.

'What am I supposed to do when you are not here?' she demanded shakily. 'Just wait idly while you search for Brigid? Have you found her?'

He shook his head. 'We followed her tracks to the mound, then lost them.' His hand pulled at his moustache before moving to scratch his head. 'Up on the mound, one can see for miles. It is a good vantage-point. But there was no sign of her.' He rammed the besom on the floor as he gazed down at it.

'What will you do? She can't have disappeared into thin air.'

'Of course she can't,' he muttered absently, bending down to pick up a knife from the floor. 'Is this the weapon she tried to kill you with?' He held it out on the palm of his hand.

'I didn't have a close look.' She peered at the knife, with its gold-like handle engraved with whorls. 'But that must be it. Is it not a warrior's blade?'

He nodded grimly. 'She could have had it for her own protection, and nothing more.'

'Of course,' she said colourlessly, not believing for one moment that Brigid would have carried such a knife. Besides, there was something in Niall's expression that convinced her that he did not believe it, either. 'What are you going to do?'

'More of what I've already done. I've got men searching for her. When she's found, she'll be brought here.' He went over to the fire, and thrust the weapon into the glowing depths. 'Grannia, go and fetch more wood.' The girl nodded, and hurried outside.

'Why are you trying to destroy it?' Constance moved to Niall's side to stare into the fire.

He glanced at her, and away again. 'That's all I can do—try. It is an evil weapon.' He crouched, and murmured words in Irish before prodding the knife in the fire with the axe he took from his belt. Constance sat on a stool, and her lips moved in prayer. There was something here that she did not understand.

Niall rose suddenly, and smiled down at her. 'I smell fresh bread!'

Her heart lifted because of the ordinariness of his remark. 'You're hungry?'

'There were only three small fishes for dinner.'

Grannia came into the hall with a bundle of firewood. Niall called to her in Irish, and she answered. 'Grannia will see to supper,' he said gravely. 'I thought you might wish to see the scrolls containing the names of the cottiers and *betaghs* here with the dues they owe you and the amounts of rents paid. You might not be able to read them, of course—you will have to take my word that they are correct.'

'If they are in Latin, I shall be able to read them,' she said softly.

He turned, half-way towards the chest. 'How is that?'

'My stepmother and father thought it wise that I should. For years, I was the heiress to a fortune, so they wanted to make certain I would not be cheated. I learnt to understand agreements and dues and charters and settlements myself, in case any man should think he could get the better of me. So many good and worthy clerics died of the plague years ago, while the rogues survived. Besides, if I could not read, how would I understand the book of simples with its herbs and medicines that Philippa gave me?' She smiled sweetly, enjoying his surprise. 'Of course I am not an heiress now, as I think I have told you. Only this . . .' her eyes roamed the rafters and walls, 'is now mine. But tell me what are cottiers and *betaghs*? Are they similar to our English serfs?'

'*Betaghs* are. Cottiers have personal freedom, but pay rent and labour service. My foster-father's ancestors were gavillers—tenants at will—as he was.' He lifted the lid, and buried his head in the chest.

She waited patiently. 'I would also wish to know what livestock we have here.' Her voice reached him as he closed the lid. 'Last time I was here, I had no mind to consider swine or sheep or cattle—ducks or chickens. Do we have many fruit-trees? Are peas and beans grown, as well as barley and oats?' She ticked the questions off on her fingers. 'I would like to know what proportion of what is mine.'

'They will be written down in the dues,' he answered shortly. 'My foster-father stuck to the letter of the law.' He handed her the scrolls.

'I do not doubt his honesty.' She looked up at him and smiled. 'But tell me where we get salt? Have we any? Do we have hives? Does a tithe of everything we have go to the priest?'

'Questions! Questions!' he muttered, throwing up his arms. 'Look in the scrolls, woman.'

A bubble of laughter formed inside her at the look on his face. Her eyes danced. 'But some people's Latin is so difficult to read. Can you not tell me? What wood may I take from the forest? I shall have some furniture made and another house built, maybe. Do all the deer belong to the king? Do sit down, man!'

Grannia, who had been watching and listening, but whom they had both forgotten, darted forward with another stool, placing it near the one already close to the fire.

Niall was suddenly aware that Constance was teasing him. There was dust on her cheek as well as a smear of flour across her forehead. What if Brigid's blade had struck? A cold hand seemed to squeeze his heart. He sat close to her as she unrolled a scroll. 'Salt we have from Dublin. It comes by ship from Chester, but you will have to confirm whether we have any. No doubt Brigid,' his voice wavered, 'will have used most of it when she salted the meat for the winter. You have certain rights to wood—they'll be listed. Deer?' He shrugged. 'Did you hunt in London?'

'Outside London—on occasions when I stayed with my father's cousin and her husband, and when I visited our manor in Kent.'

'Then, no doubt, we can find you some sport, if you wish. As for the priest, he receives a gift from you as well as from the rest of those who live in the settlement—how else would he live? He speaks no English, and the church is small, but you will be able to receive the sacrament.' His voice changed. 'My brother is a holy man, who lives in the hills in a valley—a dream of a valley.' He stopped.

Constance nudged his arm. 'Tell me about it.'

'You would have to see it to understand how beautiful it is,' he replied, a little self-consciously, flattening the parchment beneath his elbow.

'Help me to see it,' she murmured, her hand brushing against his. He looked at her, and the dusty air was suddenly charged with a tingling excitement. 'It's right in the mountains. There are two lakes in the most heavenly valley you could ever see. It's difficult to reach, but that's why Saint Kevin went there years ago. They say he was driven into solitude by the passion of a beautiful girl who pursued him relentlessly. So much so, that he turned on her and beat her with nettles.' He paused, his eyes lingering on her face.

'What happened?' she asked huskily. Somehow his hand was covering hers, and his fingers were interlaced with hers, and she felt her heart quickening. Was he aware of what he was doing?

'Her love evaporated—and she left him.' His expression was guileless. He was enjoying telling her the tale in such a way!

Her mouth formed a moue of disappointment. 'Is that all?'

'Yes, where women are concerned.' He smiled. 'He went to Gleann da Loch—that means "The place of two lakes". At first he lived in a hollow tree before he found a cave high in the face of a cliff. Eventually, other men followed him and a community came into existence. My brother lives there.' He hesitated before adding, 'I'd like you to meet him one day. I think his life would interest you.'

'I'd like to.' She thought it wise at this point to loosen her fingers and to turn the conversation to estate affairs.

It was Grannia who, during their discussion, went to fetch bacon, eggs, herbs and onions. She cut and chopped and beat them together, and when they were cooked in a small iron pot, she served them with some bread on wooden platters.

Constance and Niall ate where they sat, balancing the food on their knees, while Grannia poured ale for them. Then she sat at their side, smiling as she watched them eat together. Despite her presence, Constance was questioning the wisdom of such intimacy between her and Niall. If they had been in England and there had been trestles, she could have invited the workers to come in, and they could have eaten together, but there were no trestles.

When he had finished eating, Niall placed his cup beside his platter on the floor, and stood. 'If you'll excuse me, I'll go and see if there's been any sighting of Brigid.' He ran a hand through his hair, and a muscle tightened in his lean cheek. 'If you have a mind to, in the morning we could go for a ride so that I can show you the manor.'

'What if Brigid is not found?' she asked, looking up at him quickly.

'Then we can still ride *and* search, if that suits you?'

She nodded, considering that he looked tired. 'If you find her tonight, come and tell me. It will be some time yet before Grannia and I are finished here.'

He frowned. 'Don't work too hard in here. I'll get one of the men to clean the walls in the morning. I've told Grannia to stay here with you tonight; I thought you would not wish to be alone.'

'Thank you.' She was relieved, fearing slightly that Brigid might come back unexpectedly, and find her alone.

'I'll see you in the morning.' His lean face creased into a smile.

'In the morning,' she echoed, as he left the hall.

Constance woke early, roused by Grannia moving on the pallet on the floor. It was dull in the hall, and when she peered outside it was to see that the clear skies of the day before had vanished, to be replaced by a grey pall of lowering cloud. She determined not to let the weather lower her spirits, and dressed quickly.

Grannia watched her, touching the scarlet skirts now and again, seeming to find pleasure in the feel of the English wool. Irish wool was rougher. Constance smiled at her as she set her coif a little more firmly on her head and pulled on her riding-gloves. 'Go and tell Master Niall that I am ready. Perhaps you will find him in the stables?' He had not come with news of Brigid, and she wondered where he had spent the night. The girl scurried out. She followed more slowly, winding her veil more securely about her throat as she pondered on Brigid's strange behaviour and its possible cause. A shiver trickled down her spine as she went out into the gloomy day.

Niall came to a halt at the top of the mound. His hair was blown into a tangle by the rising wind, and he presented a rather awesome figure as Constance looked up at him. Man and horse seemed welded into one against the sky. He could have been some pagan legendary creature of old surveying his domain, but he was still searching for his foster-sister. Had he made Brigid any promises before she herself had come along? Did he care for Brigid more than he had realised? As a lover, maybe—the thought hurt. She urged her mare up the mound.

Was this another burial-mound? If so, it was a large one. There were several of them dotted about, as there were also strange stones with intricate carving and inexplicable runes. Could the dead walk again on earth? Could they really creep out of their burial-places to lure the living into their world of shadows? There were tales of such happenings. Could that have happened to Brigid? She drew alongside Niall, realising that this mound was different from the others. It was flattened on top over a larger area. She looked down the way they had come, and across the valley. One could see for miles, and the view was quite magnificent.

'Once, this was a place of safety for our people. If enemies attacked, they retreated up here. There was a fence all round, and where the gorse and brambles now grow, there was a deep ditch.'

'You speak of the English?' She tried to concentrate on what he was saying.

'No, of neighbouring tribes and the men who came from across the northern seas. They came in their long-ships and rowed up the loughs and so managed to get far inland. They were excellent seaman and doughty fighters, but eventually they intermarried with the Irish. They built towns like Dublin. We learnt from each other.' His eyes held hers, and her blood quickened. 'So it goes on,' he said softly. 'The intermingling of the races. This valley was given to the de Wensleys in Strongbow's day—that was when the first de Wensley came over with him from Wales. There was a time when the O'Mores in the east fought them over this land.'

'I did not know that!' Her dark brows rose and she was wide-eyed. 'Did you hate the de Wensleys?'

For a moment he made no answer, and he appeared so forbidding that she wished she had not asked. Then he said, 'I lived with the O'Mores only for the first two years of my life. Then my father was killed in a skirmish, and my mother returned to her own family, but she was not really welcome there and was unhappy. I was only a child when she entered the convent, and I have not seen her since. Not that I mourn her—instead of a mother wrapped up in her own misery, I had a foster-mother who loved me dearly. I make no complaint against the de Wensleys, for they did me no wrong.' He fell silent, and despite her curiosity, for there was some-thing in his words that puzzled her, she questioned him no further.

'Do we continue the search?' she asked after a long silence spent in scanning the area.

'I think not.' He turned to her hurriedly. 'I'll take you back.'

There was such an air of suppressed excitement about him, as his hand seized her bridle, that she could not remain silent. 'Have you seen something—is there danger?'

'It might be nothing.' His voice held a lilt.

'But you believe it is something?' she demanded, attempting to gain control of her own mare.

'If it is, you are playing no part in it!' he replied firmly, releasing his hold on her bridle. 'I want you at home, and with the gates shut.'

'While you go and fight for Brigid, I suppose.' Her dark eyes were stormy, and her rosy mouth set stubbornly.

'Mistress de Wensley, I believe you would like a man to fight for you.' His grey eyes suddenly gleamed like pebbles in a sunlit stream. 'Once I would have, and you did not want it.'

'I wish for nothing of the sort,' she said tartly, turning her mare's head. 'You men simply like an excuse to fight.'

'We don't need an excuse.' His eyes teased her before he slapped Maeve's rump. 'Now go for home,' he shouted, as her mare made her way down the mound.

'The nerve of the man!' she muttered, allowing Maeve her head as they came on to flat land. 'I'm not going to look back—nor am I going to care what happens to him.' Yet she wanted to—she had to fight against the desire to see whether he was fighting for his life. She groaned inwardly, wondering even now whether to disobey him and turn to see what was happening. But already the houses were looming up, and there was the possibility that nothing might be happening. Soon he would be following her, and then he would ask why she had worried enough to disobey him, and she did not want him thinking that she cared.

Once she reached the house, she changed her clothes and considered working in the garden while she waited for Niall's return. There was no sign of Grannia. Just as she was about to leave the hall, a knock came at the door, and her heart began to hammer. Perhaps it was bad news?

Squaring her shoulders, Constance flung the door open so quickly that the man there fell inside. He muttered a flurry of apologies in French, interspersed with the news that Master O'More had said that she needed some walls cleaned. He was an untidy individual, with the strings of his cap half undone and a rip in his tunic, but he appeared willing, and she left him to it after locking the chest, where she had deposited her money and the ring given to her by the king.

She took several deep breaths as she sauntered with a deliberately casual step out to the garden. It was planted with several kinds of herbs—sage, mint, thyme—and there was even some balm. They said that the juice of balm was useful for wounds. Why should she be worrying about wounds? If Niall O'More was wounded, it would be his own fault for being foolhardy and conceited enough to believe he could cope with Sil and his band of cut-throats single-handed. Why should she believe that Sil was involved in Brigid's disappearance? That was foolish! She sighed, and concentrated on the weeding. Balm was also good against a surfeit of mushrooms, not that she had seen any of them. Bees delighted in the herb, so beekeepers rubbed their hives with it. Perhaps that explained the presence of hives under some apple-trees. She knew little about bees, but supposed that she could learn.

Her eyes went on to the western mountains, she realised how threatening their presence was, and must have been for Milo's father. To the east, there was also the threat from the O'Mores. How much blood had been spilt on this land during the de Wensleys' struggle to hold it against the natives in the hills? Yet they had still been here until Milo's father had fled. She still found it difficult to accept that he could have desired a woman so badly that he had stolen her away from a husband who would surely come after him to kill him. But he had been young, and love was so unpredictable. Now she was here—surely the last of the de Wensleys, and not even of their blood-line.

She fell to weeding again as easily as her thoughts drifted. What of this woman Milo's father had slept with—could she have had a child? It was possible, but it was not as easy to conceive as some seemed to believe. In four years of marriage, she had failed to do so. Was it possible that out there in the hills there could be a half-brother—or half-sister—to Milo? Foolish thought! Even if there were, as bastards, they would have no legal claim to this land, so what was the point of thinking about it?

A few minutes later, Constance was brought to her feet by Brigid's sudden appearance round the corner. The girl smiled at her. 'I am glad to see you here, and regret not being here to welcome you. But Niall would have done that. You have forgiven him for abducting your kinsman?'

Constance eyed her warily, completely taken aback. 'It is Christian to forgive. Where have you been, Brigid? Have you seen Niall?'

'Ay, I met him as I was returning from seeing Kathleen, and I have brought you some milk.' Her eyes sparkled. 'Also I bring you news of your kinsman.'

'Of Robin?' Constance could not conceal her amazement.

'It was only by the merest chance that Kathleen saw him. She was drinking at a stream, as he and some men were crossing. At first she did not realise who he was, for he was dressed in a similar fashion to theirs. Then he slipped on a stone and his foot went in the water—and he cursed in English! At least, I'm sure he cursed—that's what Kathleen said.' Her face brimmed with mischief. 'So she realised who he was.' She scrutinised Constance carefully. 'She said he didn't look like you.'

'No, Robin is like his mother.' Constance could not believe that this conversation was taking place. 'Is he well?'

'Well, but vexed—Kathleen did not have much chance to speak with him. He was being watched carefully, but they were able to exchange a few words. He asked after you, and is wishing he could be rescued.'

'Did she tell him who she was?' Constance watched her carefully.

'Of course.' Brigid pouted. 'He did not seem pleased about Niall, but she told him that he was completely trustworthy and would see that you came to no harm.'

'And did he believe her?' she asked drily.

'I do not think so—Kathleen became quite cross, and left him.'

Constance watched her even more closely. 'When did this happen?'

A shadow crossed Brigid's freckled face. 'I cannot remember—this morning, perhaps? I have ridden fast all the way here, and now I'm hungry. Perhaps I should go and see what there is for dinner.'

'I'll come with you.' Constance brushed soil from her gloves, and followed.

Niall was in the hall, talking to Grannia, who was stirring a blackened pot on the fire. He glanced up, a worried expression on his face. He came over to Constance and Brigid. 'So Brigid found you?' His voice contained a note of forced cheerfulness.

'In the garden.' Constance's eyes scanned his face for some sign that would help her to know what had happened. 'Brigid told me that Kathleen had seen my kinsman.'

He nodded. 'So she told me. We met by the burial-mound.' He seized Constance's arm so swiftly that she jumped. 'I've been speaking to the priest. He apologised for not having been to visit you yet, but I told him that you've been busy and that you hope to see him to-morrow at Mass. I thought we could all go. That is, if you don't mind?' He had managed to draw her a little away from Brigid, who was scowling as she looked about the hall. 'He is a good man,' he continued in a loud voice, 'simple, but hardworking and honest, which is more than you can say of some churchmen.'

'I agree,' said Constance, wondering what this was all about. 'I haven't been to Mass since I've been in Ireland.' If the truth was told, she had avoided going to Mass since Milo had been killed, but she supposed she had better start as she meant to go on, by setting an example.

'Why is that?' Niall sounded interested. 'Are you accustomed to bishops in fine robes, or are your sins too few?'

'No!' she replied, startled. 'Although there are men in fine robes who make good bishops, not all bishops are good men. It's just that I have not felt inclined and that sin is difficult to confess, I find.' Why had she told him that? She must be crazed.

'Then you'll feel better when you sin is confessed,' he murmured. 'I know I will—perhaps because I am more in need of forgiveness.'

'Sin is sin.' She glanced at him, then looked away again. Was he referring to the night at the bog? 'Brigid said she was hungry, so should we not eat? Then perhaps you can show me the horses and speak to the carpenter for me.'

'Brigid can stay with Grannia and supervise the washing of the walls. She's a little effusive, my foster-sister. Really friendly, don't you agree?' he said softly.

'I can't understand it after what you told me, and from what I know of her.'

'I see. What do you think is wrong?'

'I have my suspicions, but let's talk about them elsewhere.' He took her arm and led her outside.

'Well?' said Constance, offering a slice of wrinkled apple to the black stallion nuzzling Niall's shoulder. 'I do not wish to gossip about your foster-sister, but...'

'But there's something not quite right about her,' murmured Niall, his eyes narrowing against the sun that was breaking through the clouds scurrying before the wind to reveal patches of blue. 'It's her eyes—it's as though another person were looking out of them. I've sent some of the men to see that Kathleen is all right, and to find out whether Brigid really has been there.'

'Do you suspect Sil of being the instigator of Brigid's strange behaviour?' Her emotionless voice revealed no sign of her fear.

'Why do you think that?' He looked down at her quickly.

'Because of what you said yesterday. Although, surely, someone should have seen him?' Her hand stroked the horse's mane with a controlled carefulness.

'We could have a traitor in our midst, who hides his allegiance to Sil behind a mask of friendship.' His mouth tightened.

Constance stared at him, thinking that she had never seen him looking so austere. Her fear deepened. 'How can you find out?' she asked quietly.

'Set a trap.' His knuckles gleamed white as his fingers clenched the metal of the knife he had taken from the fire's ashes that morning. 'We might not find out who he is straight away, but we'll find him!'

CHAPTER ELEVEN

'PERHAPS IT would be best if I left here?' Constance wondered. 'Maybe Sil then will release Brigid from whatever spell he has cast over her and leave you all alone.' Her eyes reflected her uncertainty.

Niall was silent, as his gaze shifted from her face to the knife in his hands. 'I would agree, except that Sil never lets go. I would have to go with you all the way, and he would have us followed. There would be an ambush in some lonely spot.' He spread his hands expressively. 'No, I would rather arrange our next confrontation on my own ground. When it takes place, only Sil or I will leave alive. The time has come for Sil's persecution of me to end.'

Constance cleared her throat. 'You want to fight him,' she stated. 'I can see it in your face.'

He smiled brilliantly. 'Do you blame me for wishing to kill him?'

'No, but he might kill *you*,' she muttered angrily. 'Is there no other way than a fight to the death?'

'Such a lack of faith you have in me, Mistress de Wensley!' There was a peculiar note in Niall's voice. 'But I swear I will not let him kill me.'

'You are so sure of yourself,' she said tersely, leaning against the horse. 'But you yourself said that he is no weakling.'

'Neither am I. I have only one weak spot, and the danger is that I believe he already has guessed it. Hence Brigid's behaviour. But you do not have to fear, for I will guard it carefully.'

She stared at him, puzzled by his words and the strange emotion—almost a pain—she experienced when looking at his profile. 'Your eye?' she said slowly. 'Is it your eye, where he nearly blinded you?' As if of its own volition, her hand reached up to touch his face.

A muscle twitched in Niall's cheek and he turned to face her. She felt a moment's unexpected headiness, of excitement—then his expression altered, and he wrenched her hand away. 'Really, Mistress de Wensley, you should not be going so close to the black stallion! He can be a devil with strangers!'

'What . . .' she began in amazement, only to be interrupted by Brigid.

'So here you are!' cried Brigid. 'I've been looking in the herb garden for you, Mistress de Wensley. I thought you might wish to come with me and see the place where the best rushes grow down by the river.' Her mouth smiled delightfully.

'Now isn't the right time,' Niall intervened before Constance could answer. 'But Mistress de Wensley might need some washing done—and as it's not a meat day, we need some fish. I suggest that we all walk that way, if Mistress de Wensley doesn't mind my company for a little longer?' His voice was smoothly polite as he addressed the latter words to Constance.

'I have no objection, Master O'More,' she said stiffly, thinking it was just as well that Brigid had come along when she had. Otherwise who knew what might have happened next?

'Then let us go.' He smiled politely, and inclined his head as he indicated with a wave of his hand that the two women should go before him. They went.

Brigid chattered brightly about the manor and the horses—and Robin. How delightful that Kathleen should have seen him, so that she, Brigid, could reassure Constance of his well-being and safety. Niall said nothing, only listening, his face expressionless.

Constance wondered if there was a threat behind the words about Robin. She had begun to accept Niall's assurances to his safety, but what if Sil had arranged for Robin to be disposed of? He did not want the exchange of hostages, according to Niall. She wished that Brigid would stop talking so that she could again broach the subject of Robin with Niall, but the opportunity did not arise.

During supper, Niall hardly exchanged a word with Constance. Instead, he addressed himself to Brigid, speaking of his plans to go to Connemara, perhaps go in a week or two. That news surprised Constance, but she kept quiet, although she would have liked to say much. Immediately supper was over, Niall disappeared swiftly out of doors, leaving Constance in the house with Brigid and Grannia.

After watching Grannia and Brigid argue over what to do with the feathers from the chicken they were plucking, Constance wandered out, but she no sooner arrived in the garden than Brigid was there. She followed her—to the horses, the stables, the carpenter's house, not speaking at all, just silently walking in her tracks. There was no sign of Niall. It was beginning to get dark when Constance went indoors, followed by Brigid.

Constance darned some stockings and then went to bed, weary and rather irritable. Brigid would have preferred Grannia to leave the hall, but she insisted on staying, and Constance was glad. She did not believe that Brigid would attempt to harm her again, but she felt much safer with Grannia there.

Sleep was elusive. Constance tossed and turned. It had been a mistake coming to Ireland. There was danger all round! How could she have believed that everything could turn out as she had wanted it? Where was Niall? Where was Sil? Were they confronting each other, even now?

Brigid shifted in her bed, and a mouse scurried across the floor. Constance stiffened, then the girl stilled. The mouse scrabbled again, and she remembered the sack of flour in the corner. They should have a cat, there was need for one here. Another problem. Tiredness began to wash over her, then she heard the rain on the roof, and she remembered the washing outside. Was Niall on the mound, watching, in this weather? She groaned, turning over to pull the blanket over her ears. Eventually she slept.

It was still raining next morning, but despite her low spirits, she dressed in a scarlet woollen gown and a cote-hardie of a paler hue. She realised that she had lost weight since coming to Ireland—but she was not going to allow that to depress her spirits further. Would Niall come to church with them, as he had promised?

He appeared in the doorway suddenly, wearing the all-encompassing mantle, and Constance could not have been more glad. The brim of his hat concealed the expression in his eyes, and when he spoke, it was to make prosaic remarks about the weather. She was annoyed. No explanation of where he had been? She had lost sleep over this man, and all he could talk about was the weather!

'I would like a cat to live in the house with me,' she said, completely irrelevantly.

'A cat, is it?' He pushed his hat further back on his head, and looked at her, and his expression was such that she felt colour warming her cheeks.

'A cat,' she repeated unevenly. 'To kill the mice. I heard them last night, when I couldn't sleep.'

'You couldn't sleep, either?' He smiled lazily. 'And there you were in a nice warm bed, and I cold and wet on the hill coming back from seeing Kathleen. It's a pity we couldn't have kept each other company.'

'I did not think that you wished for my company last evening, Master O'More,' she responded with dignity. 'I wished...'

'There you would be mistaken, Mistress Constance.' He was suddenly serious. 'Your kinsman is well, and the captain has a hand-picked guard over him—if you were worrying about him?'

'Thank you.' She smiled and he smiled back.

'It's a cat you're wanting.' His eyes twinkled. 'Then it's a cat you shall have.'

'Thank you again.' Suddenly it did not matter about the rain, or Brigid, or Sil, or anything else. Then Brigid came running out of the house. Her dark braids bounced against her small breasts, and her cheeks were rosy.

'Is that Niall's voice I hear?' she said breathlessly. Her hand went to his chest, and she gazed up at him. 'Where have you been? I've been worried about you.' Her anxiety seemed real. Some of the brightness went out of Constance's day as she stepped aside.

'I slept in the stable,' he said reassuringly, his hand covering hers. 'Now Mistress de Wensley wishes to go to church. Are you coming?'

'Church?' Brigid smiled brilliantly. 'Of course.' She tucked her hand in Niall's arm, and he stared woodenly at Constance.

'I'll go on ahead,' said Constance, turning away and walking swiftly through the rain. Her throat ached strangely as she splashed through the puddles to the tiny wooden church.

The villagers had not yet started arriving, and she felt relieved. She attempted to force all thought of Niall and Brigid out of her mind and to focus on the sin that had kept her from Mass; only to discover that the bitterness, which had festered deep inside her over the last year or so, no longer had such a strong hold. What good had it done her to bear a grudge against not only God, but Milo? He was dead. There had been times when she had wished him out of her life, but she had never consciously wished him dead—so she could not be responsible for that. Even so, she would confess her sins—her gladness that she was free of his cruelty. Perhaps, then, she could pray for herself, and Niall, and Brigid, and Robin, and a whole host of others. Later, as the smell of incense and burning tapers mingled to rise heavenwards, she was aware of a kind of peace, even if at the same time she was still unsure about forgiving and forgiveness.

After she had spoken to the young priest, Niall came up. 'Some of the people would be known to you, Mistress Constance,' he said politely. 'May I introduce them?'

She nodded as politely as he did, having been aware of people's curiosity in the church. Some she already knew by name, but others came forward now. She realised, if she were to stay, that at some time she would have to know all their names—but there were too many new ones now to remember.

Some young people spoke to Brigid, delaying her, so that Niall and Constance began to walk back together. He walked a little apart from her, aware of the interested eyes of the villagers on them. He wondered what Constance had thought about the service and the villagers, and his paying attention to Brigid. He glanced at the rain-bedewed lovely profile of the woman beside him, and wondered anew at the power of the attraction he felt. How serious she looked!

They were both startled out of their contemplative mood by a duck suddenly quacking and taking flight almost from beneath their feet. Only Niall's quick action prevented Constance from falling.

'Thank you.' Her voice was slightly breathless. 'My thoughts were far away.'

'Not in England, I hope?' He steadied her, not wanting to let her go.

'Perhaps.' After one quick glance at his face, she disentangled herself. 'I—I was mainly thinking about names. There are English and Irish here, yet the people seem content to live side by side.'

'Sometimes they can barely tolerate each other,' he said, his face expressionless, despite still feeling the sensations her soft roundness beneath his hands had roused. 'When someone's pig wanders into someone else's garden, it can cause an almighty quarrel, ending in a fist-fight, resulting in black eyes and swollen jaws.'

'That can happen in England,' she replied firmly. 'You are trying to disillusion me, Master O'More. Perhaps you would like me to return to England?' She noticed that Brigid had drawn alongside.

'This is dangerous country, Mistress de Wensley. I would suggest that, as soon as your kinsman is exchanged, you return home with him.' He smiled down at Brigid, as she tucked her hand in his arm. 'Do you not agree, little sister?'

'About this being dangerous country for Mistress de Wensley?' There was a strange glitter in Brigid's eyes. 'It is dangerous for any stranger who would attempt to take what is ours.'

Constance felt a shiver run down her spine, and she thought about how she had collided with Sil that night they had followed him. 'Perhaps I shall return home, once Robin is free.' She was certain that Brigid had seen Niall holding her a little longer than necessary. How jealous she must be! And how Sil with his magic was using that jealousy. She left the pair of them and ran the rest of the way home, glad to see Grannia when she got there—so normal, so welcoming, and so uncomplicated!

That evening Niall brought Constance a tabby, young and sleek with a huntress's gleam in her amber eyes. Their fingertips touched as he passed the cat over. A pleasant tingling passed up her arms. 'I hope you'll sleep better this night, Mistress de Wensley,' he murmured, his eyes as bright as the cat's.

'I'm sure I shall, Master O'More,' she responded colourlessly, her arms folding convulsively about the cat.

But she did not sleep well, aware of Brigid's restless movement a foot or so away. The girl sat up suddenly, and Constance's heart seemed to jump into her throat. Brigid slid from the bed and padded in her bare feet over to the door. One of the dogs uncurled itself as she opened it, and whined softly, pawing at her shift. She pushed him away, and the next moment she had vanished.

Constance did not hesitate, but flew across the hall and out of the door, but already Brigid was not to be seen. She ran to the stable, her bare feet making no sound on the grass. The dogs followed her, but the only traces of Niall were his hat, and a soiled tunic, still damp from the rain. She whirled round, her eyes spinning to take in every corner of the dark building. Nothing! Had he lied when he had told Brigid he spent the night here? Or had he heard her leaving the house, and followed?

Slowly Constance wandered out of the stable, and she reached down to the dog at her side. It licked her fingers, and she found comfort in the act. She would be a fool to carry on the search, not knowing which way Brigid had gone. With a great deal of deliberation, she turned and went back towards the house, to wait impatiently and anxiously for one or both of them to return.

It was the sound of someone knocking on the door that roused Constance from the doze she had fallen into just before dawn. Forcing her eyelids open, she stumbled to open it, even as she heard Grannia stirring on the pallet.

It was Niall. He stood leaning against the wall, his eyes half-shut, stubble on his chin and his fingers hooked into his girdle. One eye opened wide as he took in the sight of her in the thin skimpy shift. Constance's hand went to her throat, only to fall when she realised that there was no undergown there to button. She sought refuge from her confusion in words. 'Where have you been, Master O'More? Brigid is missing—but perhaps you are aware of that?'

'I'm aware of it,' he murmured, opening his other eye and rasping his chin with his fingers. 'She's as safe as she can be, with Sil at large. She's with Kathleen in the hills, but I have men watching them.'

'So that's where she went!' She felt quite weak at the knees.

'Not immediately.' He straightened. 'May I come inside?'

She nodded. 'Grannia's awake.' She thought she ought to let him know—why, she did not reason.

He smiled. 'She can make us some porridge.' He followed her in.

Grannia let out a shriek, and immediately pulled the covers over her shoulders. Niall's eyes met Constance's, and he laughed. 'You'll have to make the porridge.'

She nodded, but first went to put on her cote-hardie, needing to turn away for a moment from his gaze. She set the fire glowing by blowing on the peats after that, and was glad of the task. 'What did you mean by "not immediately"?' She kept her back to him while she found bowls and oats, and filled a pot with water.

'What I said—first, she went somewhere else, but we don't know where. For several hours she vanished. I thought that Sil might have whisked her away, so I went into the hills with some of the men. Just before dawn, she was seen wandering among the cows in Kathleen's care.'

'How strange!' Constance faced him, trepidation written in her expression. 'I don't like what's happening. How can she vanish like that?'

'It's not so strange,' he said reassuringly, coming over to her. 'In the dark, and among the trees, she could easily slip past my men and me. What I find uncanny is that she remembers nothing about being here at all.'

'Just as she didn't seem to be aware that she had attacked me with the knife,' murmured Constance, her face worried.

'We *presume* she didn't seem to be aware. We never mentioned it to her—I didn't, and I presume that you didn't.' She nodded. 'Kathleen told me that she never mentioned seeing your kinsman to Brigid, but what she said to you did take place. Kathleen has seen him since, and told me that he still is anxious about you, seeming to have no thought for his own safety.'

'*You* told me that he *was* safe.' Constance put a hand on his arm and looked up at him with shadows in her eyes.

'He is as safe as I and the captain can make him.' He smiled wryly. 'But it's possible that Sil could have questioned the men and used that information to frighten you, perhaps—even to make you more aware of his power. Brigid and Sil were close, once—it was Kathleen who told us about seeing them. My foster-father put a stop to their meetings—as far as he was able to. But Brigid has not been the same since. Your kinsman's safe, I'm sure.'

'I wish I could see him,' she said sadly, moving away from Niall.

'It's out of the question! The captain would not allow him to come down here, and I would not let you go into the hills. You're safer here in the valley.'

'Am I?' Constance tossed her head back and looked straight at him. 'If Brigid can pass out of this settlement at night, what is preventing others from passing in?'

He spoke heavily. 'We allowed her to pass out. The gate was opened for her. I told you that a watch is being kept day and night, and we wanted to follow her night or day, knowing that Sil often works when others sleep.'

'But you still lost her, and I—I never even thought of checking the gate last night,' she said angrily, ramming the pot on the burning wood and peats.

'You were awake?' He shook his head slowly. 'Do you never sleep, woman?'

'Do you? Her eyes were shadowed by anger and fear and bewilderment.

'With one eye open.' His hand on her bare arm helped her to rise from the fireside. 'Was it Brigid you still feared? I never thought...'

'You never thought that she would make the attempt again?'

'No, I never thought that you were frightened of her doing so—and I should have realised it.' He wetted his finger, and rubbed the black smear on her chin. She was suddenly still, but he seemed unaware of her stiffness. 'You have no need to fear Brigid, anyway. She will stay in the hills with Kathleen. I have made the use of her I wanted to, and she seems to be perfectly content now to stay away from here.' His fingers touched the smooth curve of her cheek, making her already rapidly beating heart increase its pace. 'Does that make you feel happier?'

'Ay,' she replied in a low voice, almost hypnotised by the little flame that seemed to be burning deep in his eyes. 'Do you always make use of women, and then get rid of them, Master O'More?' Of its own will, her body brushed against his.

His hand stopped at her throat. 'I don't think an "Ay" would raise me in your estimation, Mistress de Wensley. But don't we all use people at times to get what we want? I didn't get rid of Brigid in the way you imply, but it is safer to have her where she is now. *You* are safer.'

There was a silence, and neither of them moved. He wanted desperately to kiss her, and Constance feared his taking her in his arms in case she liked it too much. 'I don't feel safe,' she murmured. 'Was all that affection you—you showed Brigid yesterday a sham?'

'I *am* fond of her—as a brother is of a sister. But even then I was thinking of your safety. Sil's use of her jealousy might have caused her to try and harm you again.' His fingers strayed down her neck, and stilled on her shoulder. 'Your safety is my first concern.'

Constance forced herself to speak on. 'Is that because I have more to offer you than Brigid? Land and a horse, is what you said a few days ago.'

'What are you suggesting?' he said softly. 'That I have an eye on your manor? If that were all, I could have got rid of you at any time since we met, and carried on as I did before you came.' His hand slid down her arm, and his fingers caught up her hand to carry it to his lips. Her throat moved convulsively, but she could not speak the words she should have said then, because she was caught up in an onrush of longing to be able to let go of all resistance to his attraction.

Niall felt the tension seep out of her, and gently pulled her into his arms. His kiss was less gentle as he found her responsive. There was a hunger in that long kiss they shared, but he drew away first. Not too much too soon, he thought, gazing down into her dazed face. He did not want to scare her at this stage in their relationship. And, besides, he was suddenly aware of Grannia's fascinated eyes on them. He cursed inwardly. He would have to speak to the girl, otherwise the news would be all over the settlement by dinnertime. And it could get back to Sil. He wanted to keep his cousin guessing his intentions and feelings towards Constance. Thus, it would be less dangerous for her.

'I—I think the water is boiling,' said Constance, also aware of Grannia. Unless she were careful, it would be all over the settlement that Master Niall had no sooner got rid of Brigid than he was kissing and cuddling the new Mistress. She must be more circumspect—and speak to Grannia. 'Shall we have our porridge?'

He smiled, and removed the pot from the fire. She watched him, thinking that where Niall O'More, Irish horse-borrower, was concerned, she would have to be more careful, and not fall into his hands like a ripe plum in late summer. He had the ability to make her sensually aware of herself, as Milo never had. She could only put it down to their first encounter, so she must try to keep her distance.

They sat on stools, bowls in hands, and talked of affairs, of the mare about to foal, of limewashing the walls, of trestles and benches and crops—and if their knees brushed several times, each seemed completely unaware of it.

The days grew longer, and there was much to do. The villagers seemed to have accepted Constance's presence among them, and willingly co-operated with the few demands she made. On her instructions, Grannia and her mother went into Naas to purchase linen for sheets and napkins. Niall would not allow Constance to go, reminding her of possible danger.

Constance chafed at the restraints he laid on her. She was not to wander down to the river alone, or to ride without him, and then not far from the settlement. Because she had decided it was wiser not to be alone with Niall, she did not ride at all. But the carpenter had worked swiftly, and her trestles were soon made, which made her glad, because she could not enjoy eating her food on her knee for every meal. The chair would take longer, because it would be intricately carved with flowers and leaves. The walls in the hall were washed with lime, and she had plans to make a tapestry for the one that caught the most of the light—that was if she stayed, of course. She found that, as each day passed, she grew more reluctant to leave.

When one of the mares foaled a perfect replica of herself, Constance was very conscious of the plans she and Niall had discussed weeks earlier, but it was the trigger for Niall to mention his plan to go to Connemara.

'When?' she asked, her throat suddenly tight, knowing that she would miss him, and fear while he was away.

'In a few days,' he answered, stroking the new mother's mane. 'I knew that, by telling Brigid I was going, I would buy us a little time to make our own plans.' His voice sounded strained. 'Sil will act as soon as I leave. I don't doubt that.'

'You mean that he will follow you and attempt to kill you?' She did not look at him, not wanting him to guess how anxious she felt.

'Sil, or some of his men.' He forced a smile. 'Don't be afraid for your own safety, though. I shall have this place watched, and if anything were to happen, I would hear about it.'

'I'm not afraid,' she lied, rubbing her cheek against the mare's soft neck and looking down at the foal. 'But still I shall be glad when you return, and this matter is settled one way or another.'

'So shall I,' he said softly, his eyes on her face. 'Perhaps then we can concentrate on the future.'

She wondered what he meant by that, but she did not ask.

It rained that evening, and he came into the hall as he had been wont to do at such times, and played draughts with her. Grannia and her mother were hemming sheets. Constance found it unsettling having Niall just across the trestle from her. In so many ways he was a different man from the one who had pulled her from the bog and ridden to the cave near Athy with her. Had she, to him, become a different woman? They had lived soberly and sedately, taking life seriously as they performed all the mundane tasks of everyday living, yet often she had felt that tug of attraction. Niall, however, always treated her with a polite deference that at times maddened her. Now, looking at him and attempting to stamp his features on her mind, she feared that in a couple of days she might never see him again. She suddenly ached to have his arms round her and for him to kiss her, just to see how it felt—whether it still had the power to thrill her. In the last few weeks, she had become familiar with the serious cast to his high-cheekboned, sometimes haughty-looking, profile. Of late, his smile had often been missing, and that worried her. Maybe he was not as confident about defeating Sil as he had sounded?

The next day the weather was sunny again, and the air was heavy with the fragrance of early summer growth. Had everything been normal, Constance could have felt gloriously content, but something happened to brighten the day. They had a visitor. Kathleen burst in on them in the middle of supper. Her face was rosy from living so much out of doors, and her blue eyes seemed even bluer. Altogether there was a glow about her that had not been there before.

'So here you are,' she declared. 'Fancy eating indoors on such a beautiful evening.' Her arms went round Niall's neck, and she hugged him.

He kissed her cheek. 'What are you doing here?' he asked sternly. 'I thought I told you to stay with Brigid.'

Kathleen pulled a face. 'She is not alone. Some of the girls and your O'Toole friends are keeping her company. She has been her old domineering self of late, telling me that I'm doing things wrong.' A look of irritation crossed her pretty face, but it passed quickly. 'May I have some bread? I'm hungry.'

'Of course,' said Constance, delighted to see her. 'Did you ride here alone?'

Kathleen shook her head, setting her flaxen braids bouncing. 'Niall said that we were to go nowhere alone. Dara, the O'Toole dwarf, came with me, with his great axe balanced across his knee, ready to slay any of Sil's men who would dare to approach.' Her eyes danced.

'It isn't funny, Kathleen!' Niall frowned. 'Why can you never see danger?'

She wrinkled her nose, and took a piece of bread. 'Who wants to see danger behind every tree and rock on such a day?' She tore at the bread. Her eyes were suddenly pensive as they rested on Constance. 'I have come because I have seen Robin—several times. He wants to be reassured about your welfare, so I promised that I would come. Are you well?'

Niall gave a bark of laughter. 'Doesn't she look well?'

Kathleen's brows drew together as she peered more closely at Constance, who had been about to speak, but was silenced by the concentration in Kathleen's look. 'She's thinner than I remember, and her face is drawn.'

'That's only because I ate something that disagreed with me, and I was sick this morning,' murmured Constance, toying with the spoon in her bowl.

Niall glanced at her. 'You didn't say that you were unwell! If you had told me, I wouldn't have allowed you to watch me schooling the horses in the hot sun.'

'I'm all right now.' She shrugged. 'There's no need to fuss, Master O'More.'

Kathleen's warm gaze went from one to the other. 'I'll tell Robin, then, that you are all right—and happy?'

Constance smiled slightly. 'You can tell him that he has no need to worry about me, and that we hope he will be free soon, if the Earl of Ormonde has anything to do with it.'

Kathleen's face lit up. 'I shall tell him that you are happy. He already knows about Ormonde, but doesn't believe that he is working fast enough.'

'He'll have to be patient,' muttered Niall, scowling. 'Dermot's been a hostage longer than he has.'

'Robin's not a patient man,' murmured Kathleen, avoiding her foster-brother's eyes.

'Hmph,' responded Niall. 'He'll just have to try. When are you returning? I'm going to Connemara in the morning.'

'So I have heard.' Kathleen smiled at him, and picked up another piece of bread. 'I'll stay till then, and wave you off.'

CHAPTER TWELVE

'WHEN THE weather is like this, I want to peel off my clothes and kick off my shoes and dance in the grass,' said Kathleen, dancing alongside Niall and Constance as they walked to the meadow where the horses grazed under the watchful eye of the O'Toole dwarf.

'Kathleen!' Niall rebuked. 'What are you saying, girl! You speak like a pagan. We are not sun-worshippers.'

'I do not speak of worshipping the sun, but of finding pleasure in its heat. But *you* speak like an old man.' She poked her tongue out at him. 'You have forgotten, it seems, what it is like to be young.'

Niall caught her by a braid. 'And you, young woman, have taken leave of your senses,' he responded grimly. 'I think that perhaps you should return home. You are not fit company for Mistress de Wensley.'

'Oh, Niall,' her face fell, and her bottom lip quivered, 'what is wrong with you this evening?'

'There's nothing wrong with me,' he snapped, frowning. 'It is you who are in the wrong.'

'*I* consider Kathleen is fit company for me,' interpolated Constance, her brown eyes challenging him. 'At this time of year, I have often had the urge to take off at least some of my clothing. And when there's a moon sailing across a clear sky, I can believe that there is nothing more delightful than dancing beneath it. And I am not a moon-worshipper, but a true daughter of the church.'

'You've both run mad.' The heat had evaporated from Niall's voice, and he sounded amused.

'Not mad, Niall,' responded Kathleen, her smile peeping out again, 'merry! That is how Mistress Constance and I feel on such an evening. Doesn't such beauty make your blood stir? Mine is positively bubbling!' She pulled her hair free from his hold and flung her arms wide.

'Hmm! It's time I found you a husband, little sister.' His eyes narrowed as he watched her skip into the meadow.

'This evening was made for lovers,' cried Kathleen. She blew him a kiss. 'It is time you found a wife, big brother, or you'll be too old, with all your passion spent.'

'Impudent little wanton,' Niall murmured, unable to prevent himself from looking at Constance, to find that she was looking not at him, but at Kathleen. His blood stirred at the beauty of her profile. 'It's been a long day,' he said loudly.

'And you'll be leaving in the morning.' Constance turned and faced him. 'You wish to go to bed?'

Niall almost said, 'Ay, with you' but answered instead, 'It's too beautiful to sleep, although the sun is going down. See, the stars are already coming out—and you can see the moon just over the tree-tops.'

'It's lovely,' said Constance in a low voice, suddenly caught up in a mood of pure enchantment. They both looked up at the moon.

Kathleen, who was watching them, came over. 'Lovely or not,' she said, pretending to smother a yawn, 'I'm for bed. I may sleep in the hall?' addressing Constance.

'Of course. I'll be with you soon.' Why not now? A little voice asked inside Constance. She ignored it.

Kathleen blew them both a kiss and went towards the house.

'I suppose we should be going?' said Niall, his arm brushing Constance's shoulder as he began to move in the direction of the stable.

'Why?' She faced him boldly. 'Do you believe that some moon-goddess will come down and snatch you away, Master O'More?'

'My name is Niall,' he murmured. 'And I could believe that she has already come.' The back of his hand touched her cheek. 'You are beautiful.'

Her breath was almost suspended, and she had to resort to swallowing before she could speak. 'You said that very prettily.' She moved several paces forward.

'It's true.' He caught her up easily. 'Tomorrow, I'll be leaving.'

'Don't you think I'm aware of that?' Her voice quavered, and she took several more hurried paces.

'Maybe you're glad I'm going, because you've said little to make me believe that perhaps you'll miss me.' He caught hold of her arm, then stopped. They stared at each other.

'And why should I be missing you, Niall O'More?' The words came out as a whisper.

He did not answer, only reaching out to seize her arms as she would have run from him. 'You said you wanted to dance. Then dance with me.'

'Wh—What—here? We'll be seen!' Her eyes were wide as she looked into his shadowy face.

He smiled, and took her hand to hurry her away and into the trees by the river before bringing her to a halt. One arm went about her waist, while his hand clasped her fingers. His feet forced hers to move, so that she almost fell over them, and only his arm kept her upright. Her breasts brushed his chest in a sensuous buffing, and their thighs often seemed to be on a collision course as they circled in the moonlight dappling through the trees. Only when they came to a silent halt with a kind of dizzy exhilaration, did Constance look up at him.

Niall kissed her, not once but what seemed like a thousand times, one kiss tailing off to mingle with the next—each one more demanding than the one before. It was as though he could not get enough of her.

She drew a shaky breath when his mouth nuzzled her throat and his hands sought every curve moulded by the cotton gown. There seemed no danger in such gentle exploration. She did not resist when he drew her down into the long grass, sweet-smelling and welcoming.

She wanted to forget everything, despite a silent voice warning of the moon's enchantment on such a night. His fingers stroked her breast through the cotton in such a way that she gave a little moan. He said something softly in Irish, before his mouth found hers again, while he slowly began to unfasten her buttons. Part of her mind recognised that his gentleness was deliberately employed—perhaps he knew that it was a tease, rousing such desires in her as his lips moved to caress the smooth skin revealed each time a button was undone. Milo had never been gentle: his lust had been satisfied within moments. Why did she have to think of Milo now? It reminded her of how cruel men could be, and how Niall had taken her by the bog—not that his possession had been cruel. She was remembering the dream-like experiences she had felt then, and forced Milo out of her mind.

She felt a yearning in her loins, and a desire to roll over and burrow into Niall. Was it sinful to feel such a sensation in the circumstances? He pulled away, and she gasped and held out a hand to him—then she saw that he was stripping off his tunic, and a shiver raced through her. He took her hand, holding it tightly and kissing it before sweeping her fingers across his bare chest, and down. She quivered as their hands, still clasped, moved to hug her hip. Her heart had begun to beat so fast that she felt as though she could not breathe. She did not know what she wanted or what to do. Her eyes closed to shut him off in an attempt to regain control of her spiralling desire. When Niall spoke, she started. 'We have come so far. Where we go next, depends on you,' he said huskily.

Her lashes fluttered open. 'What do you mean?' she whispered.

'There is a fire in you that I could light if you wanted. If you wanted, Constance. Do you?'

Conflicting emotions tore at her. 'I don't—know— why are you asking me such things—now?' she cried, suddenly angry with him for going away from her.

'Don't you?' He bit her shoulder, and she squeaked and reared up against him and bit him back.

'So you are not so passive?' His expression was one of unholy delight. 'We are alive, Constance! Alive on such a night! I want you madly, so kiss me as you did by the bog—as if you were a plant thirsty for rain.' He tugged her hands so that her breasts collided with his chest. It hurt, and she was even more angry. 'I did not...' His mouth stopped the words, and his tongue forced her lips apart. It was a kiss that seemed to draw the soul from her body and into his control. She fought against such utter possession. He lifted his head and...laughed with pleasure, but she was in a panic.

'You raped me then,' she gasped. 'I could not have responded in the way you say!'

For several seconds neither of them moved or spoke, then Niall sat back on his heels, his naked chest gleaming in the moonlight. 'I did not force you. You might not have been fully aware of what was happening at first, but if you had resisted, I would have stopped.'

'I was exhausted,' she cried. 'You got me drunk on whiskey! I could not resist.'

'You could have struggled or pushed me away, but instead you pulled me down on top of you and welcomed me into your body,' he said softly.

'I could not have!' She sat up, her temper rising. 'What kind of woman do you think I am?'

His eyes glinted. 'Then? A tired, cold—and hungry—woman who roused my compassion as well as my desire, who was willing to be kept warm in the most enjoyable way there is. I was your heat and your bed that night, as well as your food. Because we were *both* satisfied, I considered you a fit mate for me then, as I do now. I would wed you, Constance.'

'It can't be true!' She put a hand to her head, and there were tears in her eyes. 'I thought it was a dream!' She looked at him, and what he had said at last penetrated. 'Is that how you see me, Niall O'More—as food and warmth and comfort? Well, I tell you now—that I wouldn't wed you if you were the last man on earth. I—I hate you!' She was suddenly blinded by tears, and her fingers groped for her gown as she scrambled to her feet. She turned and ran.

At any moment she expected to hear him following. Her heart was pounding as she closed the door of the house and pressed her back to it. After a minute or two, she made out the shape of the bed and the glow of the banked peats. She slumped against the door, and buried her head in her knees.

Tears trickled down her cheeks, and her fingers sought to stem them. Why had he not followed her? Did he not care about her except as a fit mate, a woman who possessed a manor that he coveted? Not one word of love from him! He could have spoken them, even if he did not mean what he said! Well, she knew where she stood—and she would be glad when he left in the morning. Perhaps she would not be here when he came back? All that talk about Sil and there had not been a sign of him or his men—she had only his word that Brigid's strange behaviour was due to Sil. Well, Brigid was welcome to him!

She heard the rustle of bedding as Kathleen turned over, and she buried her head deeper into her skirts. At last she could cry no more, and went to bed. After a long time, she slept the sleep of the exhausted.

When Constance woke, there was no sign of anybody in the hall. From outside came the sound of voices: Kathleen and Grannia. The memory of last night was vivid. A lump rose in her throat, and she swallowed with some difficulty. She felt sick. Had Niall gone already? Feeling ill, she got out of bed, fighting against nausea as she buttoned her surcote over the cotton gown. She was sick in a bowl before she went outside. Patches of blue showed between fluffy white clouds, and beneath her feet the grass was green and lush. On such a day she should have felt happy.

Both the girls turned to stare at her, accusation in their eyes. 'Niall's gone,' they cried in unison, 'and he didn't even say goodbye.'

'When?' The remains of her colour drained from her face.

'We don't know. He was gone when we got up.' Kathleen sighed. 'The dwarf said that he wasn't in a good mood.'

'He was downright surly,' muttered the little man, who was holding Kathleen's horse's bridle. 'And he had the hounds with him.'

'Did he leave any message?' asked Constance, feeling faint.

He shook his head. 'Nearly bit my head off when I asked him where he was going. Didn't like to speak after that.'

Constance nodded, and turned to Kathleen. 'Are you leaving now?'

'Ay.' Kathleen smiled. 'I promised Ro—your kinsman, that I would not be away long. I shall give him your message.' She accepted the dwarf's help to climb on the horse, and when she was up, she faced Constance. 'Don't be worrying about Niall. He can take care of himself, but you look tired, so do rest.' She waved a hand, and was soon out of sight.

Constance turned away, and without speaking a word to Grannia, went inside the house. Her world had been turned upside-down since coming to Ireland, and she had no idea what to do to right it again.

The next few days passed slowly, and the only happening of note was that she was sick in the mornings. Her suspicion of what was wrong with her was gaining ground. It seemed unbelievable that what might have made her life bearable a couple of years ago was happening to her now. Her thoughts—her emotions—were in total chaos. She went through the motions of living, without noticing what she ate or drank, or caring what clothes she put on. Sh could only think of what she should do when Niall returned. What *could* she do? He had said that he wanted to wed her—and having his child would be reason enough for him to rejoice and insist on a wedding. But she was certain she did not want him to marry her for such a reason. So he had said that he wanted her, but she had discovered that that was not enough. Had she not already suffered the depths of an unhappy marriage? She would have liked to reach the heights in the next one. She prayed for a solution to her dilemma.

The weather changed, and it rained. The tedium of staying indoors sewing linen for napkins with Grannia almost drove Constance mad. The days trickled by, and still Niall did not return, and now it was the fear that he might have been killed that tormented her.

One morning she slept late, to be woken by a sudden bustle and noise. Grannia was up, and opening the door to a tumultuous row outside. Constance flung back the covers and pulled on a surcote over her gown. Perhaps it was Niall back, safe and well! Her heart betrayed her by lifting with relief. Then Brigid entered, and her spirits fell.

Brigid came to a halt precipitately, her freckled face was scarlet with exertion, and her eyes were wild. 'She's gone!' she cried. 'Kathleen and that kinsman of yours have gone.'

'Gone? Gone where?' Constance put a hand on the chest to steady herself.

'One of the O'Tooles came to tell me. Your kinsman's horse is missing.' Brigid lowered herself on to a stool. 'I knew she would do something wicked,' she muttered angrily. 'But she won't find a decent husband now—she has ruined herself.'

Constance's head spun as she sat on the chest. 'Do you mean that they have run away? He's escaped?'

Brigid stared at her as if she had not heard her. 'I promised my mother that I would take care of her, but she's always been wayward, never obeying me, but doing what she wanted. But I never thought she would be so stupid! Serves her right if your kinsman discards her.'

'Brigid, surely they cannot have gone far! They'll find them.'

This time the girl looked at her fully. 'They think they escaped during the night. She didn't come home before I fell asleep, and she wasn't in the hut this morning. It's likely she never came home at all!'

'But Robin was watched. How could he escape?' Constance was utterly bewildered by his actions. He had never looked at a girl before, yet she could not help remembering how Kathleen had spoken of their meetings, and how *she* had seemed to glow. How often had they met?

'The guards had grown slack. He was never closely watched—they did not consider there was any danger of his escaping. They can't even understand now why he should want to, because he was well taken care of. And now...' Her shoulders sagged helplessly. 'I'll have to tell Niall. Where is he?'

'Niall?' Constance was suddenly wary. Surely Brigid knew where he had gone. 'He's gone to Connemara to see about a horse.'

'Oh, I'd forgotten! Kathleen told me. What can be done, then?' Brigid got to her feet again, and paced the floor.

'Perhaps Robin will come here for me?' suggested Constance, keeping a careful eye on the girl.

'He surely isn't such a fool! The men are already here looking for him, and planning to take *you* up into the mountains if they don't find him and Kathleen.'

'Take *me*?' Constance's voice hardened. 'Niall would not allow it.'

'But Niall is not here,' said a silky voice. Both girls whirled round to confront the man in the flowing robes filling the doorway.

Brigid gave a frightened cry, and backed away from him, but he held out an arm and fixed his dark eyes on her. After a few moments, she walked slowly towards him. Constance shuddered, but stood her ground, watching.

Sil spoke to Brigid in low compelling Irish, and she gave a moan and fell on her knees, wrapping her arms round his feet. She kissed them. He bade her to rise, and she did so hurriedly. He spoke again, and she pressed her body against his and held her face up for his kiss. Sil's eyes were on Constance's face as he kissed Brigid, and she thought she recognised triumph in their depths. A great sense of repulsion kept her sitting on the chest. Fear tightened her stomach.

Sil released Brigid abruptly, and told her to go and wait outside. She went. Then he turned to Constance again, and surveyed her carefully, his eyes passing over every aspect of her. 'You see that she is my creature,' he said melodiously. 'So shall you be.'

'I am not alone here, Sil,' she said quietly in French. 'And you surely cannot bewitch the whole settlement.'

He smiled, his black eyes glistening. 'No, but the O'Tooles will keep them in order while they search the place for your kinsman and the wayward Kathleen.'

'They are not here.' She looked down at her bare feet, already feeling the power in his gaze.

'I know it. They should be on their way to Dublin by now. Love . . . is it not a wonderful emotion? Almost as exciting as hate.' He laughed. 'Look at me, Mistress de Wensley. Surely you do not fear me?'

'I don't fear you,' she lied, 'but I have respect for your devilish powers, Sil.' She glanced at him, but immediately looked away. 'If you know that my kinsman is not here, why have you come?'

'I came for you, Mistress—and Dermot's friends among the O'Tooles will not speak a word against my taking you. They see the necessity of having another hostage in your kinsman's place. They do not realise my real interest in you.' He moved towards Constance, and it seemed to her that he glided. She closed her eyes tightly as he laughed. 'What a pretty gown you are wearing.'

Constance opened her eyes and turned to run, but he seized a handful of her long hair and dragged her to him. He forced her head back, and gazed into her face. She closed her eyes swiftly, and his laugh seemed to bounce off the rafters. 'I have been having you watched, Englishwoman,' he said melodiously, 'and your actions interest me.'

'Whom have you bewitched besides Brigid, you devil?' She struggled to free herself, but he only pulled her hair the harder until she cried out.

'What harm is there in telling you,' he murmured. 'The man who washed your walls—Grannia's mother. Just a small enchantment, that is all. But if you wish for a devil now, woman, I could summon up a devil for you.'

'Why call one up,' she hissed, tears of pain in her eyes, 'when one is already here in possession of your soul?

And you consider yourself *master*—when you are only a tool!'

'I can see that I shall have to subdue you,' he muttered, an ugly expression twisting his hawk-like features. With his free hand, he pushed her in the direction of the bed.

Desperately she tried to dig in her heels, but his next blow sent her flying on to it. She screamed as he crawled on top of her. He wrapped her hair round his wrist, so that she could not move away without causing herself great pain. He stared down at her. 'You have been in Niall's company too long, and he and his brother were always obstinate. Even as boys, they dared to range themselves against me. Me, the Great One, who will lead his people back to the old ways.'

'You're mad,' she gasped, keeping her eyes firmly closed.

'The great have often been accused of madness, because their ways are elevated far beyond the understanding of ordinary men.' He pulled her hair again, and she screamed, praying that someone would hear her and come. 'Open your eyes, woman. It will be easier for you to obey me.'

She shook her head, tears pricking the backs of her eyelids. The breath hissed between his teeth as he twisted her head this way and that, but still she did not open her eyes. Then she felt unbearable pain as he thrust his fingers against them. Instantly into her mind came the memory of how he had attempted to blind Niall, and her fear almost suffocated her. She felt the chill of metal against her cheek.

'You are a fool,' he muttered, the melody having disappeared from his voice. 'And if I did not want to possess you, I would slit your throat.' He slapped her across the face, and her eyes blinked open.

Strange coloured lights fizzed on and off in front of her. She could barely see his face through the haze. Her head throbbed. 'You will rot in hell,' she whispered, wondering why he should choose this way to have his revenge on her for spoiling his plans.

'There is the power, woman,' he answered, his voice silky again. 'Look at me! Hate is a much stronger feeling than love. And power is more exhilarating than both.'

'I despise you,' she moaned, her head swimming as she felt the power of that glistening stare. 'Love Niall. Hate you! Despise you!' She experienced a strange exultation as she realised what she had said. 'Hate what you tried to do to Niall! Hate! Hate! Hate!' She would not surrender to him.

'Niall will not come to you. He will be dead by now. My men will have seen to that. Peace lies my way. You can rest—stop struggling. You don't hate me. You desire me—you would obey me,' he said in a monotone.

'No!' she forced the words out through slack lips. 'He isn't dead. I would know if he were dead. I love him. Hate you.' She could feel his mouth pressing eagerly against her throat. 'Hate you!' she screamed. 'Love Niall!' She could feel a power growing within her, resistance strengthening. How she hated all that Sil symbolised! She recalled the pain in Niall's voice when he had spoken about his scar. 'No! No! No!' She began to wriggle, and he cursed.

Pain was her reward for resisting, but she discovered that it made it easier to go on resisting, and she knew when he decided that she was not going to submit to him. 'A different way you have chosen,' he rasped, taking a small phial from a pouch at his girdle.

She was too exhausted to move as she watched his long fingers ease out the stopper. Her tongue ran rapidly over her dry lips, and she tried to wrench herself out of his hold, but his curved nails dug into her scalp. He dragged her head back and back until it made breathing difficult, and her lips parted. Then he forced the liquid into her mouth. She choked and coughed, but still it ran down her throat. He thrust more of the liquid into her mouth until she felt that if she did not swallow or draw breath, she would die. Perhaps she *was* going to die? A mist was forming in front of her eyes, and her head spun slowly? The last sound she heard was that of Sil laughing before his laugh was cut off as the door opened.

'What do you want?' Sil snarled, as Dara, the dwarf, entered.

'Thought you should know, Master Sil, that the captain is on his way to see Mistress de Wensley.' He stared stolidly at the *filidh* and strode heavily to the bed.

Sil muttered a curse. He had never been able to do anything with the dwarf: unnatural blood there, he reckoned. 'She swooned,' he said, as the dwarf gazed down at Constance's pallid face.

'I'd better take her outside, then. The fresh air will revive her.' He scooped her up in his short strong arms before Sil could protest, and carried her across the hall and out. Sil followed him swiftly.

'I shall take her on my horse,' called the *filidh*, determined not to have his prey taken out of his control.

'The widow will go with Dara,' said a deep voice.

'But, my lord, she will be best with me,' replied Sil, facing the captain. 'The dwarf and Dermot's friends have already lost us one hostage.'

The captain squared his drooping shoulders, and his weary grey eyes fell beneath Sil's. 'Even so, Sil, she will go with Dara. Perhaps not all those about Master Milburn were my son's friends—and maybe he was not so much lost, as allowed to go free.'

'Of course,' said Sil smoothly. 'One is always inclined to blame others when something goes wrong. If the dwarf loses her...' He shrugged, and walked away from the captain to his horse.

Brigid, who had been watching, followed eagerly to paw at him. Sil spoke to her softly and stroked her cheek. She moaned, before falling back as he rode away. Hurriedly she went over to the group of villagers, and spoke to a man with a hole in his tunic and the strings of his cap untied. He pushed his way out of the huddle of people and vanished.

The captain looked at Constance in Dara's arms. His rough fingers touched her slightly damp cheek, and he sighed. 'Take her, Dara. Keep her safe.' The dwarf nodded, and moved away.

The rest of the O'Tooles mounted and rode off. Dara soon caught up. Following at a distance came the man to whom Brigid had spoken.

Once in the hills and among the trees, Dara detached himself from the group of O'Tooles. He seemed to lose himself among the gnarled trunks of the oaks, and was soon travelling terrain that seemed bleak in comparison with the greenery of the forest. After a short time, he came to a stretch of water, reed-ringed, with a small island in its centre. Only for a short distance did the horse have to swim before its hoofs were scrabbling for a firm footing on land again. Though the island covered only a small area, it was populated with bushes and saplings and a couple of fully grown alders. The horse was soon out of sight of any watchers on the far shore, and then it was as though he and the riders had vanished from the earth.

Constance woke slowly. The afternoon sun was slanting in through the woven branches that served as a roof for the crude hut, washing the interior in a wavering green light. Where was she? Something moved to her right, and her head turned quickly as remembrance flooded through her. But it was not Sil—it was a little man with a long beard and concerned, bright, hazel eyes. Kathleen's O'Toole dwarf—but was he a friend or a foe? Her fear must have showed in her face, because he spoke.

'You are safe, Niall's woman. Sil will not find you here.'

'What happened? I...' Her hand went to her head, which felt strange. He told her, and relieved, she sank back on the bed of moss and grass, her eyes on his gentle face. He seemed completely different from the time she had seen him with Kathleen. And what had he said about her being Niall's woman? Was that how some of those who knew Niall saw her? 'What now?' she murmured, glad to rest.

'I shall go and tell Niall where you are.' He sat cross-legged on the ground. 'But first you must have a drink and some food. I shall be some time, but you must not worry.'

'But you said you did not know where he had gone!' she exclaimed, watching him fill a wooden cup from a flask.

A smile creased his leathery face. 'Even the trees might be listening, Niall's woman.'

'So you do know, and he's not dead?' She took the cup.

'He is not dead. Wounded, ay! Or he would have faced Sil by now.' A napkin was placed by her side. 'Bread and fish,' he said. 'Now I must go.' His hand touched her sleeve. 'You are on an island, but you must not wander round it in case you are seen. Keep hidden within the trees and undergrowth.'

She nodded, and took a sip of water. He patted her arm, and with a 'The saints will guard you', he left the hut. For a moment she stared at the fluttering leaves, and then unfolded the napkin.

Dara caught his first glimpse of water in the valley below, and knew that he would soon see the tower of St Kevin's fine stone building. There were robed figures ahead on the lower slopes. As he neared them, heads turned, and he recognised first the handsome man with a strong chin and far-seeing eyes, and then Niall with his thatch of tawny hair not quite concealed by the monk's cowl.

'Friend! What brings you here?' Niall's expression was anxious, for it had been agreed that Dara was not to risk being followed unless Sil made a move that put Constance in danger.

'She is safe,' Dara assured him, dismounting. 'At least for the moment. But I bring you bad news, Niall.' He inclined his head to Niall's companion. 'Brother Michael.'

Niall had gone pale, and clutched at the horse's bridle. 'How can you say in one breath that she is safe, and then tell me you bring bad news?'

'It is her kinsman and Kathleen. They have run away— allowed to escape, is what the captain believes.'

Niall's brown clouded, and he muttered under his breath, his bound hand clenching. 'And Mistress Constance?'

'I have her safe on the island, but for how long I do not know. Sil made sure that your woman's estate was searched. He disappeared inside the house just as I reached it. Your foster-sister came out—and I heard your lady scream, and went in.'

'What had he done to her?' demanded Niall unsteadily.

'She was unconscious. That foul liquid he used on Dermot when he was taken by the English, I don't doubt.' He squeezed Niall's arm reassuringly. 'He has not possessed her body or her mind, if that is what you fear. There is no sign of it in her eyes—and, besides, he would not have needed to drug her if he had. But you must come! I do not trust Sil, even though he rode before me and could not have seen me leave. Come, Niall, come!'

CHAPTER THIRTEEN

'I SHALL come as well,' said Brother Michael, his mouth firming. 'Your wound is not quite healed, Niall, and you might have need of my skills.'

A slight smile eased Niall's lips. 'We go to face Sil together as in the old days, Dougal—is that it?'

'Not quite as it was then,' replied his brother. 'We are not children now.'

The dwarf nodded. 'It is good. We shall get the horses and dogs?'

The brothers agreed, and followed Dara down the hill.

Constance woke, and the hut was filled with dusk. Something had disturbed her, but was it only a bird settling for the night? Or maybe the dwarf was returning with Niall! Her heart gave a leap, and she rose hurriedly as a rustling came from the undergrowth. It was possible that it was neither, but Sil. Her blood chilled as she remembered how Brigid had behaved towards the *filidh*. Poor Brigid! She could not help pitying her.

A voice suddenly spoke, and her spirits soared. 'Niall!' she cried, stumbling in the direction of the sound.

'Why, I do believe you are glad to see me.' He scanned her face as he seized her outstretched hands.

'Of course I am!' She was forgetting in that moment how they had parted. 'I thought you might be that terrible Sil.' Her fingers laced feverishly through his as she stared into the lean scarred face she had come to love.

'Then at least I'm preferable to him,' he said lightly.

She frowned. There was something in his voice. 'A thousand times a thousand,' she replied extravagantly.

'A thousand thousand? Sweet Jesu, you must hate Sil!'

'Hate! Loathe! Despise!' She lowered her voice. 'If you could have seen the way he made Brigid kiss his feet.' She gave a shudder.

'I don't doubt that he has possessed my sister,' he said harshly. 'Another reason why I have to kill him.' His bound hand curled stiffly about her wrist as he pulled her to the low doorway. 'Did he hurt you?'

It sounded to Constance as if it were an afterthought, and a great ache caught her throat. 'Nearly tore the hair from my head,' she said brightly.

'Nothing more?' he asked tautly as they came out into the open.

'He threatened to slit my throat if I did not submit.' Her voice was still airy. 'He slapped my face quite hard. Cut my mouth.' Her tongue licked the inside of her cheek. 'And poured some foul liquid down my throat.'

'Anything else?' Niall's breathing sounded loud.

'Isn't that enough?' she said quietly, dropping all pretense. 'I was terrified.'

Niall made no answer, but he was almost choked with fury as he pulled her on towards where the lough gleamed in the starlight. Dougal and Dara waited there with the horses. 'This is my brother Dougal,' said Niall, releasing her hand. He watched Constance's face, feeling slightly anxious as she looked up at Dougal.

'It is a pleasure to meet Niall's brother.' Constance made the sketchiest of reverences, uncertain how to address him. She could not see his face properly, shadowed as it was by his cowl. Why was he here?

'I am pleased to meet Niall's mistress.' His voice was deep, and it seemed slightly familiar. 'But let us not delay here,' he added. 'Even the night has eyes when creatures like Sil are about.'

'You have seen something?' asked Niall sharply.

'Only shadows,' Dara replied, stroking his beard.

The hounds whined softly, and Niall's hand took hold of Constance's again. She was glad of the contact. 'You consider them more than shadows?' whispered Niall, his eyes narrowing as they searched the water and the far bank.

'It's possible.' Dara reached for the axe at his girdle. 'It might be wiser to wait out the night and cross the lough with the dawn light.'

'Then we shall wait,' said Dougal, lowering himself to the ground, and sitting cross-legged.

'I'll set the dogs to roam,' murmured Niall. 'We'll take turns at watching.'

'No,' said Dougal, looking up at him. 'Your wound is not yet healed, and you need more rest than I do. I am used to keeping all-night vigils, brother.'

Niall would have protested, but Dougal and Dara insisted that he took some rest. 'Take your mistress with you,' said Dougal, 'and go to my hut.'

Constance was about to say that she had been sleeping on and off most of the day, but Niall pulled on her hand and she was forced to go with him. She wondered what a man of the church was thinking of, telling his brother to take his woman with him to rest, and part of her was hoping that the dwarf at least would come with them, but he did not.

'You don't have to be nervous,' muttered Niall, as they retraced their steps back to the hut. 'I won't touch you. I'll be acting as your guard.'

Constance made no reply. She felt like laughing, and saying: It's too late for that, Niall O'More, I'm having your child! But now was not the time. Her fingers were warm inside his, and she could feel the binding about his wrist. How bad was his wound? The tips of her fingers sought to find the extent of the bandaging.

'Don't do that,' he ordered, wriggling his arm.

'Is it very painful?' Constance's thumb stroked the back of his hand, and she looked up at him. 'Was it a bloody fight?'

'Very bloody,' he said roughly, stilling her thumb with his thumb. 'But there are three less on Sil's side.' Their thumbs rubbed up against each other. 'You realise I'll have to let the captain exchange you for Dermot?'

'I know,' she murmured. 'It's a pity Kathleen couldn't have been a little more patient.'

'Kathleen? It was your kinsman who couldn't wait,' he snapped. 'He's ruined her reputation; you realise that?' His index finger tickled the palm of her hand.

'He'll marry her. If nothing else, Robin is a gentleman.' There was a quiver in her voice.

'I'll make sure he does,' said Niall in a stern voice, bringing her to a halt outside the hut. 'You'll sleep inside, and I'll sleep outside.'

'Of course,' she responded in a dignified voice. 'And if I scream, you are not to enter.'

'Why should you scream?' he demanded impatiently.

'I can't abide spiders!' Constance shivered. 'Or anything else that creeps or crawls—such as Sil.'

The corner of Niall's mouth quivered. 'Sil's not going to get you, because he'd have to do so over my dead body—and I've no intention of dying yet.'

'How chivalrous of you to guard me with your life,' she said, smiling sweetly.

'Isn't that what you employed me for?' he said sternly, pushing her towards the doorway.

She went inside, and for several minutes sat silently, pondering over what to do next. Then she screamed. Niall jumped out of his skin, but stayed where he was, leaning against the side of the hut. She sighed. It was going to be a long tedious night if he did not come inside. They could at least talk. She wanted to know about the battle.

Niall was just dozing when he was suddenly disturbed by singing. He groaned, and pulled his mantle about his ears. What was wrong with the woman to be singing at this time of night? The singing stopped after several minutes, and in its place began a moaning. He smiled, and poked his head through the doorway. 'Are you in some kind of pain?'

'I'm cold,' she said in a woebegone voice. 'And the ground is hard.'

Niall was tempted then to forget the hurt that her parting words had inflicted. But she needed a lesson, he decided. He pulled off his mantle and threw it at her. 'That should keep you warm.' His head withdrew just as Constance picked up his mantle to throw at him. Furious, she was silent after that.

The grey of dawn was in the hut when Constance woke, and she had scarcely left the hut when she felt the familiar sense of nausea. She dashed round to the back, and when she appeared again at the front, she was pale and trembling.

'How long have you been like that?' Niall's grey eyes scanned her face. There was a peculiar sensation in the pit of his stomach. She made no answer, only wiping her mouth with the back of her hand. He seized her by the shoulders. 'You were sick the morning before I left! That's over two weeks ago—three, maybe.'

'And what if I was!' She did not look at him as she tried to wriggle out of his hold.

His hands were suddenly shaking on her shoulders. 'Have you been sick every morning since I left?' She was silent. Niall swallowed convulsively. 'I—I didn't see my foster-mother sick in the morning several times without realising that a child was on the way. A few she lost, but that means—you must be...'

'What, Master O'More?' she asked coolly, lifting her head and staring at him steadily. 'That I'm carrying your bastard?'

'Ay!' he exclaimed with a note of exultation in his voice. 'We'll have to wed now. Sweet Jesu, to think...'

'We don't have to do anything of the sort!' Her tart voice cut through his like a whiplash.

Some of the wonder evaporated from his face. 'I know that you said you'd rather wed any man but me—but I don't believe you really meant it,' he said in a low voice.

'Why should you think I didn't mean it?' she demanded unevenly. 'I want my child's father to be respectable, not—not a horse-thief!'

He pulled her into his arms. 'I'll become respectable. Don't fight me on this. I'll be the only father my son shall have—unless you would deny that he is mine?' His penetrating gaze scanned her face.

Her eyes widened. 'You insult me again! Do you think I lie with men from here to Dublin? How can I deny that you are the only man who could have fathered this child?'

'So you'll wed me?' he said roughly.

'For the child's sake, I suppose I'll have to,' she murmured, not looking at him.

For a moment he was silent. 'For the child's sake,' he said drily. She looked up at him then and their eyes held, and she wondered why there was no sign of triumph in their steely depths. 'You don't have to,' she said uncertainly. 'I'll go home to England, and...'

'I do,' he interrupted inexorably. 'We can't have your good name ruined, Mistress de Wensley—I would make a respectable woman of you.' Then he kissed her in such a way that he crushed her lips, and left them feeling bruised, and she wondered what had happened to the gentle man who had made such sweet love to her under the moon.

'We'll wed now—today!' declared Niall, lifting his head.

'But...' She stared wide-eyed at him, feeling as though her life were being taken out of her control and into his.

'But yes!' He slapped her bottom lightly. 'The dawn has come, if you haven't noticed. Dougal can marry us.' He took her hand to lead her back to the shore.

Constance resisted. 'It is too soon!'

'Not in your condition,' he retorted in a honeyed tone.

She felt like screaming, but the sight of Dougal and Dara sitting in the lee of a bush out of the wind calmed her.

'Any sign of movement?' whispered Niall, dragging Constance with him as he knelt on the ground.

Dara shook his head. 'That doesn't mean that there's nobody about. We could try leaving from the other side of the island, but the water's deeper there.'

'No,' said Niall, glancing at Constance, 'we'll go back the way we came.'

Dougal nodded. 'It is safe, I think.'

Niall reached out and touched his arm. 'But first, brother, I want you to make Constance my wife.'

Dougal's eyebrows lifted slightly, but that was the only sign of surprise he showed. 'If you are both willing,' he said, 'and you'll help me with the words. I have not performed many weddings.'

Constance was tempted to say that she was not willing to be wed in such a manner, but Niall's hold on her hand was firm and she did not doubt, looking at his stern profile, that even if she did, he would still be able to persuade his brother. 'I know some of the words,' she offered calmly.

'There you are,' said Niall. 'And I know enough.'

Dougal threw back his hood and indicated that they should kneel before him. Constance could not help thinking that she ought to recognise his face, but perhaps it was only because he resembled his brother, although Niall was fair and Dougal dark.

She stumbled her way through the wedding service, taking Niall for fairer for fouler, for better for worse, in sickness and in health—till death did them part.

When it came to the ring, Niall pulled Milo's ring from her finger and tossed it in the lough. 'A new life—a new symbol,' he said quietly, taking the ring from his little finger to hold it over her thumb in the name of the Father; over her index fingers in the name of the Son; and over her middle fingers in the name of the Holy Ghost. As the Amen sounded, he slipped it on her third finger. His kiss was cool as they sealed the ceremony, and within moments she was up on his horse and they were leaving the island.

Soon the horses were swimming through the water, and now Constance could feel the tension mounting in Niall's body. Her feet and the hem of her gown were soaked, but she was almost unaware of the coldness, for her eyes were searching the bank of the lake. The hounds, which had been able to swim faster, were already on land and shaking themselves, and within minutes the horses were following them out.

The three men looked about them; Niall and Dara with their axes to hand, while Dougal held the knife at his girdle. 'Someone's followed our tracks,' said Niall, carefully dismounting and inspecting the ground. He sat back on his heels. 'Someone riding our black stallion has been here. He cast a shoe before I left, and I meant to tell you, Constance, to see that it was replaced.'

'None of the captain's men took any of your horses,' said the dwarf.

'Then it must be either Brigid, or——' Constance's brow wrinkled with concentration, '—that man who washed the walls, or Grannia's mother. Sil said that they were his creatures,' she murmured.

Niall glanced up quickly. 'It surely couldn't be Grannia's mother! But whoever it is, it's likely that they have gone to inform Sil where we are.' He straightened up. 'Let's go swiftly, for I want you safe before we confront him.'

Was it her he cared about, she thought sadly, or was it the child she carried? Even so, she found herself suddenly fiercely protective towards the baby inside her.

It was as they entered the oak-grove that they were attacked by Sil's followers, by a handful, no more, of O'Tooles that he had won to his side. Of Sil himself, there was no sign. It was a fierce fight, and Constance was aware from its beginning that she and Niall were the main targets.

The dwarf fought like a man possessed, swinging his axe as though it were a scythe cutting corn. He disposed swiftly of one man, while Dougal stabbed another. The dogs dealt with the one who had washed Constance's walls. Despite Niall's wounded arm, he killed his attacker, but the last man was attempting to drag Constance from the horse behind him. The dogs barked madly.

All would have gone well had another six men not burst through the trees. Constance called a warning while she rained blows on her assailant, and immediately the three defenders turned to face the fresh attack and Niall set the dogs on the reinforcements. But as he turned his horse to face the men, Constance was dislodged from her perch and dragged down. Screaming and kicking, she was pulled through the trees before any of the men could prevent it.

Sil appeared suddenly in front of her, staring at her with glistening triumphant eyes. Then he hit her across the head, and she collapsed on the ground.

Desperation served Niall and the others well, and with the dogs' help, the six men were despatched swiftly; but already it was too late to see in which direction Constance had been taken.

Chest heaving with exertion, Niall faced his brother and Dara. 'We've got to find her soon, or...' He could not finish.

'Where do you think he'll have taken her?' Dougal gazed into his brother's anxious face and wiped his blade on a fold of his habit.

'Not to the captain's settlement or to her manor, certainly,' grunted the dwarf, swinging his axe absently.

Niall's lips were compressed tightly. 'There is a place—I found Brigid wandering near it when she went missing,' he told them.

'Then let us go,' said Dougal, putting away his knife. 'And let us pray that we are in time.'

Constance ached all over. It was dark—darker than she had ever known it to be—as she opened her eyes wide. Where was she? Sil! She had seen Sil coming through the trees. Niall! Sweet Jesu, where was Niall? He had been fighting for his life! Despair clutched her heart.

She scrambled to her feet, and immediately banged her head on a low roof. If she had been fearful before, it was little compared with how she felt now as her hands searched for a wall or furniture—anything that spoke of human habitation. But there was nothing, only air and a noisome odour. Her fear was such that her knees suddenly gave way and she sank to the ground to huddle in a tight ball. What if Niall were here, but he was dead! 'Sweet Jesu! Sweet Jesu! Don't let him be dead—don't let me be—where I think I am.' The sibilancy of the words seemed to hiss back at her: 'am—am—am.'

All her fears about burial-mounds, and of the dead stealing away the living, clawed at her mind, so that somehow she managed to get to her feet and run—run as fast as she could into the darkness, not knowing where her fear would take her. She fled up a passage, some instinct keeping her from hitting the sides or from falling, only to be brought to a halt when she ran into something solid directly in her path. Panting, she drew back and fell to the floor. Nausea doubled her up, and she sat trying to calm herself, as she fought against the sickness and feared for the baby. Then she heard a noise, so muted at first that she thought she imagined it. Until it came again.

The breath caught in her throat as she saw a glimmer of light edging round what must be a door in front of her. Then it was thrust open, and a figure in flowing robes stood there.

'No!' Constance whispered. 'It can't be you. I want Niall, not you.'

'How did you get as far as this?' Sil's eyes snapped cold fire.

She did not answer; her head was aching and she could not bear to look at the *filidh*.

'No matter,' he muttered, gazing down at her, 'you can forget Niall. He might have escaped my creatures once, but he will not do so again. They will bring his body here, and I shall put it among the dead.'

'He *can't* be dead,' said Constance in a thread of a whisper.

Sil smiled mirthlessly. 'I will have you come to me, then I will possess your willing soul and body utterly. I shall wed you, and we shall reign in power.'

She stared at him in fascinated horror. 'You will never have me willingly! As for wedding me, I am already wed to Niall. On the island, I became his wife.'

His mouth twisted into an ugly grimace. 'You wed that cur? Have you lain with him yet?'

'That is none of your affair.' She laughed suddenly, a slightly hysterical laugh. 'But, ay, I have. We shall have a son, and live happily together.'

'Never,' he snarled. 'He shall not have you! At every turn, that dog of an O'More has confronted me and spoilt my plans.' His hand went to the sickle at his waist.

She backed away from him hurriedly. 'You are quite mad! Why do you hate Niall so much? He is your kinsman!'

'He is an O'More, and he would dare to defy me. His mother was a whore, who slept with the English—an Englishman that you surely knew—your having wed his son.'

Constance could not speak, neither could she move because of the shock of his words. Sil smiled. 'You did not know? He did not tell you that his mother and de Wensley...?'

He laughed when she still did not answer, and his voice was almost gentle as he fingered the blade of the sickle. 'You chose to take sides with Niall against me, and for that you will pay the price. Did you know that, in the old days, women's heads were greatly prized? They joined in the battle alongside their husbands, and it was a risky affair whether they survived or not.' He lunged towards her, but she rolled over swiftly and he missed her—to fall over her feet. Suddenly she heard the baying of hounds.

It was a sound that was enough to freeze the blood, and it had its effect on both of them. Constance scrambled desperately to her feet and ran for the opening. Sil rose, his hand searching for his sickle. Again the hounds bayed, and suddenly she laughed, because now she was out of Sil's range and in daylight. 'The hounds of hell are after you, Sil!'

He spat a curse at her, but she did not care, for already she could see the wolfhounds loping towards her. Behind them, she could see Niall just a little ahead of what appeared to be the whole clan of the O'Tooles. As he came, he swung his axe. She had wanted him to come, but now she wished he had not. His aim was to fight Sil; she had no doubt about that because it was written in his face. Why had he not told her that he was Milo's half-brother? That must have been the reason why he had taken her by the bog: revenge for what a de Wensley had done to his mother! And surely it was the compulsion behind his wanting the child to be legitimate. Yet, if he was

Milo's half-brother, surely their marriage was not acceptable to the Church? Her heart sank.

The whole band of men halted suddenly, and Niall called sharply to the dogs, who had bounded within striking distance of Sil's upraised sickle. Across the short distance, she and Niall gazed at each other. 'Has he harmed you, wife?' he called harshly.

'He has threatened to take my head from my shoulders and bury me in the mound.' The horror of that moment was apparent in her voice.

'That's not polite, Sil.' Niall's voice was suddenly unemotional. 'Because it means that I am going to hack *your* evil big head into the nearest bog!'

Sil spat out a string of obscenities before shouting in his rich voice, 'Are you going to allow this man—this son of a whore—to speak for you? Or are you...?' He got no further, because Niall ran towards him, whirling his axe.

Constance drew back hurriedly as Sil brought his arm back. The blade of the sickle shone in the sunlight as it swept a circle and down, but it did not find a target. After that first rush, Niall and Sil became more wary. Not one of the watching men made a sound as they circled each other. There was an other-worldliness about the scene that struck Constance vividly, even as fear for Niall tensed every muscle and sinew in her body. It was as though a scene from the old tales of battle and glory was being relived. The men were silent, and no birds seemed to sing beneath the shadow of the burial-mound.

The men's weapons suddenly caught and locked—were somehow disentangled—to begin again the macabre sweeps in the air that were part of this dance of death. Constance found that she could not bear to watch, yet not watching was as terrible as recognising the danger that stalked her husband. Her imagination could so easily convince her that a sudden grunt or stumbling foot belonged to the man she loved. Love! She had known there was pain in it.

The fighting seemed to take an enormous amount of leaping and dodging and ducking as well as swinging, and when the end came, it was swift, taking them all by surprise, because it had seemed that Sil's swinging sickle would take Niall's head. However, he ducked in time and darted back before sending his axe whirling through the air to catch Sil in the neck.

There was a stunned silence before a cheer went up. Slowly several men came forward to crowd about Niall and slap him on the back. Constance, as if pulled by a string, moved forward to force her way through them to reach him. The men stepped back, so that she faced Niall alone.

A cut on his cheek bled sluggishly, and there was soil smeared across his chin. His mouth was taut and his eyes unreadable. Hot tears trickled slowly down her cheeks and she would have gone into his arms, but at that moment the captain pushed his way through to stand between them.

'So you have killed Sil, Niall,' he said in Irish, 'and I cannot blame you for wanting to do so. Perhaps it is best for all of us, although the *filidh* had a magical way with words when it came to telling a tale. But what about Dermot? Your woman's kinsman has gone. She will have to be exchanged for my son despite your having wed her, for there is no other.'

'There—must—be another—way,' panted Niall, wiping the blood on his cheek. 'If I went to Dublin, I might be able to find Kathleen and Master Milburn and bring them back.'

'You might—and then you might be captured yourself.' He nodded gravely. 'But if you wish to try...' He shrugged.

'I'll try.' Niall freed a long breath.

Constance touched his arm in frustration. 'Tell me, Niall, what is being said?'

He covered her hand with his, but did not reply. Instead, he addressed the captain again. 'My wife—she may go home?'

The captain frowned. 'I am not certain that can be allowed. She might try to escape, as did her kinsman.'

'You can place some of your men to watch her, although I doubt she will try to escape. She is in need of rest. The last two days have been arduous for her.' Niall's arm went about her shoulders.

The other man nodded. 'So be it, then. I shall set men to watch her.' He turned away and shouted something in Irish.

Constance looked up at Niall, and said quietly, 'Tell me, Niall.'

He rubbed his moustache. 'Let's go home. You don't realise how tired I am, wife. And I think my wound is bleeding again.'

Immediately she was all concern. 'Is it very painful?' She gasped when she saw the blood soaking through his sleeve. 'You should have said so... The captain could have waited.' She put her arm round his waist. 'Lean on me.'

A tired grin lit his dust-begrimed face. 'No, you lean on me. Call Dougal, and let him come with us.'

'You're a stubborn man, Niall O'More,' she said crossly, 'if you think you're going to do any more fighting...!'

'Not at the moment. I'd probably fall flat on my face, Mistress O'More.' He kissed her cheek, and his eyes closed.

She shouted, 'Dougal!'

When they entered the house, there were already a couple of O'Tooles inside. Constance glanced at them, but said nothing; she had more important things on her mind. She ordered Dougal to put Niall to bed.

'Dammit, woman,' said Niall, his face twisted with pain, 'I'm not going to bed. I've got to go to Dublin.'

'Dublin?' she cried. 'You aren't going anywhere, Niall, even when that wound has been seen to.'

'I'll have my wound seen to—and then I'll go,' he muttered, gritting his teeth as Dougal helped him on to the bed. 'I'm not dead yet,' he added angrily.

'You soon will be,' intervened Constance, taking the mantle from his shoulders, 'if you don't do as you're told. Now take that tunic off, or I'll do it for you.' She stood, hands on hips, staring at him sternly.

Niall's eyebrows lifted. 'Would that be part of your wifely duties now?' They were both speaking in English.

'I could make it so, if you want that in front of your brother and the O'Tooles.' She attempted to prevent the colour from flooding her cheeks.

'Well, now.' His eyes twinkled. 'I think I'd prefer it when we are alone. But I see what you meant by the need for screens in here.'

'I'm glad you're going to be sensible,' she said cheerfully. 'Although what all this talk about going to Dublin is about, I don't know.'

'It's about fetching your kinsman and Kathleen back—that's what it is,' he murmured, and smiled faintly. 'I don't think I can get this tunic off. You'll have to do it.'

Constance sighed heavily, but she was anxious. 'Get into bed. Kathleen and Robin can wait—I doubt you'll catch them now.'

'I'll have to—there's no other way.' Niall's eyes were on her face. 'I'm certainly not letting the captain hand you over to the English. It's just possible that they might not like handing you back to me. I have to get to Dublin, Constance, and the sooner the better.'

She pulled the covers back. 'You're not going,' she muttered, and threw the covers over him.

CHAPTER FOURTEEN

GRANNIA SUDDENLY appeared, as though she had come as soon as she had heard her mistress and Master Niall were there. 'What can I do?' she asked, her face beaming as she stared at them both sitting on the bed.

'Light the fire,' ordered Constance, 'and kill a chicken. We need broth.'

'Find some whiskey,' Niall commanded. 'I'm in pain.'

Grannia nodded vigorously, and moved away. Constance could not help being glad that it was not Grannia who had fallen under Sil's spell. She wondered what would happen to those who had, now that he was dead. Where was Brigid? She was concerned about the girl. She turned back to Niall. 'Have you pains other than that in your arm?'

'I ache all over,' he replied promptly, 'but mostly *here*.' He surprised her by catching her hand and pressing it against his heart.

She flushed. 'There's no need to pretend, Niall.'

'Who's pretending? You're a lovely brave woman,' his smile wavered, 'but are you going to tend my wound before I faint from loss of blood? Dougal's waiting.' His head fell back against the pillows, and his eyes closed.

'Oh, why must you jest?' cried Constance, wringing her hands.

'I think he really has swooned,' said Dougal in a worried voice.

'Give me your knife then, brother!' she demanded, holding out her hand. Dougal smiled slightly, but complied, sitting on the side of the bed to watch her slit up the sleeve of the tunic. She began the task of unwinding the blood-soaked binding.

'Sister, let me finish that,' said Dougal. 'You can find me some clean bandages.'

Constance nodded and rose swiftly, only to sway once on her feet. At that moment, Grannia rushed in with her arms filled with kindling, took one look at Constance, and dropped it all. 'Now you lie down,' she ordered in a soothing voice. 'It's quite seemly to be there with Master Niall, because they say you're wed. Not that anyone seems to know when that happened.'

'This morning,' murmured Constance, obeying Grannia's command, while she tried to keep her eyes open long enough to say that under no circumstances must Niall leave the house to go to Dublin. 'He might die on the way,' she muttered, 'and I couldn't bear that.' Her head slipped back on the pillow, and she surrendered herself to the waves of weariness that swept over her.

When she woke, it was to a sense of well-being. Warmth and comfort wrapped her round and there was a smell of food, which made her mouth water. Remembrance flooded over her, and she sat up.

'So you're awake at last,' said Niall, looking sidelong at her. 'I wish you'd slept on.'

'Why?' she asked, although she knew the answer. She could see his face, pale and earnest.

'You know why!' he said roughly. 'I'm going to Dublin. Any more delay, and Kathleen and your kinsman could be on a boat to England.'

'They could be on a boat now.' All traces of Constance's sense of well-being vanished. 'It's stupid of you even to think of going to Dublin!' She put a hand to her head. 'How long have I slept? What time of day is it?'

'Early morning. We both slept all evening and through the night.' He grimaced. 'I've already lost too many hours.'

She pursed her mouth. 'Too many to make it worth your while to risk your life.' Her hand touched his shoulder. 'You're not well enough.'

'I'll do.' He set his jaw determinedly. 'My brother is making a search for Brigid, and will follow on. A holy man is always useful.'

She nodded. At the moment she was not really interested in Brigid or Dougal. 'And if you're captured? What then?'

He raised his eyebrows. 'I've no intention of being captured! I've entered and left Dublin safely before, Constance.'

'But your face is known now! What if Ormonde is there, and sees you? He would imprison you as soon as look at you,' she said angrily.

'That's a chance I'll have to take. I'll use his horse. It just might stand me in good stead!' He smiled faintly, touching her hand. 'Trust me.'

'You've told me to trust you before, and look where it led us!'

He smiled slightly. 'It hasn't been all bad. We're here safe—both of us. I am glad to see this day. There's food cooked, and a drink to be had together before I go.' His fingers toyed with hers. 'If we were alone...'

'But we're not,' she murmured, not knowing whether to be sad or relieved. Sil's words were suddenly vivid, and it was in her mind to ask Niall for the truth—except that Grannia came over to them, bringing a salver with food and drink, and the moment passed.

It was with a sense of foreboding that Constance stood in front of the house, watching Niall depart. If she believed that begging him not to go would have done any good, she would have tried to do so.

'Don't look so forlorn,' he said, punching her lightly on the chin. 'I'll be back.'

She forced a smile and nodded, but could not rid herself of her depression. She felt that something was coming to an end. For a moment, she thought he would kiss her, but he mounted the chestnut horse, raised a hand, and was gone.

She stood watching until he was out of sight, feeling utterly bereft. A furry head stropped her skirts, and she bent to pick up the tabby and rubbed her chin on its soft head. Somehow, it helped to ease her desolation to have her arms filled. That night, the cat slept on her bed.

Three days after Niall had departed, she woke up and immediately went outside. The sky was a creamy pearl, and mist hung on trees and bushes. A sheep coughed somewhere, and a man whistled, a hen brooded in a patch of grass, its feathers damp and bedraggled. For a moment she thought the O'Tooles had deserted her when there was no sign of them, and her heart lifted, for she had a plan. Then they came round the side of the house, accompanied by Niall's brother.

'Sister!' Dougal hurried to reach her. There was a smile on his normally serious face. 'I have good news for you.'

'Niall?' Her expression brightened.

He shook his head. 'No, alas, it is Brigid. She is now her normal self. I have spent much time with her in prayer and talking to her, and she is repentant. Not that all the blame was hers, poor girl. She has decided to enter a convent, but wishes to see you before I take her there.'

'I see.' Constance felt relieved, but she wondered how Niall would react to the news. 'Where is she?'

'At the hut in the hills. She said that it would make her sad to come back here, so, if you would not mind...'

Constance shook her head. 'I do not mind. I shall come with you, if the O'Tooles will allow me.'

He smiled. 'I have already asked them. They will accompany us.'

She nodded. 'Then I shall make ready.'

The journey was accomplished at a leisurely pace, so that she wondered whether Dougal knew about the child she was carrying, and if he did, what he thought about it. He had showed no sign of censure, only of caring.

When they reached the hut, it was just beginning to rain; soft misting rain that swept like a grey curtain over the landscape. Brigid appeared in the doorway of the simple wooden hut, and immediately Constance could see that whatever had possessed her had departed.

'You forgive me?' Brigid asked her. 'Brother Michael told me of the terrible act I performed when I was in Sil's power.'

Constance dismounted, and took her hand. 'Of course I forgive you! It was not the real you who did those things.'

Brigid smiled. 'You will come in and have a cup of buttermilk?'

Constance thanked her. 'The men—can they come inside also? It is so wet outside.'

Brigid nodded, and they all crowded inside, and cups of milk were passed round.

'So Niall has gone to try to bring back Kathleen and your kinsman,' said Brigid, her freckled face suddenly moody. 'I hope he can.'

'He has been gone three days—surely he would have found them by now? It's possible that they have already left.' Constance drained the cup.

'Niall will be annoyed if they have. He might try to do something foolish—a rescue! He thinks himself invincible.' Brigid fiddled with her girdle.

Constance paled. 'He wouldn't do anything so foolish, surely? Isn't Dermot in Trim Castle? What hope has Niall of entering there and getting out alive again?'

'I didn't say that he *would* attempt a rescue,' said Brigid, making a helpless gesture, 'only that he might.'

'I must go home,' Constance said. 'Niall might have decided to leave Dublin already.' She looked down at the ring on her finger, the one the king had given her. Perhaps she should put her plan into action. She lifted her head. 'Thank you for the milk. I hope you'll be happy in your new life.'

Brigid shrugged. 'Brother Michael thinks I shall.' She smilingly held the door open for Constance. 'I wouldn't worry too much about Niall. He generally gets what he wants, and he had his eye on you and your manor as soon as he realised who you were.' Her smile slipped. 'Goodbye, Mistress—Constance—O'More.'

Constance's face was drained of colour as she pulled on her gloves. 'Goodbye, Brigid,' she said through stiff lips, realising now just how much the girl resented her. Maybe it was because a vestige of the evil that Sil had wrought remained? Or perhaps she could not help feeling slightly jealous? But she had told her nothing that she did not already know. Constance stepped out into the rain, and the O'Tooles followed.

'I'll see that the cows are looked after,' Brigid surprised her by saying. 'Brother Michael said that Grannia and her mother are willing to come up here when I go.' She slammed the door in Constance's face.

A moment later, it was opened again, and Dougal's head popped out. 'Forgive her, sister, but she was fond of my brother,' he said in a concerned voice. 'I'll come back as soon as I can.' The door closed again.

Constance suddenly had a wild urge to laugh, but instead accepted a hand to mount, and soberly made her plans. If only she could escape the watchful eyes of her guards, she would make her move!

It was still raining at suppertime when they arrived back at the house, so after she had changed her clothes, Constance called to the O'Tooles to come inside out of the rain. They came, huddling near the door, dripping water on the floor. All their faces expressed their misery. Then suddenly bliss showed on their faces, and their noses wrinkled as they sniffed the rabbit stewing in the pot.

After several minutes, she told them to come closer to the fire. They came, standing with their mantles steaming, watching her ladle stew into bowls set on the new trestle table. When she indicated that they sit down on the benches, they hurried forward.

She sat opposite them and took up the first man's cup. 'Whiskey?' she offered, holding up the container that Grannia had brought a few nights earlier for Niall. The three of them nodded, thanking her as their faces brightened.

Constance left the pitcher on the table, and later, after finishing her meal, she went to the chest and took out a pair of Niall's old trews. Then she took up her needle, and sitting on a stool near the fire, she mended a tear in them, pushing to the back of her mind any second thoughts she might have of wearing them herself.

The dangers of travelling alone had made her remember how she had worn the page's clothes and given her the idea of wearing Niall's trews and tunic and mantle, even though they might be on the large side. She watched the men out of the corner of her eye. An hour must have passed before she heard them singing and clashing their cups together. How powerfully strong a whole pitcher of whiskey was! The men were lolling over the table, their eyes bleary.

She rose, and going over, peered inside the pitcher. 'More whiskey?' she asked, holding the pitcher upside down to show them that it was empty.

They nodded, and the middle one put his arm about her waist. Gazing into her face, he began to warble. A bubble of laughter surfaced inside her because he looked quite ridiculous, but she hoped that her opinion did not show in her expression. She knew too well how violent men in drink could be if crossed. So she removed his hand, smiling, and tapping the pitcher with her finger, repeated the words, 'More whiskey?'

He laughed, and slapped her bottom as she moved away. One of the others called something, and she caught Niall's name. She was half-way to the door, Niall's trews and a tunic over her arm, when the little man got to his feet and followed her. She quickly swallowed a groan and left the door open.

The rain had stopped, but it was still a grey evening, although there were several hours of daylight left. She had to get rid of the man. She came to the store-hut and swiftly filled the jug with whiskey. The man smiled at her, as sweetly as one of the cherubs painted on the church wall at home in England, indicating that he would carry the pitcher for her. She had no intention of hurting him.

It was a hen that saved her a lot of bother. One suddenly seemed to lose its way as it scattered with the others out of their path, and the little man's legs buckled as he fell over it. But in the end it was his reluctance to let go of the pitcher that proved his downfall. Still holding the vessel aloft, his head hit the side of the house and he slumped, stunned, to the ground.

Constance did not linger to see what might happen next, but ran round the house to the stable. Her search for a bridle was frantic, as was her hunt for one of Niall's caps. She found one perched on a hook, and swiftly changed her clothes. Fortunately, because of the weather, there were few people about. She spared a second's thought for her manor. With luck, it would remain dry after this for a while, so that the hay could be cut. She climbed on to Maeve, and headed across the field.

The sun was having an unexpected final burst of glory before sliding into darkness as Constance came to Naas. As she entered, she could not help recalling how she had met Brandon here and thought him her saviour. How wrong she had been, where he was concerned! Perhaps he was still alive, and maybe in England by now? She decided to seek lodgings at the inn where she had stabled her horse last time. To her surprise, Pat, the ostler was there. Forgetting her disguise, she waited for him to recognise her, but he was aware of her horse first.

'Now where have you got this beauty from, lad?' he demanded, eyeing her suspiciously. 'Last I remember seeing her, she was in company with a friend of mine.'

'A horse-thief, you mean,' she said. 'Master Niall O'More! And if you are a friend of his, Pat, you would help me.' She pulled off her cap. 'He has gone to Dublin, and I need to find him.'

His eyes widened. 'You're Mistress de Wensley! There's a man here—Master Upton—who is looking for you.'

'Master Upton!' Her voice rose with gladness. 'He is just the person I need to escort me!' Even as she spoke, the shutter overhead flew open and a head appeared in the opening.

'Did someone mention my name?'

'I did, Master Upton. Come down, I must speak with you.'

'Mistress de Wensley?' His eyes seemed to start out of his head as he gazed down into her upturned face. 'By all that's holy! I'll be down right away.'

He was as good as his word, and within minutes he lumbered into the stable where the ostler was making Maeve comfortable. He eyed Constance speculatively. 'Did you have to escape the rascally O'Tooles dressed like that? What's Master Niall thinking of, leaving you to go to Connemara?'

'Mind what you're saying, man,' said the ostler indignantly, 'or you'll be gettin' a biff on the snout!'

'Hush, Pat!' Constance pressed his arm. 'Have you seen Kathleen and my kinsman, Master Upton?'

'That I have. On a ship Liverpool-bound he is, with the young wench.' He scowled at Pat.

'He has departed already?'

He nodded. 'Thought he should.' He rubbed the back of his hand across his chins. 'I have bad news for you, mistress.'

'Bad news?' A muscle tightened in her throat. 'Is it Master Niall?' she said huskily.

'Indeed it isn't; I haven't seen a sign of him! No, 'tis your father. He's been imprisoned on a charge of heresy, and your stepmother fears for his safety. She wants you to go home to be with her.'

'Oh no!' The stable seemed to swim round her, and she swayed. Pat caught hold of her as Master Upton put out a hand.

'You shouldn't have told the lady the news like that, man,' scolded Pat, easing Constance on to a pile of straw.

'There's no easy way of telling bad news,' Master Upton grunted, slowly getting down on one knee and taking her hand in his chubby one. He patted it gently.

Constance took a deep shaky breath. 'Oh, what am I to do?'

'There's only one thing for you to do,' said Master Upton, 'and that's to return to England. Your family have need of you.'

'But—But you don't understand!' She tried to sit up, but her head spun, and she desisted. Pat put his arm round her and eased her against his knee so that she was in a sitting position. She thanked him, before addressing Master Upton again. 'You don't understand,' she repeated. 'Niall's life is in danger, too! And I am married to him.'

'Married!' Pat and Master Upton exchanged looks.

She nodded. 'He has gone to Dublin in search of Robin—but I fear that when he finds he has gone, he will do something foolish such as going to Trim and attempting a rescue.'

'It's Dermot O'Toole he wants to set free?' muttered Master Upton, rubbing his chin.

'Of course it is,' said Pat. 'And once Niall's mind's set on a path, there'll be no changing it.'

'That is what I believe,' cried Constance, starting up. 'He'll do something foolish if I'm not there to prevent it. But it could be that he hasn't left for Trim. He would have to work out some plan, and he surely won't have done that already.'

The two men made no answer, but she could guess what they were thinking—that she clutched at straws. But what else was there for her to do but hope, and pray that they were wrong and she was not? In the morning she would go with Master Upton to Dublin, and one way or another she would find Niall and tell him of her plan.

Constance was very much aware of how much Dublin had sprawled beyond its city walls. If Niall was still there, it would not be an easy task to find him. They had come to another of the guarded gateways, which went some way to recognising the need for defence. Beggars huddled there, just as they had at the other gates. She tossed several small coins, and caused a scramble. Then they were through, and heading towards the city and its main gate.

She could see the castle, its massive bulk forming the cornerstone of the city walls pierced with gates and towers. When they were almost there, they came to an enormous ditch that reeked of rotting offal and vegetation. She wondered how the beggars clustering about the main gate could bear the stench.

'Master Upton,' she murmured, 'could you give me a couple of coins?'

He grunted, but gave her more than she asked. She was aware of eyes watching them, and was glad of the guards at the gate. As they passed through the gateway, she saw a shambling figure detach itself from the group scrambling for the money, to follow them into the city.

Master Upton had decided that they should first go to her father's agent's house, where he was certain she would be welcome. She had managed to buy a gown from Pat's wife, and for that she was glad, having no desire to arrive at the Larchers' house in Niall's clothes. It was well on in the evening, but despite that, the narrow streets were bustling with people.

She looked about her as they travelled the High Street past Christ Church Cathedral. She had visited it when she had come here in Robin's company, and had seen the tomb of Strongbow, the first Norman invader, who had come from Wales by order of Henry II. Perhaps there would be opportunity to pray there in the morning, if she rose early. She was relieved when they came to the house not far from the city wall.

They were made welcome, and it was not too long before she was ushered into a bedchamber overlooking a walled garden, which she was to share with their host's three daughters. They would have chattered half the night, but she was much too tired, and soon she was asleep.

Constance rose early, woken by the sound of activity below and the sun filtering through the horn window. She presumed it was Mistress Larcher, and that soon she would be calling her daughters. Not wishing to be questioned any more about her affairs Constance got up quickly.

Mistress Larcher seemed to understand her desire to go alone to pray in the cathedral, and as there was no sign of Master Larcher or Upton, she left the house without hindrance to make her way to the cathedral. Her heart was only a little lighter when she emerged. The two men she loved were in danger of their lives, and she could only see vaguely a way to help one of them out of his difficulties.

She had not walked far when she heard footsteps behind her. Not an uncommon sound at that time of morning, but there was a beat in their pacing that she recognised. She whirled round just as a hand seized her arm. Niall swore fluently as he looked down at her.

For a few seconds, Constance barely recognised him. Gone was the moustache, and his shoulder-length hair had been bobbed neatly to just below his ears. It gleamed dull gold in the morning sun. He no longer wore trews and a tunic, but some kind of livery of red and gold. She quickly blinked back the tears of relief that pricked her eyes. 'Why are you dressed like that?' she asked huskily. 'I feared you might be already captured or even dead!'

He stared at her, a sudden awareness in his face. 'Why should you fear that I would be dead?' He reached out to brush away the tear at the corner of her eye.

She caught his hand quickly, and forced a laugh. 'You don't have to pretend to me that you haven't some pre-posterous plan to free Dermot now that you have discovered that Robin and Kathleen have already left Ireland! But there's no need for you to go to Trim.'

He shook his head slowly. 'Did you come all this way just to tell me that?' She nodded, and he groaned. 'How did you escape the O'Tooles?'

'I gave them your whiskey.' Her fingers of their own accord were lacing through his.

He groaned again. 'How much?'

'At least two pitchers.' She giggled suddenly, remembering how the men had looked. 'It worked beautifully.'

'They'll be furious!' He grinned, then his expression grew serious. 'You shouldn't have come here. The journey must have been arduous for you.' He moved her swiftly out of the path of a wagon, and nearer to the High Cross set at the crossroads.

'I'm perfectly well.' She tilted her head to look up at him. 'You should be worrying about yourself, not me.'

He shook his head. 'You should have stayed at home, because there's nothing you can do here. If Ormonde should see you...!'

'Ormonde is here?' she exclaimed. 'Never mind me, what if he sees *you*?'

'He has seen me,' he said drily, 'and he didn't know me. Neither did you!' He squeezed her fingers. 'It is a generous nature you have, Mistress O'More, the way you give to the poor beggars. We'll have no money to buy horses if you go on giving it away.'

Her eyes widened. 'You were at the gate? I thought someone was watching me.'

'I thought my eyes and ears were playing tricks on me, because I've looked at many a face in the last couple of days. What are you doing here with *Master Upton*?'

She was suddenly at a loss whether to tell him about her father and her need to go to England. He might make it more difficult for her if she did, and she had decided that she must leave. 'He came with a message from Robin,' she said brightly. 'He was sorry not to be able to see me before he went to England. Since I was concerned that you might do something foolish, like attempting a rescue at Trim, I asked him to escort me here.'

'I see,' he said with a touch of humour. 'Well, you could have stayed at home, because I'm not going to Trim. Dermot is here in Dublin Castle. It's too late, now that your kinsman has gone, but it seems that Ormonde kept his word. If only it had been a week ago, I wouldn't be here now. As it is, Dublin's a place I know. It shouldn't be too difficult for me to attempt a rescue.'

She stared at him. 'Have you considered that, now Sil's dead, there is not the same need for you to risk being captured?'

He frowned. 'Of course there is. I want Dermot free! Besides, now that you've tricked the O'Tooles, while it might raise you in their estimation as a worthy wife for me, it means that we can't go back until we do have Dermot.'

She bit her lip. 'There is another way than your endangering your freedom.'

His mouth set stubbornly. 'If you're going to suggest that we exchange you for Dermot, I won't do it. If Ormonde knew that we were married, he'd probably ship you off to England simply to spite me. I'll do what I think best.'

'Oh, Niall, won't you ever listen to me!' she cried with a touch of asperity. She pulled the king's ring from her finger. 'Remember that I saved the king's life? You helped also, so surely that must count for something. A boon! I will ask him for a boon.'

He made an incredulous noise. 'That's your plan? He won't grant it.'

'Why shouldn't he?' she demanded. 'He's not a hard man.'

Niall folded his arms across his chest. 'He was the justiciar for years! I'll follow my own plan.'

She stamped her foot in frustration. 'It's because you want to play the hero, and storm the castle! Because Dermot helped you in the past, you have to help him now.'

'That's right, and losing your temper isn't going to prevent me from doing it.' The grey eyes glinted. 'Surely you can understand that?'

'Ay! But you play a fool's game,' she said crossly. She humped her shoulder and turned a little away from him.

'You don't have to worry about me. Show concern for our child, and go and rest.' He seized her by the shoulders. 'Please don't tell Master Upton about any of this.' She nodded. 'If all goes well, I'll call on you tomorrow.'

'And if it doesn't?' she asked in a small voice.

'Then you must go home.' He kissed her averted cheek, and turning on his heel, left her standing in the middle of the road. She swiftly walked away, her face set.

'You say that you don't want me to search for Master O'More?' said Master Upton for the second time.

'That is correct, sir,' she replied quietly, gazing beyond him to the roses filling the air with their fragrance.

He stroked his chins. 'Why is that? I ask myself. And I come back with the answer that perhaps you have already seen your husband.'

'Master Upton,' she replied coolly, looking straight at him, 'I have appreciated all the help you have given me since I came to Ireland, but I ask you most earnestly not to interfere in this matter. If you want a reason for my not searching for Niall, believe me when I say that I realise that my father and family need me more than he does at this moment.'

'Wouldn't listen to you, would he?' murmured Master Upton.

'Sir,' she cried indignantly, 'will you say no more! Tell me, when has Master Larcher arranged for me to sail for Liverpool?'

'Day after tomorrow. There's a ship sailing then.' His face was worried. 'Is there naught I can do for you?'

She half smiled. 'Just be patient with me, and tell me if you have any more details about my father.'

'I have told you all that I know. You will go to your stepmother, who is staying with his cousin Beatrice in Southwark, so that she can be close to your father.'

She nodded. 'And my brothers?'

'They are with your stepmother. If she has opportunity, she will take them to see your father, before...' He coughed, and said no more.

Tears itched Constance's eyes, but she blinked them back. What was the point of crying? It would not serve Niall or her father. She felt as if a great weight rested on her shoulders. She might never see her father or her husband alive again, and she could not bear the thought that there was not much she could do to help either of them, but pray.

CHAPTER FIFTEEN

IT SEEMED to Constance that tomorrow would never come, but at last it dawned. If Niall did achieve that which he had set out to do and came today, she would tell him about going to England. Surely he would understand and not mind too much. He had her manor!

She went with Master Larcher down Winetavern Street, which ran steeply to the River Liffey, to Merchant's Quay, where she met the master of the ship she was to sail on. Later, after dinner, she was persuaded to go shopping with one of the daughters of the house, but all the time she fretted in case Niall called while she was out. When she returned, it was to find Master Upton waiting for her.

He greeted her cheerfully before asking if he could have a private word with her in the garden. She agreed, wondering if what he had to say concerned Niall. With a fast beating heart, she followed him outside and faced him. 'What is it you have to say, Master Upton?'

He cleared his throat and rubbed his hands down the sides of his surcote. 'There's been an escape from the castle. A prisoner—one named Dermot O'Toole. Yesterday evening it was, and the hue and cry raised immediately, and the gates of the town shut tight.' He nodded his head several times, a twinkle in his eye.

'And?' She held her breath, her stare fixed rigidly upon his face.

'A search has been made of part of the town this side of the river—and they started on Oxmantown on the other bank this afternoon. So far, it is rumoured, they have not found the man they're seeking. It's likely that they will continue their search here later in the day. No doubt the Earl of Ormonde knows by now who is responsible, but he will not understand why. He knows that your father has an agent here, and once he discovers your kinsman has left for England—Master Larcher is sure to tell him—he *will* know why.'

'Do you consider that His Grace will come here himself?'

'It is possible. You must deny any knowledge of Master Niall's presence in Dublin. Show surprise—horror, even! Rejoice in your kinsman's escape and—you have a valid reason—tell him that already you are preparing to leave for England because of family matters. Fortunately, you never told the Larchers about your marriage to Master Niall—and I have not mentioned it, either.' He beamed at her. 'Now you can leave Ireland, knowing he isn't dead or even a prisoner.'

'But he might yet be caught!' she cried, twisting her hands.

He scratched his head and winked at her. 'A resourceful man, Master Niall. Don't you be worrying. You get on the boat in the morning and leave the rest to me.' He nodded sagely, his jowls wobbling.

She eyed him thoughtfully. 'You will help him, Master Upton?'

'Now, if I see the man—and I won't say that I haven't been making a search of my own—maybe I'll be helping him out of trouble.'

Constance held out a hand. 'You are a friend indeed, Master Upton.'

He took her hand and patted it. 'You take care of yourself, Mistress Constance, and don't be worrying about anything. It does no good at all. No good at all!' Then he left her in the garden to gaze unseeingly at the roses, wondering if she would ever see Niall again.

* * *

Constance stood on the deck of the ship, watching the shores of Ireland recede into the distance. Her eyes reached beyond the huddle of Dublin and the plains— to the hills that lay fold upon fold, some long and of gentle outline, others sharp and conical. Perhaps Niall and his cousin were there, even now? She had no way of knowing. The Earl of Ormonde had come, as Master Upton had predicted, and spoken with her, and she had obeyed Upton's words. Ormonde had seemed convinced of her sincerity. She could only pray that Niall would continue to elude him. Turning away with tears blurring her vision, she collided into someone.

'Mistress O'More,' said a sombre voice, 'you really must be more careful.'

Constance blinked and rubbed her eyes, hardly able to believe that it was Niall standing in front of her. 'How...?'

He shrugged. 'Master Upton is a resourceful man.'

'He said the same about you.' She gripped the side of the boat firmly as the deck slanted. 'But, even so...'

'Why did you not tell me about your father?' He looked angry.

'I thought you might not let me go, and I have to go.' She had known it would be difficult to tell him, but she wished he would not be so vexed.

'You consider me such a selfish man? I understand your concern for your father.' He sighed. 'Or did you not tell me because you had it in mind to return to England anyway?'

She was silent a moment. 'I do miss my family at times—and because of the child, I thought I should go home.'

'Why?' he said forcibly. 'Do you not wish to be married to me, even for the child's sake?'

'I did not say that! Let us forget about the child for now. I am no longer sick in the mornings, and I can almost believe that it was all a mistake.' She laughed.

'A mistake! You would wish it to be a mistake?' He seized hold of her. 'Do you detest me so much?'

'Of course not.' Tears suddenly clogged her throat, and she had to swallow. 'Let's forget about it now. I can think only about my father. I might never see him again,' she whispered unsteadily. She clutched at his surcote as the deck tilted again. It was rather large, and of a sober hue. Master Upton's, she presumed.

Suddenly the anger died in his face and he wrapped his arms round her and pressed her head against his shoulder. 'You are imagining the worst again! You thought that I would be captured—killed—yet I'm here.' She sniffed to stem her tears. 'Have faith,' continued Niall. 'Together we will save your father. As you once suggested asking Ormonde for a boon—Dermot's freedom—might it not be possible that King Richard could grant you a boon? You have his ring—a life for a life?' He hugged her to him. 'It's worth a try.'

She lifted her head, and smiled. 'Of course it is,' she said cheerfully. Strangely, she was comforted by his words, even though she remembered that he had not had much faith in the idea of a boon where Dermot's freedom had been concerned. But she was soothed by his just being with her. For a while she would pretend that theirs was an ordinary marriage, and forget what Sil and Brigid had said. She stretched up and kissed his cheek. 'Thank you, Niall. I feel better now.'

'Good.' He smiled, and his finger traced a path down her cheek where a tear had fallen. Then he turned to her, and they stood side by side looking towards Ireland.

'What happened to Dermot?' she asked suddenly.

Niall grinned. 'On another boat that will take him down the coast and hence home. And Ormonde has his horse back, so perhaps he will let the matter drop when he doesn't find us.'

'I hope so.' Her brow wrinkled. 'Brigid is going into a convent. Your brother thinks it best for her.'

He nodded. 'I thought Dougal might persuade her. The nuns might calm her, and good deeds will help her to forget.'

'I hope so,' murmured Constance, glad that he did not seem concerned about Brigid. He nodded, and they were both silent as they watched the coast of Ireland until it vanished from their sight.

Constance could not help a rush of emotion when she saw the shores of Liverpool, with the beacon plainly visible on Everton hill. She had hopes of finding Robin and Kathleen at his father's house in Dale Street, only a short distance from the market place near the castle.

Robin opened the door to them, and she did not know whether to laugh or to scold him. He spoke first in an incredulous voice mixed with delight and trepidation. 'Sweet Jesu! I hoped, but I never believed, that you would get here, Con. Kathleen said that she thought you and O'More,' he cast a wary eye in Niall's direction, 'might make a match of it, but I couldn't quite believe it.'

'Then you can believe it now, Master Milburn,' said Niall drily. 'Constance and I are wed—which is more than can be said for you and Kathleen, I suppose.'

Robin grinned. 'Well, you'd be wrong there. We were wed as soon as Mother was told what was happening and how far we'd travelled alone.'

Constance laughed at the look on Niall's face. 'I told you that Robin was a gentleman—and he would deal with Kathleen properly!'

Niall grunted before giving Robin his hand. 'Shall we be friends, Master Milburn, for it seems that we are kin?' They shook hands. 'Now where's that sister of mine?'

'I'm here,' said a quiet joyous voice, and Kathleen pushed her way past her husband and threw herself into Niall's arms. 'Oh, 'tis so good to see you both! And you

have caught us just in time, because we are on our way
to London.'

Immediately the atmosphere changed, and they all
became serious. 'Tell me,' demanded Constance, 'have
you more news of my father?'

Robin sighed heavily. 'Only that he is being kept in
prison, kicking his heels, because he won't recant when
Sir Richard Stury and the others have done so—with the
threat of the foulest death hanging over them if they
break their oath.'

Constance sighed with relief. 'At least he's still alive—
and Niall and I have a plan for his release.' She began
to tell the others about it, and it was with some hope
that they all set out for London later that morning.

London Bridge was crowded with wagons and carts,
walkers and riders, so that it was slow work making their
way across to Southwark.

Niall's eyes idly scanned the crowds; he had never seen
so many people, even in Dublin. Suddenly his gaze fixed
as he thought he recognised a figure in the throng. He
glanced at his wife and saw her weariness, then turned
to Robin and murmured a name in his ear. Immediately
Robin looked up, and followed his eyes. For a moment
he was silent, and then he said, 'Ay,' softly.

'Constance!' called Niall quietly.

She broke off her conversation with Kathleen. 'What
is it?' Immediately she sensed the suppressed excitement
within him.

'I think I have seen someone we know, who might
make our case with the king. You'll make Robin's and
my excuses to Master and Mistress Wantsum?' He
covered her hand with his.

'Who?' Her eyes were curious.

'Later!' He raised her fingers to his lips and kissed
them, before riding back with Robin the way they had
come.

'Well, who can it be?' said Kathleen with a frown. 'I hope Niall will not get Robin embroiled in one of his escapades!'

'It was you who once said that with Niall around, life is never dull,' stated Constance absently, her eyes following Niall's back. 'I think Robin is about to find out that that is true. Myself, I have known it for a long time! Come, Kathleen, let us go and make their excuses to cousin Beatrice and my stepmother, and pray that they won't be long.'

'Love, I never expected to see you so soon.' Philippa Milburn held out her arms to Constance as she entered the large, comfortably furnished hall. 'But I am so pleased that you are here.' The two women who loved Guy Milburn most in the world hugged each other and burst into tears. They were a foil for each other. Constance, dark-haired and olive-complexioned, her stepmother, silver fair, with a skin as delicate as a rose.

'He is still alive?' Constance demanded in a trembling voice, as they drew apart.

'Praise Jesu, yes,' she replied with a bright smile that did not quite reach her eyes. 'But the king's moods are changeable, and he considers your father a traitor.'

'But Father isn't a traitor!' cried Constance. 'He is the king's most loyal subject.'

'I know,' said Philippa in a soothing voice, leading her over to a settle in front of which played two small boys, dark-haired and blue-eyed images of Constance's father. 'It is because the Lollards' aims were pinned to the doors of St Paul's, and written in the common tongue. They stressed that to slay one's enemy in warfare is directly contrary to Jesus' teachings. And what king doesn't have his enemies slain?'

'I understand.' Constance's legs suddenly gave way and she sank onto the settle. 'I think that the sooner Niall and I see the king, the better it will be.'

'Niall?' questioned Philippa, her green eyes curious.

'Niall O'More is an Irishman,' said Constance, flushing, 'who has a habit of rescuing people from seemingly impossible situations.'

'Tell me more,' demanded Philippa, noting her blushes. 'He sounds like the answer to a prayer.'

Constance hesitated, and then decided that the time to unburden herself had come, although she did not plan to tell all and shock the woman who, while she had behaved unconventionally in the past, might not look too kindly on Niall because her stepdaughter was involved. But she would have her advice.

'You love this Niall O'More, don't you?' said Philippa after Constance had finished talking.

'Ay,' said Constance in a low voice, 'strange as it may seem in some of the circumstances.' She gave a reluctant laugh. 'He believes that we were fated to meet.'

'Perhaps you were. It would make some sense of your disastrous marriage to Milo.' Her white forehead knitted. 'Concerning what this terrible man Sil said about him being Milo's half-brother, I would suggest that you ask your husband whether it is true.' She shrugged. 'It could be that he said it just to upset you—you said yourself that the tale of the abduction was known by Desmond. Possibly this Sil knew of it, too.'

'I never thought that he might be lying,' murmured Constance. She squared her shoulders. 'I will do as you say, although it will not be easy to ask such a thing.' She smiled at her stepmother and touched her hand. 'I should not be burdening you with such matters at this time. We shall forget it until Father is with us once more.'

A shadow crossed Philippa's face, but she only took Constance's hand in her gentle hold, and said, 'Of course.'

Philippa had been prepared to be polite to Niall for Constance's sake, although she had concealed extremely well her reaction to parts of her tale. She knew how lusty some men could be! What she was not prepared for was the sheer charm of the man, and his handling of Constance. Immediately she understood how Constance had succumbed to him. Even so, she allowed none of this to show in her face. Her husband, when—if—he was freed, would decide what attitude they would take concerning his daughter's marriage. But she might speak in his favour, for it was obvious to her that Niall cared for her stepdaughter.

'Constance said that you had a plan to persuade the king to set my husband free, Master O'More,' she said gravely, as the three of them sat on the settle. 'I pray it is one that will work!'

Niall smiled at her, and then flashed a particularly mischievous grin at his wife. 'I think so. It involves a man who has a taste for extremely long, pointed, shoes.'

Constance's eyes widened. 'Brandon?'

'The very man! He's here in London, and I know exactly where to find him.' His hand covered hers and he squeezed her fingers gently. 'All we have to do is gain access to the king.'

'That should not be too difficult,' interpolated Philippa, her spirits lifting. 'Master Wantsum is a member of the council, so he will be able to arrange it quite easily, I should imagine, especially if you give him the king's ring to pave the way.'

'Then it's as good as done,' said Niall confidently.

'You understand, Constance and Master O'More,' murmured Master Wantsum, as they walked side by side along the passage in the Tower, 'that the king can be as obdurate as your father when it comes to one of his subjects deliberately defying him.' He shot a quick look at the servant who was escorting them to the king's chamber.

'We understand,' said Niall, easing the high collar of the blue houppelande that Constance had persuaded him to wear for the occasion, having informed him that Richard laid great importance on dress. Earlier her eyes had teased him and he had longed to make passionate love to her, but always in his mind was the remembrance that she had wed him only for the child's sake. There was a kind of loving between them, but his desire had never been given full rein, for he feared wrecking what they already had. He only hoped that it would grow into something more, that would be able to take all the knocks that life inflicted.

'I shall, perhaps, cry,' said Constance, disturbing his thoughts. She smoothed the scarlet skirts of the satin gown lent to her by Philippa. 'Do you think that it would move the king?'

'It might,' said Master Wantsum with a small smile. They approached the great oak door.

The servant knocked on the door, and opened it wide at the invitation of a voice within.

Richard sat at a table, writing, and did not look up for several minutes. Then he set the scroll aside and gazed at them from his heavy-lidded eyes. 'Master Wantsum, Master and Mistress O'More—you may approach.'

Constance thought the servant scowled, but she could spare him no more than a quick look. Surely Niall was right in his assumption?

She went forward with Niall and Master Wantsum, and sank into a billowing curtsy. Richard signalled for them to rise. 'You saved my life, Mistress O'More, I remember that.' He turned the ring she had presented to Master Wantsum round the tip of his middle finger. 'You, Master O'More, killed one of the men who plotted against my life, so I have been informed. But,' he addressed Constance again, 'your father is an obstinate man—a traitor and a heretic! I cannot disregard such blatant disobedience. Does he count himself higher than Stury and the others that he still defies me?'

'I am certain that my father intends no disloyalty to your noble person, my liege,' said Constance in a quivering voice, and she allowed the tears to fall.

Richard stared at her uneasily, but said nothing. Niall felt his temper rising, not enjoying the experience of letting his wife behave thus in front of this man whose life she had saved. 'Lord Richard!' he cried, 'my wife's father is as loyal to you as she is, but there is a man in this building who even now plots to kill you, as he did in Ireland!'

'What's this?' Stark terror suddenly gazed out of Richard's eyes and he clutched at the arms of the chair. 'Who are you talking about?'

Niall moved swiftly towards the servant, whose hand was already on the door, and seized him by the back of his tunic and spun him round. 'Master Brandon, I believe,' he said cheerfully.

The king let out a roar. Brandon snarled and spat in Niall's face, struggling furiously. Master Wantsum pulled Constance swiftly back. Suddenly Brandon broke free, and she heard the hiss of Niall's indrawn breath and saw the blood on his hand. She wrenched herself out of Master Wantsum's grasp, as Brandon dragged the door open and fled up the passage, with the dagger still clutched in his hand. 'After him!' yelled the king.

Niall wiped the blood on the blue houppelande, and took to his heels. Constance ran out of the doorway and would have followed them, had Master Wantsum not seized her arm and dragged her back.

'Not this time!' he said firmly. 'Master O'More stressed that you were to be looked after if anything like this happened.'

Tears sparkled in her eyes. 'But what if something happens to him? More than it has already? You saw that dagger!'

'I know.' He patted her shoulder. 'But your husband knows that the dagger is there now. Brandon had it hidden inside his tunic before.' He led her back into the chamber where the king stood, seething with rage over how close he had come to death in one of the most strongly guarded fortresses in the kingdom.

It was not long before Niall appeared, dragging an unconscious Brandon by the hood of his tunic. His eyes were alight with satisfaction. He dumped Brandon in front of the king. 'An exchange, Lord Richard,' he cried in ringing tones. 'Master Milburn for this traitor!'

Richard gazed at Brandon's limp body, then at Niall. Suddenly he laughed, and held out his hand. 'Well done, Master O'More! You may tell Master Milburn that my enemy's life has bought his. But this enemy will die!' He kicked the man on the floor, and nodded his head several times, a smile on his face.

'So, Master O'More, I owe you my life,' said Guy Milburn, his bright blue eyes on Niall's scarred profile. 'That is what my wife tells me.'

Niall and Constance turned from their contemplation of the scene outside Master Wantsum's hall window and looked at him with his wife on his arm. It was the afternoon of the same day, and they had not yet changed out of their fine clothes. 'Oh, Father, it is so good to see you!' cried Constance, starting forward to meet him. 'I have missed you so.'

Guy caught hold of her hand and held her from him for a moment. His eyes went from her face to Niall's behind her. 'I would have thought, from all I've heard, that you would have been too busy to think of your aged parent,' he said drily.

Constance moistened her mouth, but Niall moved to stand by her side. 'I crave your forgiveness, sir. There was no time to ask for your daughter's hand, but I swear that I shall always cherish her, and protect her with my life if need be.' His bandaged hand sought Constance's to clasp it firmly.

'Very nicely said, Master O'More,' stated Philippa with a smile. 'Don't you think so, Guy?'

'I couldn't ask for a better vow,' murmured Guy, returning her smile, before facing Constance and Niall again. 'But that is not to say that I approve of your behaviour towards my daughter, Master O'More.' He paused, and stroked his cheek. 'Still, I did not always behave circumspectly in my younger days, so I shall not judge you.' He smiled austerely. 'Now, Constance, you may kiss me. I consider in the circumstances—I believe Beatrice is going to have a feast to celebrate my being freed, and yours and Robin's weddings—that you should both change out of your clothes,' he groaned, 'which have blood on them.'

Constance smiled. 'I'm sorry, Father.' She kissed him. 'Your best blue houppelande too.' Another kiss. 'And I hope I do not upset you, but we need to borrow more clothes, for ours are in Ireland.'

'I thought as much.' Guy sighed, and rested his cheek against hers. 'Philippa has put some clean garments in your chamber—but no more venturing while you wear them, or I doubt that I will forgive you!' He released her. 'Now go and change.' She kissed him again, and suddenly too shy to look at Niall, although she allowed him to take her hand, she did as her father had told her.

'I doubt if Richard even noticed my fine blue houppelande,' said Niall, stripping it off carefully.

'I noticed how well it became you,' murmured Constance, deliberating what to say as she unfastened the scarlet gown. 'But I was wrong to borrow father's best houppelande for you to get blood on it. It's ruined, I fear. It would not be so bad if it was Brandon's blood, but...'

Niall turned to look at her. 'But...?' There was something in her voice.

Her eyes met his. 'But I don't doubt that it is yours! Do you know how many times I have seen you bleeding?' she said unsteadily. 'How many times you get hurt? Such as the time you fought Sil, after rescuing me from the burial chamber. How did you know I was there, by the way?'

'I believed that Sil took Brigid there when she went missing. I found her near there, if you remember?' He sat beside her on the bed, his eyes never leaving her face. 'Do you keep a count of the times I get hurt?' He smiled slightly.

'Of—Of course not.' She presented him with her profile and undid another button. 'But I know it's more times than I like to remember. But—But to get back to Sil.'

'I don't want to talk about Sil.' He caught her hand, holding it tightly. 'I'd rather talk about us. We are going back to Ireland, aren't we?'

Her throat moved, and her fingers curled inside his hand. 'That depends on whether our marriage is lawful...or not.' She was finding it very difficult to get the words out, and really, she thought, it did not matter what he said, because she did not think she could let him go without her. She loved him too much to relinquish a life with him.

'Do you mean because Dougal performed the ceremony on the island?' He was suddenly pale. 'You want to get out of it—is that what it is? Well, I won't let you go, Constance.' He pulled hard on her hand so that she fell against him. His arm went round her. 'You're mine, and I would not give you up to the devil himself! I said that it's useful to have a holy man around, and if Dougal had not been taking Brigid to the convent, he might have been here to tell you that it was perfectly legal—but if you have any doubts, we'll get married again.' He rammed her hard against his body and she clung to him. Then he drew back slightly. 'Remind me another time

that there's something I must tell you about Dougal.'
He bent his head to kiss her, but now she warded him
off with both hands against his naked chest.

'That wasn't what I meant, Niall.' There was a faint
smile on her lips. 'And, I suppose, if you feel so strongly
about everything being legal, what Sil said couldn't be
true.'

His fair brows drew together and he rubbed his scar
against her arm. 'What did Sil say?'

'That you were Milo's father's son.' There it was, out,
and she felt greatly relieved.

'He said that? Are you sure?' He grinned.

Constance wrinkled her nose. 'I'm reasonably sure.'

'Are you certain that he didn't say that my mother
was a whore who slept with an Englishman?' He removed his hands from her chest and brought her close
to him and pressed his cheek against hers. 'Sil was always
saying that to Dougal and me when we were young. And
my mother did sleep with de Wensley. It's Dougal who's
his son, not I.'

Constance's eyes were shining like stars. 'Are you
sure?'

'Do you doubt me, woman?' He kissed the tip of her
nose. 'I wasn't born until three years after de Wensley
fled. I think I remember my father, but I was only young
when he died. He was fair. I look like him, so my mother
told Dougal. Dougal's like de Wensley—my foster-father
swore to the likeness.'

Constance's breath came out in a rush. 'That's a relief!
I was afraid we might have to part.' She rubbed gently
at the hairs on his chest, not looking at him.

'And you did not want—that?' There was a deep note
of tenderness in his voice. She shook her head. 'What
do you want, Constance O'More?' His mouth teased her
earlobe.

'I—I want you to love me,' she said shyly. 'And for
us to live happily in Ireland, breeding the best horses in

all of Ireland and England.' Her arms went about his waist.

'That can be,' he kissed her gently, 'if you can love this barbarian, who knew as soon as he saw you riding out of the mist that you were the woman of his dreams.'

She pressed her body against his and planted kisses on his chin, nose and mouth. 'You were terrible to me.'

'I wanted to make sure that you'd never forget me.' He pulled her down on top of him on the bed.

'That's so,' she whispered, letting the passion within her flow out to him. 'Was it not fated to be so?'

'We are fated to live happily—that's so,' he murmured against her mouth. 'Now kiss me, woman.' And she kissed him.

BETRAYALS, DECISIONS AND CHOICES...

BUY OUT by David Wind   £2.95

The money-making trend of redeveloping Manhattan tenement blocks sets the scene for this explosive novel. In the face of shady deals and corrupt landlords, tenants of the Crestfield begin a fight for their rights – and end up in a fight for their lives.

BEGINNINGS by Judith Duncan   £2.50

Judith Duncan, bestselling author of "Into the Light", blends sensitivity and insight in this novel of a woman determined to make a new beginning for herself and her children. But an unforeseen problem arises with the arrival of Grady O'Neil.

ROOM FOR ONE MORE by Virginia Nielsen   £2.75

At 38, Charlotte Emlyn was about to marry Brock Morley – 5 years her junior. Then her teenage son announced that his girlfriend was pregnant. Could Brock face being husband, stepfather *and* grandfather at 33? Suddenly 5 years seemed like a lifetime – but could the dilemma be overcome?.

These three new titles will be out in bookshops from MAY 1989

W♥RLDWIDE

Available from Boots, Martins, John Menzies, W.H. Smith, Woolworths and other paperback stockists.